Cal caught her hand and held her cold, trembling fingers in the warm fold of his own.

The heat and strength in his grasp were almost enough to drive away the doubts chilling her to the marrow. His grip felt safe. Steady. Solid.

But the last time she'd needed him to be there for her, he'd abandoned her. Shattered her faith. Broken her heart.

The judge pronounced them man and wife and turned to Cal with a grin. "You may kiss your bride."

Libby's stomach pitched.

No way.

Cal had accepted her terms. He'd agreed to keep things strictly hands-off. He'd promised. So he wouldn't…he couldn't…he—cupped her cheek in his palm and tipped her chin up.

Libby gawked at him, her heart thumping.

His piercing gaze zeroed in on her mouth like a heat-seeking missile. And ka-boom.

Dear Reader,

Let April shower you with the most thrilling romances around—from Silhouette Intimate Moments, of course. We love Karen Templeton's engaging characters and page-turning prose. In her latest story, *Swept Away* (#1357), from her miniseries THE MEN OF MAYES COUNTY, a big-city heroine goes on a road trip and gets stranded in tiny Haven, Oklahoma...with a very handsome cowboy and his six kids. Can this rollicking group become a family? *New York Times* bestselling author Ana Leigh returns with another BISHOP'S HEROES romance, *Reconcilable Differences* (#1358), in which two lovers reunite as they play a deadly game to fight international terror.

You will love the action and heavy emotion of *Midnight Hero* (#1359) in Diana Duncan's new FOREVER IN A DAY miniseries. Here, a SWAT cop has to convince his sweetheart to marry him—while trying to survive a hostage situation! And get ready for Suzanne McMinn to take you by storm in *Cole Dempsey's Back in Town* (#1360), in which a rakish hero must clear his name and face the woman he's never forgotten.

Catch feverish passion and high stakes in Nina Bruhns's *Blue Jeans and a Badge* (#1361). This tale features a female bounty hunter who arrests a very exasperating—very sexy— chief of police! Can these two get along long enough to catch a dangerous criminal? And please join me in welcoming new author Beth Cornelison to the line. In *To Love, Honor and Defend* (#1362), a tormented beauty enters a marriage of convenience with an old flame...and hopes that he'll keep her safe from a stalker. Will their relationship deepen into true love? Don't miss this touching and gripping romance!

So, sit back, prop up your feet and enjoy the ride with Silhouette Intimate Moments. And be sure to join us next month for another stellar lineup.

Happy reading!

Patience Smith
Associate Senior Editor

Please address questions and book requests to:
Silhouette Reader Service
U.S.: 3010 Walden Ave., P.O. Box 1325, Buffalo, NY 14269
Canadian: P.O. Box 609, Fort Erie, Ont. L2A 5X3

To Love, Honor and Defend

BETH CORNELISON

Silhouette®

INTIMATE MOMENTS™

Published by Silhouette Books

America's Publisher of Contemporary Romance

SILHOUETTE BOOKS

ISBN 0-373-27432-7

TO LOVE, HONOR AND DEFEND

Visit Silhouette Books at www.eHarlequin.com

Printed in U.S.A.

BETH CORNELISON

started writing stories as a child when she penned a tale about the adventures of her cat, Ajax. A Georgia native, she received her bachelor's degree in public relations from the University of Georgia. After working in public relations for a little more than a year, she moved with her husband to Louisiana, where she decided to pursue her love of writing fiction.

Since that first time, Beth has written many more stories of adventure and romantic suspense and has won numerous honors for her work, including the coveted Golden Heart Award in romantic suspense from Romance Writers of America. She is active on the board of directors for the North Louisiana Storytellers and Authors of Romance (NOLA STARS) and loves reading, traveling, Peanuts' Snoopy and spending downtime with her family.

She writes from her home in Louisiana, where she lives with her husband, one son and two cats who think they are people. Beth loves to hear from her readers. You can write to her at P.O. Box 52505, Shreveport, LA 71135-2505 or visit her Web site at www.bethcornelison.com.

This one is for Jeffery—who has big dreams
of his own. You can achieve anything in life with faith,
a firm foundation, a good attitude and
dogged perseverance. I love you!

Acknowledgments

Many thanks to Lt. J. E. Via, retired Investigator
and Major Case Supervisor for the Criminal Investigation
Division of the Ouachita Parish Sheriff Department,
for answering my many questions and letting me
know about Louisiana Act 894, which will allow
Cal a happier ending!

To Christy Hughes, sales manager for Kone, Inc.,
for her helpful information about elevators.

To Anna Destefano and Winnie Griggs,
my dear friends and critique partners on this book.

To Lucienne Diver, my wonderful agent,
for her assistance, friendship and
unflagging support through the years.

To Paul, for putting up with this zany writer
while I followed my dream.

Prologue

"All rise. The Honorable Judge Thomas Fitzpatrick presiding."

Showtime.

Cal Walters shoved stiffly to his feet. He knew what was coming—two years in prison before he was eligible for parole.

Tension vibrated in the silent courtroom and through Cal's taut muscles as he waited for the judge to rule on the plea agreement. He glanced behind him, where the guys from his fire station had come out in a show of support. His fellow firefighters had been at the bar with him the night he'd spotted David Ralston in the back hall using a woman as a punching bag. They'd stood with him as he'd come to the woman's defense.

And his buddies had peeled him off Ralston when his defense of the woman had turned into something more, when the past and present had blurred and Cal had gone a little crazy.

He drew a deep, fortifying breath as Fitzpatrick settled at the bench.

Maybe, just maybe, the judge would agree that the deal the district attorney's office had offered was unreasonable. Maybe the judge wouldn't make him serve time once he considered the circumstances surrounding that bar fight.

Sure. And maybe Assistant D.A. Libby Hopkins's presence in the courtroom meant she still had feelings for him and wanted to pick up where they'd left off three years ago.

In your dreams.

Regret sliced through him, sharp and merciless.

"Counsel, I've reviewed the plea agreement reached in this matter." Judge Fitzpatrick shuffled his papers then addressed the lead prosecutor. "Mr. Moore, do you have anything that needs attention before I make my ruling?"

"No, Your Honor."

Cal turned, staring past the tall, bearded assistant D.A.

When his gaze locked on the brunette in the first row of the gallery, his gut rolled. Libby stood with her back rigid, buttoned down in her pinstriped suit. She'd slicked her shiny chestnut hair into a neat bun. Her cool, crisp courtroom dress didn't fool him. He remembered the feel of that silky mane, unbound and tumbled around him during the hottest sex he'd ever had. Even now the memory made his body ache and pulse, his heart clench. They'd shared something special. Something intense.

Something he'd ended after a precious few months to marry a former girlfriend. Renee had discovered, weeks after they'd parted company and he'd later met Libby, that she was carrying his child. Cal wanted his baby to have his name, but giving Libby up had left a hole in his heart.

Seeing Libby walk into the courtroom today had been bittersweet. She hadn't been a member of the prosecution team, but that didn't allay his suspicions about her contributions to his lynching. Watching her repeatedly confer with the prosecution made it clear where Libby's loyalties lay.

"Mr. Walters, do you understand the terms of this plea and accept them without coercion or duress?"

Hell, no! I don't understand why any of this has happened, how my life could have gotten so far off track.

Cal's chest contracted, filled with a dull ache. If he went to prison, he wouldn't see his daughter for months. Two-year-old Ally meant the world to him. He'd given up Libby to be Ally's father, and now he felt his baby girl slipping away, too. He choked back the bitter frustration and defeat and nodded solemnly. "Yes, Your Honor."

"You understand that your attorney has asked that you be allowed the provisions of Act 894? That if you maintain a clean record for five years after serving your full sentence that these charges will be expunged from your record?"

"Yes, Your Honor." He was grateful for that ray of hope in this nightmare.

"Would you like to address the court before I rule on this plea agreement?" Judge Fitzpatrick asked.

"Yes, Your Honor." Cal knew that what he had to say wouldn't make a bean's difference. He'd pleaded his case to his attorney, to the police, to Renee. So why repeat himself now? Libby lifted her dark brown eyes to his at that moment, and he knew. He was appealing to her. Maybe *she* could dismiss all they'd shared, but their months together meant something to *him*.

"I deeply regret everything that has happened. If I could change things, I would. Many people have been hurt by my actions, and for that I'm sorry."

Libby shifted her weight, her hard, all-business facade cracking. She knew he was addressing her, their history. He could see it in the flash of vulnerability and sadness that drifted over her face. Then she glanced to the spot behind him where Renee sat, and Libby's sadness morphed into something hard-edged, cold. And vengeful?

Cal's pulse jumped. He knew he'd hurt her when he'd married Renee, but he never imagined Libby would retaliate. Had Libby played a part, behind the scenes, in the D.A. office's tough negotiations on his plea?

A chill snaked through him. The glint of anger and distrust in Libby's glare was unmistakable. The acid bite of betrayal gnawed inside him. Didn't she know how it had killed him to leave her? Didn't she understand why he'd made the choices he had?

Cal's attorney cleared his throat, and Cal realized he'd lapsed into an awkward silence. His muscles tense, he tore his gaze away from Libby and addressed the judge again.

"My father raised me to respect and defend women." He took a slow breath to keep the pain of Libby's injustice out of his voice. He saw the stiff penalty the prosecution had demanded in a new light, and his gut twisted. "I couldn't sit back and watch Ralston hitting a lady." Cal took a deep breath and shook his head. "As a firefighter, my job is to protect and save lives. Ms. Dillingham was in danger, so I stepped in. I regret crossing the line with Ralston, but in the same situation, I would still defend any woman."

Judge Fitzpatrick arched a bushy eyebrow. "Anything else?"

Cal clenched his teeth, glanced at Libby again. "No, sir."

The judge unfolded the document in front of him and read, "Calvin Rutledge Walters, in accordance with the plea agreement reached with the Lagniappe, Louisiana, District Attorney's office, this court accepts your guilty plea to the charge of aggravated battery and sentences you to serve no less than two years and no more than five years in the parish correctional institution."

Cal's knees almost buckled, but he stood firm by sheer will.

He couldn't be certain, but Cal would have sworn Libby flinched when the gavel slammed down, sealing his fate. Yet while the bailiff snapped handcuffs on his wrists, she congratulated her colleagues on a job well done.

Renee marched up and shot him a disgusted look. "I'll be filing for divorce tomorrow. I should've done it long ago."

"Fine," he said, still watching Libby revel. "As long as you let me see Ally. You can't keep me away from my daughter."

Renee snorted. "Watch me. You're hardly in a position to fight for custody."

A tremor twisted through Cal as he met Renee's sneer. What if he lost his rights to see Ally while he was locked away? Ally was all he had left.

The cold steel handcuffs jerked his arms up as the bailiff led him out of the courtroom. Cal found Libby again as he shuffled toward the door. He gritted his teeth and kept an icy stare pinned on the woman he'd once believed he loved. Libby Hopkins had betrayed everything they'd once shared. He had no doubt she'd encouraged her colleagues' merciless dealings with him. Her vindictive glare confirmed that she'd sought revenge on him for her broken heart.

She'd helped destroy his life.

Chapter 1

Two years later

Another letter. Her stalker was nothing if not persistent.

Libby Hopkins's hands shook as she stared down at the telltale blue envelope. Dread twisted her stomach, but perverse curiosity, a need to know what she was dealing with made her open the letter and read.

To the bitch who ruined my life,
That was an ugly blue suit you wore yesterday. Made you look like a man. Under those suits, I bet you have a hot body. You should dress to show off your assets. Better yet, you should stay home, where a woman belongs, and stop playing the tough lawyer. Do you get a thrill destroying people's lives? You ruined my life, but I'll have the last laugh. When you least expect it.

Shuddering, she crunched the letter in her hand. He knew what she'd worn to court yesterday. He was watching her.

"Libby?"

She gasped, and the letter fluttered to the floor. Clapping a hand over her racing heart, she turned toward her office door and flashed an embarrassed grin at her colleague from the D.A.'s office.

"God, Stan, you scared the daylights out of me." She stooped to retrieve the letter and tossed it on her desk. "Try to make more noise when you sneak up on someone."

Stan Moore grinned and shoved his hands into his pressed and pleated khakis. "Like wear a cowbell maybe?"

She dropped into her chair. "There's an interesting idea. You could start a Lagniappe fashion trend."

Stan scratched his ear and grimaced. "I'll pass, thanks." He nodded toward the letter. "So what had you so engrossed that you didn't hear me sneaking up? Something break in the Chandler trial?"

Libby shook her head. "See for yourself. That's the fifth one I've gotten. Same handwriting, same stationery, same language. I'm beginning to take this guy seriously. I admit, I'm spooked."

Frowning, Stan took the letter from the desk and read. "Have you reported this to the police?"

"Yeah. A couple weeks ago. They can't tell me much. No prints on the letters, and the stationery is pretty generic."

He grunted. "And this one? You called it in yet?"

"Not yet." Libby rubbed her temple. "I've been so tied up with the Chandler case, I hadn't realized how out of hand this guy had gotten. I've had hate mail before—people letting off steam. No real substance. But this guy…" Libby bit down on her bottom lip as she thought back to the earlier letters. "His threats are escalating."

Stan tossed the letter onto her desk. "This is way beyond venting steam, Lib."

She shivered. "Yeah. I know."

"So…" He lifted the receiver of her desk phone and waved it at her. "Shall I report this letter or will you?"

Sighing, she pried the phone from his hand. "I'll call it in. But not now. I'm exhausted. Too tired to deal with police questions and protocol." She hung up the receiver, and Stan frowned. "When I get home. I promise. First, I just want a hot bath and a couple aspirin."

Pushing away from her desk, she collected her briefcase and brushed past him. Stan turned as she marched toward the door and continued glaring his disapproval. "You taking home the brief I gave you on the Browning case?"

She raised her overstuffed briefcase and nodded. "Got it. I'll go over it tonight and get back with you in the morning."

"That's what I was afraid of. If I know you, you'll put it first and forget about calling the cops."

Her shoulders drooped. "I won't forget."

"Promise me. 'Cause I *will* call if you don't. This guy sounds serious, and you know how dangerous he could be."

She shuddered. Yeah, she knew. The wackos she'd helped put away never ceased to amaze her with their capacity for evil.

"I'll call. I swear." She gave Stan an affectionate pat on the shoulder then headed out to the long, dim hall.

"Let me at least walk you out to your car." Stan kept pace beside her.

She grinned and shook her head. "No need. I've got Old Peppy with me." She held up the pepper spray on her key chain. "And I'm parked in the garage. Security's got cameras there. I'll be fine. Go back to whatever's got you here burning the midnight oil."

Stan hesitated, but finally shrugged and waved her off. "Just be careful."

"Always am." Despite her bone-deep weariness, she headed toward the elevator with a brisk stride, her head high and her eyes scanning her surroundings. As usual, she and Stan weren't the only ones working late, but the majority of the offices along the spartan corridor were already dark and empty. Her low-heeled pumps clicked on the linoleum floor, the sound reverberating in the deserted hall. Libby had walked this hallway at night for years. Yet tonight, with Stan's warnings fresh in her ears and the newest letter from her stalker tugging at her thoughts, the isolated corridor seemed gloomy. Unsettling. The spiders-on-your-skin feeling of having someone unseen watching you.

Libby jabbed the elevator call button with more force than needed, irked that she let herself get spooked so easily. Just the same, she repositioned her keys so the pepper spray was more accessible and ready with the flick of a finger.

She pulled in a cleansing breath while she waited for the elevator and mentally reviewed her schedule for tomorrow. In addition to the Browning hearing, she had depositions for the Gulliver case and motions to file with the Chandler case. Another twelve-hour day at least.

The elevator rumbled and groaned in the shaft, but the doors never opened. *Hadn't Sally Hickson spent two hours stuck in the elevator last week?*

Libby gave the elevator doors one last withering glance before she headed for the stairs. The exercise would be good for her. By working late, she'd missed her three-nights-a-week kickboxing class twice this week already.

The emergency exit door clanged closed behind her as she trudged down the first of twelve flights of stairs, lugging her overburdened briefcase. Until the Chandler case was settled, she'd probably be missing a lot more than just aerobics classes. Like a personal life.

When was the last time she'd gone to dinner with a friend?

If she couldn't remember, it had been too long. And forget about dating. A relationship took too much time and energy. She didn't need another demand on her day.

Or another broken heart. Libby's steps faltered. Where had that thought come from?

Easy. Her assistant Helen's little aside in their morning meeting that Cal Walters was out on parole.

Cal Walters. The memory of his laserlike blue eyes drilling into her from across the courtroom still haunted her. He hated her. He'd made that much clear with his icy glare. But why?

So much history…

Squaring her shoulders, she plodded on down the steps, shaking off the melancholy that settled over her whenever she thought about Cal. No point dredging up the *if onlys.*

As she reached the ninth floor, Libby heard a door a few floors above her open and close. She grinned wryly. Someone else had tired of waiting on the decrepit elevator.

The heavy, low-pitched thud of a man's footsteps joined the clack of her own shoes on the concrete steps. An uneasy jitter crawled up her spine. She was so isolated in the stairwell….

She pushed the nagging sensation aside, blaming Stan for making her too jumpy. Pausing at the seventh floor, she shifted her briefcase from one hand to the other. When she stopped, the heavier footsteps fell silent, too.

Libby furrowed her brow. Odd.

She started down the next flight. The man's footsteps resumed.

A prick of alarm nudged her to a faster pace. The person behind her matched her speed.

Don't panic. Clamping down on the swirl of jitters that skittered through her, she leaned over the railing to look up. "Stan? Is that you?"

No answer.

"Hello? Who's there?"

Silence.

She slowly took a few more steps. The thuds echoed her progress, but she saw no one.

"You're not funny, Stan!" She picked up her pace, wishing she'd accepted his offer of an escort.

The rasp of labored breathing wheezed behind her, growing louder—the ominous hiss of a viper waiting to strike.

Libby took the steps as quickly as she could without tripping. Her briefcase slapped her legs. Her heartbeat matched the frantic rhythm of her feet. Her pursuer kept time.

"I'm gonna get you, bitch!" His hoarse voice scratched through her like shards of ice, chilling her to the marrow. She swallowed the whimper that swelled in her throat.

Stay calm. Think.

With a sweaty hand, she clutched her pepper spray, flicked off the safety catch. Racing to the fifth floor, she mentally prepared for an attack. No one would hear if she screamed.

She was alone. On her own.

She could head for the lobby instead of the garage, but the night watchman's desk was down several long corridors.

No. She'd parked right across from the stairs. Much closer. If she could just reach her car and get inside…

His footsteps sounded closer. *Oh God, no!*

Move faster! Panic hovered in her chest.

She had to keep her head.

Turning at the third floor, her heel snagged. She stumbled. Her hip smacked the steel bar. Pain snaked down her leg, and she yelped. The misstep cost her valuable seconds. Ignoring the throb in her hip, she plowed on.

He was gaining on her.

Breathing raggedly, Libby bolted down the next set of stairs. It was him—the crazy who'd sent threats on blue paper. Her gut told her so.

Terror clambered up her throat, choking her. The heat of his breath scorched her neck, but when she turned, no one was there.

Don't look. Just run.

Second floor. First. Faster!

Libby slammed through the door at garage level. Steel bands of terror strangled her lungs. A white-hot sting speared her hip as she sprinted across the deserted parking area. Gasping in pain and panic, she frantically mashed the remote to unlock her Camry. The headlights flashed on, blinding her briefly as she neared the driver's side.

Her fingers fumbled with the ignition key. Cursing the shadows that cast the parking lot in darkness, she groped for the door. She jerked the handle of her Camry. The door didn't budge. Her head swam dizzily, and her hands shook as she tried the remote again.

Metal screeched, followed by an echoing boom. The stairwell door. He'd reached the garage. She sensed her stalker zeroing in on her, heard the shuffle of feet on concrete....

Please, please! Finally her door lock clicked off with a *snick*. Her knees wobbled with relief. Snatching the door open, she threw her briefcase inside.

She smelled him first.

The unmistakable scents of male sweat, deodorant soap and pine. An instant later, a large hand closed around her arm.

"Lib—"

She gasped and jerked against the man's grip. Spun. Raised the can of pepper spray.

With lightning speed, he knocked the vial from her hand. She screamed. Fought. Flailed at him with her fists.

He clamped a hand over her mouth. His long, hard body pinned her against the side of her car.

Still, she struggled, but her captor was an immovable wall of muscle.

The prosecutor in her cut through the haze of fear. Look at his face. Make a mental picture so you can give a description.

Assuming she got away.

Her stubborn will rejected the voice of doubt. She *would* get away. *No way* would she become a statistic.

Fighting his hold on her mouth, she angled her head. The light from her Camry spilled through the open door and illuminated his chiseled jaw, raven hair and laser-blue eyes.

A face she knew. Intimately.

"Hello, Libby," Cal drawled. "Long time no see."

Libby's face, already pale with fright, blanched a shade whiter. Cal frowned and eased his grip on her arm. Something had her spooked. Badly. She'd bolted through the door from the stairs as if she had the hounds of hell on her heels.

"Are you all right, Lib?"

The bedroom-brown eyes he remembered were now bright with fear and glanced nervously around the empty parking garage. But was she looking for someone to help her or searching for whatever demon had had her racing for her car?

The idea that she could be afraid of him gnawed his gut. No matter how much he hated what she'd done to his life, the years she'd stolen from him, the job he'd lost, he wasn't the kind of man who'd harm a woman. In all the months they'd spent together, hadn't she at least learned that about him?

"Mmmr wwrm," she mumbled from under his hand.

His scowl deepened, and he nailed her with a no-nonsense glare. "I'll let go of your mouth if you promise not to scream again. That last screech busted my ears."

Her dark eyes flashed indignantly.

Oh, yes, he remembered her stubborn pride. A steel will ran through her, equal to her passion. And her compassion.

He needed to reach her tender heart and her inordinate sense of responsibility today. She was his last hope, his only hope. Besides, she owed him.

Slowly he pulled his hand away, keeping a wary eye on her.

"How *dare* you scare me like that! What were you thinking? You deserve a face full of pepper spray for that stunt! Of all the—"

She swung at him.

But twenty-four months in prison had sharpened his reflexes, taught him to be quick on his feet and have eyes in the back of his head. He easily blocked her fist and pinned her wrist to the car. "Whoa! Settle down. What stunt are you talking about?"

She rolled her eyes then turned an icy glare on him. "On the stairs? The 'I'm gonna get you, bitch' crack? Following me, hiding from me, purposely freaking me out?"

The stairs? He thought about the terror that had filled her face when she'd burst through the garage door and run for her car. Unease jerked a knot in his gut. He cut a sharp glance to the stairs then back to Libby. "Someone followed you on the stairs? Did they hurt you?"

What had she said about a comment using the term *bitch?* His disquiet ratcheted up a notch.

She yanked her arm from his grip and righted her silk blouse. The soft fabric clung to her curves and made no secret of the feminine body beneath. "You're not funny. What were you trying to prove?"

"It wasn't me."

"Yeah, right." As she moved to climb into her Camry, he grabbed her arm and brought her dark eyes back to his. She pressed her lips in a thin line of irritation.

"I've been over there in my truck waiting for you for over an hour." With a hitch of his head, he directed her gaze to his dilapidated Chevy.

Suspicion narrowed her eyes but soon gave way to the pale, shaken look she'd worn when he'd first approached her. "You weren't just on the stairs? You swear?"

He snorted. "Not that my word has ever carried any weight with you, but…yeah, I swear." He felt the shudder that raced through her, and his chest tightened. Releasing her arm, he cast another look toward the stairwell door. "Want me to go check it out? See if anybody's in there?"

Stiffly she shook her head and sank onto the front seat. "I'm sure whoever was there is long gone now."

Her cheeks had regained most of their color. She pulled her lips into a pinched frown and raised her chin. "If I find out you're lying, I won't hesitate to have you hauled in for harassing an officer of the court."

Clenching his teeth, he fought down the rise of bile that rose in his throat. The last thing he needed was to give his parole officer an excuse to send him back to prison. "I thought you'd already done that. Isn't that what the last two years of my life have been about? Your revenge for my leaving you to marry Renee?"

Her eyes flickered with shock, and her lips parted in protest. "I didn't—"

"Trust me, marriage to Renee was a punishment in itself. Ally's the only good thing to come from that mistake."

Libby's expression softened a degree at the mention of Ally. Maybe his mission wasn't a lost cause.

As quickly as the tenderness appeared, it dissipated, replaced with hard-edged anger. "Your prison time had *nothing* to do with us and *everything* to do with the fact that you attacked a man!"

"My actions were justified! Was I supposed to stand back and let him beat the hell out of that woman?"

Libby threw her hands up and shook her head.

She jabbed a well-manicured finger in his chest and drilled

him with a stony glare. He remembered that stare from the courtroom two years ago. Cold. Flat. Void of emotion. "Save it. It's over, and I won't debate this with you."

She tried to close her door, and he blocked it. "Hang on. There's something else we need to discuss."

With a trace of suspicion still coloring her expression, she tipped her head. "What?"

Cal straightened and met her eyes. This was it. Everything he cared about rode on convincing Libby to go along with his plan. Drawing a deep breath, he plunged in. "I need your help."

She scoffed. "My help? Why?"

He crouched down to her eye level. When he braced a hand on the headrest by her cheek and leaned toward her, she stiffened. He moved close enough to smell the subtle musk scent of her perfume, close enough to feel her breath on his face, close enough to hear the sexy catch in her breath. His own pulse scrambled from the proximity.

Damn! She still affected him. Mesmerized him. Tortured him.

"Because the way I see it, you owe me."

She frowned and rolled her shoulders, clearly struggling to keep her cool. "I don't owe you squat, Walters."

He tensed as if she'd kicked him in the teeth. He'd expected this reaction from her, but that didn't make it easier to take. Curling his fingers into fists, he plowed on, struggling to rein in his temper. It wouldn't serve his cause to blow up at her now, put her on the defensive.

"Look me in the eye and tell me you didn't have anything to do with your office's hardball negotiation on my plea agreement. Tell me that during my sentencing you didn't once think about how I hurt you when I married Renee."

Surprise flitted across her sculpted, heaven-sent face.

"Yeah," he whispered. "I know I hurt you. And I'm sorry."

She knitted her brow and turned away, but not before he

glimpsed the pain in her eyes. Taking her chin in his hand, he angled her face toward him, felt her tremble.

The wall of her defenses came up in her eyes. The cold, blank prosecutor look returned. "What do you want, Cal?"

"I want my daughter. I want custody of Ally, but my prison record and my being a single father work against me."

"You want me to take your case? Is that it? Sorry, I don't do custody cases, but I'll be happy to recommend someone—"

"I have a lawyer."

She huffed. "Then why do you need me?"

"Respectability. Stability. Image."

Her face darkened. "I don't follow."

But the wary glint in her gaze said she did understand. The fluttering pulse at her throat gave away her panic.

"Hear me out, Libby." He ran his thumb along the line of her jaw, and heat flared in her eyes.

Good. He still affected her, too. He tugged his mouth sideways in a satisfied grin.

"You see, Renee's got a bum for a boyfriend and a new drug habit. She's neglecting Ally. I want to make a home for my daughter, a better one than the hellhole she lives in now. You can help give me that edge."

She was already shaking her head. But he wouldn't take no for an answer. Libby was his last chance.

"I want you to marry me, Lib. I need a wife."

Chapter 2

"This is insane! You can't be serious." Libby paced across the black-and-white-tile floor of her kitchen and sent Cal a dubious look.

"I'm dead serious." The penetrating blue of his returned gaze echoed his resolve. He'd sprawled casually in one of her antique ladder-back chairs, making himself at home. As if he thought he belonged in her kitchen. As if five years and so much painful history hadn't come between them.

While they waited for the pot of coffee she'd started, he propped a booted foot on another chair and watched her pace. Jewel, her gray cat, rubbed against Cal's leg, and he reached down to scratch her head while clucking his tongue. His calm repose stood in sharp contrast to the jitters dancing along Libby's nerves.

If Cal's crazy proposal weren't enough, she still heard the hiss of her stalker's voice echoing in her head. She shivered.

Had Cal not been in the garage, would the creep have caught her? Killed her?

The sooner she dealt with Cal, the sooner she could get rid of him and report her stalker's latest stunt to the police.

"I wouldn't be here if I weren't serious."

When Cal spoke, she snapped her gaze to his.

Cal. In her kitchen again after all these years. And back in her life, if he had his way.

Seeing his long, muscular legs stretched out comfortably at her table filled Libby with a déjà vu that swirled like warm honey in her blood. The sight was so familiar. So inviting.

So…wrong.

She shook her head briskly, clearing it of cozy memories and renewing her protest. "No. There are so many reasons why it's a bad idea, that—"

"Name one." He dropped his boot to the floor and stood. Moving to the gurgling coffeemaker, Cal poured himself a cup then leveled a challenging gaze on her as he sipped.

"It's just…wrong. It's—"

"Why?" He stepped closer to her, and her pulse scrambled. "Why is it so wrong?"

Angling her head to meet his gaze, she noticed the thin, pale scar on his square chin, nearly hidden in his bristly black stubble. She remembered that scar, remembered tracing it with her tongue in the heat of lovemaking. Catching her breath, she averted her eyes, struggled to calm her runaway heartbeat. "Because I…I—"

She couldn't think straight with all his raw male sensuality towering over her and the pine scent of his cologne teasing her senses. Rather than let him corner her, either with his body or his arguments, Libby ducked away, rubbing her arms.

"Are you sure you're all right? You were pretty shaken up earlier, and you still seem…edgy."

The concern in his tone unnerved her as much as the lingering thoughts of the man on the stairs. "I'm fine. Really."

She didn't want to discuss her stalker with Cal. That was her problem. She'd deal with it in her own way.

As she crossed the room, she turned the tables, wanting, *needing* to stay in control of this discussion. "Why marry me? Surely you have plenty of other women you could choose from."

"No one else has your power and prestige in court," he said. "Which I'll need to counter my prison record. And no one else owes me like you do."

Her spine stiffened. "I owe you nothing! Get that through your thick skull."

His smoldering stare closed the distance between them. Pitching his voice low, he said, "No one else got under my skin the way you did. We were good together, Lib. You know that. Not even prison could make me forget the way we burned up the sheets."

His husky tone slid over her like a lover's callused hand, rough yet gentle. Her skin tingled in response. Grasping for control, she swallowed the hitch in her breath and crossed her arms over her sensitized breasts so he wouldn't see how his words had affected her.

Her traitorous body's reaction to him was just one more reason why she couldn't afford to let him back in her life. Sure the sex had been good. Mind-blowing even. But the last thing she needed was another broken heart thanks to Cal Walters.

"You're crazier than I thought if you believe for a second that I'd ever sleep with you again."

He arched a dark eyebrow. "You sure about that? Your eyes are telling me you remember just how good it was between us. I'll bet that chemistry is still there."

He gave her an impudent grin, and she gritted her teeth.

"That's not lust, hotshot. It's shock. I can't believe you have the gall to ask anything of me considering our past." Drawing on her practiced courtroom control, she marched across the kitchen to him, her shoulders back. "We had great chemistry in bed. I'll give you that. But sex wasn't enough to save our relationship when you found out Renee was pregnant. You stood right here in my kitchen and told me it was over without so much as blinking. 'See ya later, Libby. It's been real. Gotta go marry someone else now.'" She gave a jerky wave, her hurt and anger coiled inside her, ready to spring.

A muscle in Cal's jaw twitched. "It didn't happen like that. You make it sound like I cheated on you. I never—"

Libby lifted a palm to stop him. "I know you were faithful, that it was over with Renee long before you met me. I've never questioned that. But one day everything was great, and the next you came by for five minutes to pick up your things and break my heart. Just *boom,* you're gone."

"Maybe I was a little quick in leaving, but I'm not good at goodbyes. I don't do big, emotional scenes. I honestly thought a clean break would be easier for both of us."

She flicked a hand and shook her head. "Whatever. It's over. Just forget it." Calming herself with a deep breath, she added, "Regardless of how you remember our breakup, the point is, we're history. You've got a lot of nerve coming to me, using our past as leverage to make demands and accusations. Get this much straight—I had nothing to do with the prosecution of your case. Zilch."

"Right." His features hardened, and the blaze in his eyes now had nothing to do with desire. "You just came to my sentencing to gloat, I suppose? I saw you conferring with the lead prosecutor."

"I came to your sentencing. But not to gloat." That he'd believe such a petty thing of her hurt. More than she cared to admit. His opinion shouldn't matter anymore. "And if I did talk with Stan, it was something personal, like, 'Where are you going for lunch?' Not anything about your case. Like I said, there are ethical canons that prevent—"

"Then why couldn't you look me in the eye? You knew I was getting railroaded, didn't you? I had six witnesses who said I was justified in defending that woman's life!"

"*Defending* her, yes. But the prosecution found just as many people who said that even after the threat had been contained, you kept hitting the guy. Your excessive force landed you in jail. Not me."

He'd made his bed, and he'd had to sleep in it.

Heat flashed over her skin. Bad analogy. Best not to think of *Cal* and *bed* in the same breath.

"Why don't you own up to your actions instead of pointing the blame at everyone else?"

He stiffened, and a muscle in his jaw ticked. "I owned up to my actions when I married Renee, didn't I? I wanted my daughter to have my name, to have a father."

"I understood the choice you made and why. It was the way you handled things between us that I have a problem with." *Like the way your leaving ripped my heart out.*

When Jewel mewled at her from the floor, Libby picked up her cat and cradled her, seeking solace in Jewel's gently rumbling purr.

More composed, she regarded Cal with as much dispassion as she could muster. "I've put you in the past and moved on. I suggest you do the same."

He narrowed his gaze on her and raised a black eyebrow. His piercing eyes stirred a quiver in her belly, and she hugged Jewel tighter.

Oh God, he always could see through her bravado. *That* was why she'd avoided looking at him at his sentencing. She couldn't let him see how much his ordeal hurt her, how frightened she was for him.

Obviously she needn't have been scared. He had an uncanny way of scraping past danger and landing on his feet. Like a cat with about nine hundred lives. She and her staid, black-and-white life were better off without him.

"Believe me, Lib, I've tried to move on. Unfortunately, you're kinda hard to forget."

"That's your problem. Not mine."

As she turned away, he caught her shoulders in a firm grip and stared into her eyes with his laser gaze. "No, Lib, my problem is, my daughter is living in a cesspool of an apartment with a mother who's turned to arm candy for recreation and deadbeat scum for company. I want Ally out of there. Permanently. And you're gonna help me get her."

Libby stroked the cat's head, thankful she had something to do with her restless hands. "And if I don't?"

Cal angled his chin, assessing her. "You may hate me, but I know you'd never refuse to help a four-year-old girl. Ally needs you. She needs *us* to get her into a safe home. Thanks to my criminal record, the only way the court will give me custody is if I can prove I'll provide her with the stability, safety and love she's not getting now. The love part I've got covered." Cal paused and rubbed the scar on his chin with his thumb, his jaw tight and his shrewd eyes gauging her reaction. When she continued to stare at him without speaking, he added, "I just need your co-operation, as my wife, for a couple years. Just until all the legal matters are settled and I have Ally free and clear. Then, if it's what you want—" he pressed his lips in a frown and sighed "—I'll let you walk away. No strings. Please, Libby, Ally is my heart, my everything. I'll do whatever it takes to protect her."

"Even marry a woman you don't love? Oh, wait…" She raised a finger as if struck by inspiration. "You already did."

Cal's jaw tensed even further, and his glare narrowed. "You know what it's like to live with an addicted mother."

Her lungs seized, and her grip on Jewel tightened.

"How dare you use my past against me," she whispered.

"You know how it feels to be—"

"Stop! I don't want to talk about my mother. When I told you about her, I warned you not to mention her or my past ever again." Her voice cracked, and she spun away from him.

Why had she trusted him with even a glimpse of her painful childhood? Just another mistake she'd made with Cal, another example of how she'd given too much of herself away. But never again.

Jewel squirmed and jumped down from her arms.

Libby fought to plug the wellspring of painful memories Cal had tapped. *Control.*

"Cal, we can't even be in the same room for five minutes without arguing. What kind of home will that be for Ally?"

"A whole lot better than the one she's in now. I didn't say I had all the answers. It'll take effort from both of us to make this thing work. But I'm willing to do whatever it takes, for Ally's sake."

Libby opened her mouth to tell him there were other solutions to his quandary that didn't involve her and a marriage of convenience. Social workers, counseling for Renee, another candidate to be his temporary wife—anything!

She dusted cat hair off her work clothes and pushed aside the uneasy prickle at the thought of some other woman marrying Cal.

Whipping out his wallet, he flipped to a picture of a blue-eyed cherub with her daddy's inky black hair.

A sharp pang pinched her heart.

Cal must have seen her weakening. He circled and moved in for the kill. "Can you tell *her* no? She's an innocent in this whole mess. She deserves better than roaches in her bed at night and going to day care with no breakfast."

Libby scowled and marched to the refrigerator, where she yanked out a quart of milk. "It couldn't be as bad as that. Renee would never—"

"Renee doesn't even know the day of the week most times. She and her live-in dirtwad are usually too stoned to take care of themselves, much less Ally!" He slapped his wallet shut and jammed it back in his pocket.

Setting the milk on the counter by the coffeepot, Libby straightened her back and lifted her chin. "There are laws to protect children in cases like this. Someone from Child Welfare should—"

"No! Not the courts. Ally doesn't need bureaucracy or some government yahoo. I'm her father. *I* want her. She needs *me!*" He thrust his hands through his hair and growled his frustration. The muscle in his jaw jumped wildly as he ground his teeth.

The passion saturating his tone and the worry creasing his face reminded Libby of the man she'd grown close to, fallen in love with, five years ago. For all his machismo and toughness, his tender and compassionate side had touched her heart.

"When Renee and I divorced two years ago, I was awarded visitation rights. Every other weekend, Ally is supposed to be with me. While I was in prison, I obviously couldn't take my weekends, and since my parole three weeks ago, I've only had one weekend with my daughter. But I saw enough that weekend to convince me Ally was in jeopardy. My lawyer filed the petition for custody Monday. I have to do this soon or I could lose my case." He gave her a pointed look. "Again."

She blinked back the sting of tears, the pain of all they'd lost and her own concern for his daughter. Pulling in a deep breath, she battled the turmoil rolling through her. *Stay in control.*

How could she do it? She had enough to worry about with a stalker following her. How could she tangle her life up with Cal's again?

"So what'll it be, Libby? Will you help us? I give you my word, you'll be free to go, to file for divorce, once I know my rights to Ally are secure."

A throwaway marriage. Just as their first relationship had been disposable to him. She rubbed a throbbing ache growing at her temple. "I don't know, Cal. I need time to think."

Why were personal decisions always so difficult? What if she made the wrong choice and screwed up her life or someone else's? She thought she'd outgrown the nerve-racking responsibility of no-win choices that had been her mother's legacy.

She needed black-and-white. Clear-cut answers and certainties. Someone she could count on. Especially now while this stalker was out there watching her. But nothing about Cal was black-and-white.

He spread his hands in supplication. "Ally and I need your help stacking the deck in our favor. I don't want the court to have any reason to deny my motion for custody."

Gray. That's what Cal was. Or rather, he was passionate shades of red and green and gold. A confusing blur of color.

As if to punctuate this fact, his eyes turned the shade of a stormy azure sea, brimming with heartbreaking desperation. Desperation she'd seen too often in her mother's eyes while growing up.

"Please?" The whispered plea, reverberating with a father's love and a proud man's struggle with humility, twisted inside her.

"I'll think about it."

But she knew she'd lost.

The man behind her quickened his pace. She heard his ragged breathing, smelled his fetid breath. She tried to run, but her mother held on to her feet, sobbing. "Help me, Libby. I don't know what to do!"

"I'm going to get you, bitch," her pursuer growled from inches behind her. But she couldn't see him. It was dark. So dark.

His footsteps pounded on the stairs. Louder. Louder.

"Libby!"

She woke with a gasp and jackknifed up in her bed.

But the pounding continued. She swept a glance around her dim bedroom, orienting herself. Jewel slept draped over her legs, a feline deadweight. Seven-oh-three glowed from her bedside clock. She'd only been dreaming about her stalker, but the person beating on her front door was real.

"Come on, Lib! Open up!"

Cal. He may have stayed away yesterday, given her a little room to think, but danged if he wasn't back, bright and early, barely thirty-six hours later—no doubt to demand an answer. Honestly, she was surprised he'd given her breathing room all of Friday rather than pressing her for a commitment last night.

Groaning, she scooted Jewel aside and dragged herself from her warm covers. She hurried to the door before Cal's yelling woke the neighbors.

"Do you know what time it is?" she snapped, still edgy from her nightmare. She poked her arms in the robe she'd snatched from the foot of the bed and finger-combed her hair with jerky swipes.

He quirked an irreverent grin that shot a sizzle straight to her core. "And good morning to you, too, sunshine."

Morning light cast his face in a golden glow, and his tight T-shirt delineated every muscle in his chest and arms. There should be a law against him looking so delicious at this hour. Grumbling, Libby rubbed her sleep-blurred eyes. "Geez, Walters! Roosters aren't even up yet."

She tried to slam the door on Cal, but he caught it with his boot toe. Tugging her robe closed at the throat, she frowned. "Go away! Saturdays are for sleep."

"Not this Saturday. This is my weekend with Ally, and you and I are going to pick her up. So go get dressed and I'll start some coffee."

"Why?"

"Because you look like you could use a strong cup."

She flashed him a dark scowl. "I mean, why am I going with you to get Ally?"

"Simple. I want you to see for yourself the conditions she lives in."

Libby shuddered. She didn't need to see. Ever since Cal had described Ally's living conditions, she'd replayed memories of her youth, of surviving similar circumstances. "Forget it. I'm not going. Damn it, Cal! I haven't even agreed to your crazy marriage plan."

"But you've thought about it, right? Thought about what it would mean to Ally?"

"Oh, I thought about it, all right. I spent most of the night rehashing all the reasons why a fake marriage would be a mistake." Libby marched toward the kitchen, needing something to do with her hands more than she needed the hot coffee she started.

"Not fake, Lib. The marriage would be very real." He stepped up behind her, close enough for her to smell the crisp scent of his deodorant soap over the rich aroma of coffee grounds. The tantalizing smell brought to mind thoughts of Cal in his morning shower.

"So…if you haven't made up your mind, then I still have a shot at convincing you?"

Libby gritted her teeth as she scooped coffee out of the canister into the filter basket. Whenever she closed her eyes, she saw the angel-sweet face of Cal's daughter.

Can you tell her no?

Cal was right. She knew how it felt to be neglected, how lonely and frightened Ally had to be.

When sleep had finally come last night, Cal's voice had become her mother's. An echo of the past. Memories she couldn't outrun.

You have to help me, honey. I can't do it alone.

You've ruined everything, Libby! How could you do this to me?

She flinched when Cal touched her arm and stopped her from dumping another load of coffee.

"Just how strong do you intend to make that?" Amusement laced his tone and chafed her raw nerves.

When he took the scoop from her hand, she realized she'd been dumping grounds into the filter without measuring. Irritated by her inattention, she flipped the top down on the machine and jabbed the start button. "I can't marry you. I can refer you to people who will help with Ally's situation, but I—"

"No!" Cal touched a finger to her lips to halt her argument. Even that mild contact made Libby's heart jump, and the spike of adrenaline left her trembling.

Geez, that dream had left her jittery, reviving the terror she'd known on the stairs. The stairs…

Libby's thoughts snagged on the memory. What was she thinking? How could she consider bringing Cal and his daughter into her life while she was being stalked?

She schooled her features as Cal leaned toward her, his arm braced on the counter.

"Go with me this morning and see for yourself what I'm talking about. See for yourself how much she needs our help."

"It's not that I don't care what happens to Ally—I do! The thing is…I'm embroiled in a touchy situation."

Cal raised one dark eyebrow. "What kind of situation? Are you involved with someone else?"

She sighed. "No, it's nothing like that. I…someone is watching me. Sending me letters. Trying to frighten me."

Cal drew himself to his full, impressive height. "Watching you? Like a stalker?"

Libby stalled, turning to pour a cup of coffee. She didn't

want to sound like an alarmist. And she really didn't want Cal meddling in her affairs, which she was certain he would do if he knew the whole truth. "He's more of an annoyance than anything. It's no big deal, but I can't justify bringing you or Ally into the mix right now."

She gazed at him over the rim of her mug as she sipped, trying to act as unconcerned about the stalker as she claimed.

A dark shadow crossed Cal's face. "The other night in the garage… Is that what had you spooked?"

She nodded and glanced away from his incisive stare. "I thought I heard him following me."

"What do the cops say about this? You have reported this guy to the police, right?"

She snorted. "You sound like Stan. Of course I've called the cops. As soon as you left Thursday night, I called, and they came to take my statement about his latest ploy. They're working on it, and they'll catch him. Soon."

Please, God. Her nerves couldn't handle much more of the creep's scare tactics.

"Has he ever hurt you? Do you think he's dangerous?"

I'm gonna get you, bitch. She suppressed a shudder.

"No." *Maybe.* "Look, I know his type. Hateful letters are part and parcel of my job. He probably just wants to scare me, but I won't let him. If I refuse to let him manipulate me, eventually he'll get tired of his games and go away."

Cal frowned. "You don't really believe that, do you?"

"Yes." *No.* But maybe if she kept telling herself she had no reason to be worried, she would eventually believe it.

He arched his eyebrow again, clearly unconvinced. "Seems to me this guy is another reason you *should* marry me."

She choked on her coffee. "What?" she sputtered.

"I can protect you."

She thunked her mug down on the counter. "I don't need

protection. Besides, what about the potential danger you'd put yourself in?"

Cal brushed a wisp of hair from her cheek, tucking it behind her ear. "I can take care of myself."

"So can I." She ducked away from his hand. The mere touch of his finger against her cheek curled her toes, sent ribbons of pleasure swirling inside her. Damn it, spending any length of time with this man threatened her libido. And the shabby patchwork of her reconstructed heart.

"What about Ally?" she asked. "Aren't you worried about her being at risk from this guy?"

"He'd have to come through me to get to Ally. Or to you. I would never let that happen. She's at far greater risk as long as she's living in that dump with Renee. That's the problem I'm concerned with."

Cal slid warm hands over her shoulders and gripped her arms, pinning her with an intense blue gaze. "Please, Lib. Go with me to get Ally. It's important to me that you understand what's at stake."

She knew the stakes better than he did. To her heart. And to Ally. She'd lived it.

The answer wasn't clear-cut, black or white.

As much as she wanted to tell him no, the incident on the stairs, her nightmare had rattled her more than she cared to admit. Maybe having Cal around *would* give her more protection. And a little peace of mind.

But protection wasn't justification for getting married. Especially not to Cal. Letting Cal back into her life posed a far more imminent danger to her heart. Her throat tightened. Damn it, he'd already made a riot of her emotions.

"If I go…" she began, hating the seductive rasp in her voice.

The smoky haze in his eyes told her he'd noticed, too. His gaze locked on her mouth, and she fought the urge to retreat a step. Or to lean in and kiss him. She cleared her throat before she went on. "If I go with you now, you'll take my no for an answer and leave me alone?"

"You won't tell me no." His grin was confident and disarming. "As I recall, you never could."

Libby scowled at his back as he sauntered toward her living room. Maybe the *old* Libby never could tell him no, but since he'd walked out on her five years ago, she'd changed.

Chapter 3

Nothing had changed at Renee's apartment since he'd been by earlier in the week. Except perhaps a few more crusty dishes were piled in the sink and on the coffee table. A stronger stench of rotten garbage permeated the air.

Cal watched Libby react to the scene. With her eyes wide and her stance rigid, she pressed a hand over her mouth and took in the chaos of clutter and filth.

"You're early." Renee stumbled back from the door, tripping past the spot where her boyfriend Gary—or Jerry, or whatever the creep's name was—lay passed out on the floor. Judging from Renee's glazed expression, she was high again. Surprise, surprise.

"Actually I'm not. It's past nine. Where's Ally?"

"Asleep, I guess. Try her room." Renee rubbed her face hard and winced. Black circles ringed his ex's eyes, and baggy clothes hung on her rail-thin frame. She'd lost too much weight in the last few months. Cal's stomach knotted. Renee had been vibrant and beautiful when they'd first met. Her mind had been sharp. He hated seeing her like this. If Renee took such poor care of herself, what did Ally endure?

"Renee, look at this place. Don't you understand that the authorities could take Ally away, put her in foster care, if you don't get your act together?"

Renee scoffed. "I'm her mother. They can't take her from me. And neither can you. I have rights."

"They *can* take her away, and they will. What about Ally's right to have a clean home? To have someone love her and take care of her?"

"I love her!" Renee wobbled, and Cal steadied her with a hand on her arm.

He mustered every ounce of his patience. "Then get clean. I'm not fighting for custody to hurt you, Renee. I'm doing it because I love Ally. I don't want to see her suffer."

Renee pulled free of his grip. "She's fine."

Grunting his disgust and frustration, Cal stalked toward the back of the tiny apartment and nearly collided with a scruffy man who came out of the bathroom, zipping his pants.

"Look where you're going, man," the hoodlum grumbled, bumping past Cal on his way back to the front room.

"Who the hell are you?" Cal followed the man into the living room and divided a glare between the man and Renee.

"Who's askin'?" The stranger gave Libby, who still hovered by the door, a suspicious look. "Hey, do I know you?"

Cal tensed, ready to intervene if the scumbag took another step toward Libby.

She raised her chin and appraised the man with a honed look, one that doubtlessly brought hostile witnesses to their knees. "Not unless you've had a reason to appear in court recently."

Cal felt a quick tug of pride. Libby personified strength under fire. Cool and poised. Other than two nights ago in the parking garage, when she'd been so uncharacteristically rattled, he'd only seen her experience meltdown between the sheets. During sex, she let go, burned hot and fast like a forest fire in a drought. When his libido pulsed to life, he firmly pushed thoughts of tangling limbs with Libby aside for another time.

"That's right." The slimeball wagged a finger toward Libby. "You're the skirt from the D.A.'s office." When the disheveled man stepped toward her, Cal instinctively moved to Libby's side.

"So, you're familiar with the prosecutor's office, Mr.—" Libby tipped her head, tapping a finger to her lips as if trying to remember something. "I'm sorry, who did you say you were?"

The bum flashed an oily smile. "You can just call me Roach, lawyer babe."

"Roach, huh? Interesting. Family name?" Libby parried.

Roach chortled and flopped back onto the stained cushions of Renee's couch. On the floor, Gary/Jerry/whatever-his-name-was, stirred, coughed then lurched for an empty glass as he retched.

Cal felt Libby's shudder only because he'd put his hand on her arm to guide her away from Roach. "Come on. Let's find Ally and get the hell out of here," he said under his breath.

With a nod, she followed him back to the corner bedroom, where Ally's toys littered the floor.

The bed was empty.

Anxiety flashed through Cal with the force of a backdraft. "Ally?"

Darting forward, he ripped the covers from the bed, searching for his daughter, even though the girl clearly wasn't there. He cut a sharp glance toward Libby, whose face reflected the same concern and confusion that knifed him.

"Renee!" He stormed out to the living room, his body tense with fury, his stomach knotted with dread. "She's not there! Where the hell is my daughter?"

Renee clutched her head and slouched in her seat, curling into a tiny ball. "Don't yell! Damn, my head's gonna explode."

"Where's Ally? She's not in her room!"

His ex sighed heavily. "Have you looked in her closet?"

Beside him, Libby gasped. He spared her only a brief I-told-you-so glance as he rushed back to look for Ally.

When he snatched open the closet door, the flood of light from the bedroom revealed hidden horrors in the small, dark space. Cal winced as the odor of urine hit him. A spider scurried under a box in the corner.

A raven-haired moppet raised bleary eyes to squint at him. "Mommy?"

Emotions slammed into him. A tangled mix of relief, outrage and anguish squeezed his heart and brought him to his knees. "Oh, baby girl. It's Daddy. Why are you in here?"

Ally whimpered when he leaned down to scoop her up in his arms. "No! Leave me alone!"

"It's all right, Ally. It's Daddy. Remember last weekend when we went to the park, I asked if you'd like to come visit me sometime? You said you did."

Ally nodded.

"Well, I'm here so you can visit my apartment, stay with me for the weekend. Would you like that?"

"Can we go to the park again?"

"Sure, kitten. Whatever you want." He tucked Ally under his chin and turned to carry her out. Her clothes were damp. "Ally, what happened to your nightgown? It's wet."

Ally sniffed. "I'm sorry. Didn't mean to."

"Didn't mean to what?" Cal coaxed.

"Wet my pants," she whispered. "That man was in the potty, and I had t'go."

"Aw, sweetie. It's okay. We'll get you cleaned up. C'mon."

Libby stood two paces from the closet door, her face white

and her features a mask of horror. He'd never seen Libby cry, but tears filled her eyes now. Her whole body shook.

"Still think you can tell us no?" he rasped, wishing he could cry, too. Wishing he could throw back his head and howl for the suffering his little girl had endured without him.

Sucking in a harsh, strangled breath, Libby bolted from the room.

Libby sat inside Cal's truck and wrapped her arms around herself. She concentrated on calming her ragged breaths and erasing the ugly memories that had chased her from Renee's apartment. When a movement outside the pickup caught her eye, she jerked her gaze up, her pulse jumping.

Deep breaths. Don't lose control.

Cal approached the passenger's door, carrying his daughter on one shoulder and a duffel bag slung over the other. Libby climbed from the truck on shaky legs and pulled the seat forward so he could put Ally in the back. A biting January wind whipped around her, and she shivered.

"Thanks." Sparing Libby a quick glance, Cal settled Ally on the back seat and gently tucked his jacket around her. "Sorry we took so long. I had to pack her things and get her changed into something clean."

"Mmm," she hummed in acknowledgment, certain she couldn't speak yet without her voice cracking. Bad enough she'd lost it in the apartment and fled like a startled doe. *Way to keep it together, Counselor.*

Libby avoided Cal's eyes as he lifted Ally's small duffel into the truck bed. She'd seen his haunted despair when he'd found his daughter, and she couldn't face his tormented gaze again. Not until she'd gotten a firmer grip on her own composure.

Ally leaned against the far side of the truck, her eyes squeezed tightly closed. Too tight to truly be asleep. Libby recognized Ally's game of possum for what it was—avoidance. How many times had Libby pretended to be asleep to avoid facing her mother's drinking and boyfriends?

A rock settled in Libby's chest, choking her. An oppressive omen. The weight of dread.

She was going to tell Cal yes.

Damn it, she knew marrying him, for whatever reason, was flirting with disaster. But the ghosts that had rattled their chains in Renee's apartment could not be ignored. The past could not be repeated. She couldn't leave Ally to endure what she herself had barely survived.

Even if it meant putting her heart on the line with Cal.

Despite any possible threat from the stalker, first and foremost, Ally needed protection from her mother's bad habits and neglect.

Turning from Ally, Libby fastened her seat belt as Cal climbed into the truck. She felt his gaze on her, but kept her attention focused on the apartment stairs.

Roach ambled out wearing a long trench coat and lighting a cigarette. The scruffy man, whose bleached hair spiked in all directions, seemed vaguely familiar. After a while, though, the parade of deadbeats through the court system began to blur. Still, she searched her memory for a previous run-in with Roach.

Cal touched her arm, and she flinched as if burned. Her emotions were too close to the surface. Even the comforting graze of his hand triggered an electric reaction that crackled along her raw nerves.

"You okay?"

No, she longed to wail. *I've just revisited my childhood and really need for you to hold me for a minute. Or a week.*

She gave him a curt nod. "Fine."

"You know, Renee hasn't always been this way. When I met her, she was perky and intelligent. She had so much potential. Seeing her like this…"

Judging from the grim set of Cal's jaw and his white-knuckle grip on the steering wheel, he had plenty he wanted to say but couldn't because of the four-year-old in the back seat.

As they headed out of the parking lot, Cal's eyes shifted to Roach, and a growl rumbled from his throat. "That guy's trouble. I don't want Ally around creeps like him. Before Renee got involved with Gary/Jerry/what's-his-name, before her next hit was more important than our daughter, she wouldn't have been caught dead hanging around with a jerk like that."

Libby cut her gaze back to the man in question. "The fact that he knew I was from the D.A.'s office tells me he's had a few scrapes with the law. I'd be willing to bet he's her dealer."

Dismay filled Cal's face then shifted to cold determination. "Great. Renee's consorting with criminals. More ammunition for my case."

Cal gunned the engine and peeled out of the parking lot. He drove in stony, brooding silence.

She stole glimpses of his hard jaw and the unshaven shadow of beard that gave him a dangerous look. His appearance belied the gentle soul she knew lived beneath the rough-edged exterior. Her fingers itched to comb back the black hair curling over his collar and savor the rasp of his stubble beneath her hands. Five years ago, that weekend beard had abraded the tenderest places of her body, left his brand on her skin. The way his memory left its mark upon her heart.

She swallowed hard, forcing down the knot in her throat. He'd made his choice. He'd left her, thrown away what they'd had together. Only a fool would set herself up for that kind of fall a second time.

After a few minutes, the tense quiet in the truck became almost more unbearable than the thought of rehashing what had just happened, than facing the inevitable question: *What are you going to do now, Libby?*

She couldn't walk away. She never could. Not from her mother. Not from Cal. And certainly not now from Ally.

She glanced into the back seat where Ally slept. The picture of this frail angel huddled in the back of her closet amid the filth was an image burned forever in Libby's mind.

"All right," she said without looking at Cal. She turned to watch the stark, winter-bare trees pass outside her window and shivered. "I'll do it. I'll marry you."

Cal darted an uncertain look across the front seat then gaped as if he thought he'd heard wrong. Finally, he nodded.

"Good." He sighed wearily and rubbed the scar on his chin with his palm. "Thank you."

"But I have conditions."

He chuckled wryly. "Figures."

"Our marriage will be in name only. Separate beds."

Scoffing, Cal shook his head. "No way. The court has to believe I'll give Ally a *Leave it to Beaver* home life. Ward and June didn't keep separate quarters."

Libby snorted. "Pal, if you're looking for June Cleaver, you've come to the wrong woman."

She turned to check on Ally again, in time to see a pair of curious blue eyes snap shut. A grin ghosted across Libby's lips, and she faced the front again, giving Cal's daughter the privacy she wanted and the freedom to observe her father and his friend uninterrupted.

"I'm not asking you to make meat loaf and vacuum the house in high heels and pearls," Cal said. "But I have to show the court that Ally will have a stable, two-parent home where she'll be safe and loved."

"This one's a deal breaker. You're in the guest room, or I walk. I'm *not* sharing a bed with you."

A muscle in his jaw twitched, and he sent her a hooded glance. "Good enough. For now."

He turned back to stare out the windshield, and a strange

hollowness poked at her. Irritated with her reaction, she squeezed the door handle even tighter. She was *not* disappointed that he'd accepted her term of celibacy so readily.

"Fine." And she was fine, too. Getting into bed with Cal Walters again, no matter how tempting, would be the height of stupidity.

At a traffic light, Cal drummed the steering wheel with his fingers. "But you'll need to keep up appearances in public. The world, the judge, has to believe we're happily married… in every way."

"Fine." Libby pressed a hand to her stomach, hoping to calm the swirl of apprehension growing inside her.

Happily married? To Cal?

Not so many years ago, sharing her life with Cal had been her greatest hope, her dream. Now the proposition seemed more of a nightmare. A recipe for heartbreak.

"All right, then. Make time on your calendar first thing Monday to get the license." Cal cut a sideways glance at her. "With the three-day waiting period, the soonest we can get married is Thursday."

She shook her head. "I have a case going to trial Thursday. I'll be in court all day."

"All day?"

"There'll be a recess for lunch, but—"

"Good. We'll just grab a judge during your break and do it then."

"Cal, I—" She stopped, unsure what her objection was. But she couldn't shake the foreboding sense that she was making a terrible mistake.

He hoped to God he wasn't making a terrible mistake. Having listened to his mom and stepdad bicker over everything from scrambled eggs to the electric bill, he knew what it was like to grow up in a house rife with hostility.

An all-too-familiar prick of guilt needled him. Hell, the hostility should have been a clue to what was really going on. He should have known. Should have done something sooner.

One thing was certain—Libby would never endure from him what his mother had with his stepfather. Never.

He watched from the door of his bedroom as Libby stroked a gentle hand over Ally's cheek and tucked a teddy bear under his daughter's arm. Libby had dived right in beside him, helping with Ally's bath and fixing a hot brunch of pancakes and bacon before they shuffled his drowsy daughter off to nap.

Despite her kindness to Ally, the silent treatment and physical distance Libby kept from him conveyed her feelings about their relationship loud and clear. Not exactly the parental atmosphere he wanted for his daughter.

He'd hoped the warm, compassionate Libby who had stolen his heart years ago would be his wife. Every night of his incarceration, he'd dreamed of the woman who'd made him laugh, who'd kissed him in the rain and made s'mores with him over the fireplace flames. After three passionate months together, they'd been on the verge of taking their affair to a deeper, more personal level when Renee had called to say she was five months pregnant with Ally. He never got the chance to probe the deeper layers of the fun-loving and complex woman Libby was, the woman he'd started to love.

He sighed his regret. Maybe he'd never regain what he'd lost with Libby. She could resent him all she wanted as long as Ally had the love she deserved.

He stepped out of the way so Libby could back from the room and pull the door closed.

"I have to leave."

He cocked his head. "Excuse me?"

She gave him a pointed look. "Leave. Go home. Your little field trip this morning has put me behind schedule." She squared her shoulders and jutted out her chin. "I have things to do today."

"Yeah, things like making plans with me about how this arrangement will work. Spending time with Ally. Getting to know her." He hooked his thumbs in his jeans and frowned.

"No…like researching an important case at the library. And taking Jewel to the vet for her shots." She brushed past him and began gathering her coat and purse. "I have to pick up my dry cleaning and get the oil changed on my car and—"

"I can change your oil. No point paying someone else to do it."

She paused in the middle of pulling on her coat. "I don't need you to change my oil. I'm perfectly happy having my mechanic take care of it." She jabbed a finger in his direction as she slung her purse over her shoulder. "I agreed to this plan of yours, and I'll do what I can to help you get custody of Ally. But that doesn't mean you can come in and dictate my life."

"I don't intend to dictate your life, but if this marriage is going to work, if it's going to look convincing, you're going to have to find time for us. You can't bury yourself in your job to hide out from us."

As soon as the words left his mouth, he wished he could reel them back. For Ally's sake, he needed to work on smoothing the rough edges in his relationship with Libby.

She pulled herself to her full height and pressed her mouth in a taut line. "What's wrong with working hard at a job I enjoy?"

He shrugged and stepped closer. "Nothing at all. It's great you enjoy your work."

Her dark eyes sparked with suppressed pain and anger. "At least I can count on my job being there when I need it. That's more than I can say about some people."

Her gibe sliced deep, a direct hit to ancient guilt. But she had no way of knowing about his mother. Did she? As close as they'd been, he'd never shared his darkest secret with her.

He determinedly kept his expression neutral, giving away none of his rioting emotions.

"I help get criminals off the street," she added. "It's satisfying."

Moving within inches of her, he reached for the lapel of her coat and smoothed a wrinkle. Beneath his touch, she stiffened, drew herself up a notch tighter, like a coil ready to spring.

"More satisfying than your personal relationships?" *Damn it, why did he keep goading her?*

Despite his efforts to set his feelings aside for Ally's sake, the hurt and anger he'd nourished through his incarceration bubbled to the surface. "I had a job I loved, too, you know."

She stopped on her way out and cut a startled glance over her shoulder.

"I loved being a firefighter. Loved knowing I was making a difference, saving lives, helping my community the only way I knew how. But when I was convicted, I lost my firefighting credentials."

He saw the question in her eyes and her reluctance to ask it. "No, I can't get my old job back," he volunteered. "But I've taken a job my parole officer found for me, working road construction with the highway department. I had to have some income, some employment, if I wanted to fight for Ally."

Libby closed her eyes and turned away. "I'm sorry."

"Are you?" He hated the resentment that slipped into his tone when he considered all he'd lost. A loss she'd played a part in.

Pivoting to face him, she straightened her spine and raised her chin. "Yes, I am sorry you lost your job. I know what it meant to you. But sometimes our actions have consequences that reach further than the here and now. If people would stop and think before they went off half-cocked, it would sure make my job simpler."

He braced a hand on the door frame and leaned closer, breaching the breathing space she'd kept between them all morning. "Libby, you and I both know I don't do *anything* half-cocked."

Color flamed in her cheeks, and though she pursed her lips in a scowl, a flicker of desire danced through her mahogany eyes. *So she did remember.*

The floral scent of her shampoo tickled his senses, and he battled the urge to kiss her firmly set mouth. He could so easily shock that smugness from her expression, stoke the passion he knew lurked just below the surface.

He settled for giving her a knowing grin. He had time. Time to remind her of the heat they'd once shared. Time to smooth away her prickly edges and find the soft, willing woman he'd known.

Time to warm her back into his bed.

She took a slow, deep breath before answering, clearly composing her reply, struggling to remain calm. With her cool detachment back in place, Libby buttoned her coat. "You know how to reach me."

By phone maybe, but how did he reach her heart again? How did he break through the stony walls of resistance to find the flesh-and-blood woman he had once loved?

When she opened the door, he caught her arm and turned her to face him. "If Ally feels up to it later, I thought we'd go to Tony's for pizza. Go with us. I think you should spend a little time getting to know her before we get married."

She opened her mouth, ready to protest, but finally sighed and gave a quick nod. "I'll meet you there. Call me when you're ready to go."

She shrugged out of his grip and backed out the door. He told himself his disappointment in her abrupt departure had more to do with Ally's needs than his own. Forget the fact that he'd spent the past two years in prison waiting for his chance to look Libby in the eye and ask her, Why? How did we end up like this?

They'd lost precious years together, but now he had a second chance.

This time, he wouldn't let her get away.

She couldn't wait to get out of there.

Libby shifted on the vinyl booth seat and cast an uneasy gaze around the pizzeria.

The atmosphere at the family-oriented restaurant was too…*familial.* To the casual observer, she, Cal and Ally probably looked like just another happy family enjoying a Saturday night out. Certainly that was the effect Cal was after. But Libby wore the role like outgrown shoes. Playing Cal's wife pinched and rubbed uncomfortably.

"When you finish eating, we can play some of those video games, if you want," Cal told Ally, who huddled in the corner of the booth clutching her teddy bear. He flashed Libby an awkward smile. "I'm glad you made it."

Cal gave a meaningful nod in Ally's direction.

Libby searched for some gesture to reach the shy girl, when what she wanted was to tell Cal she'd changed her mind. She couldn't go through with his marriage plans, couldn't pretend domestic bliss when the concept was so foreign to her. Acting the part of his partner, his friend, *his lover,* struck far too close to the memories she needed to keep at bay. Letting Cal anywhere near the vicinity of her heart was trouble.

But she had only to look at Ally, still silent, still withdrawn, still watching her and Cal with caution and curiosity in her cerulean eyes, and Libby knew she had no alternative. She had to help Ally.

For once she wished the choice weren't so clear. The black-and-white of Ally's situation only made things with Cal more gray. More confusing.

"So, Ally…" Libby studied the tiny girl and floundered for something to say.

How could she face down the most hardened criminals in the courtroom every day, pry confessions out of the most tight-lipped conspirators, yet be left tongue-tied by this wide-eyed child? "Do you think Mr. Bear is going to eat much pizza? I hear that after sleeping all winter, bears can get really hungry."

Ally hugged her bear tighter, as if she thought Libby would try to steal her stuffed friend.

Libby glanced at Cal and immediately wished she hadn't. The eager hopefulness in his expression, the desperation and pure love for his daughter, wrenched something deep inside her. Cal stroked Ally's tumble of raven curls, pushing strands behind her ear with a gentle finger.

His daughter whimpered and turned her face. He backed off, pulling his hand away, palm up, in surrender. The pain that skated across his face sliced through Libby with a jagged edge.

"She barely remembers me," he whispered darkly. Frustration corded the muscles in his shoulders and arms, and on the table, he balled his hands in tight fists. When he met Libby's eyes, raw emotion swirled in the piercing blue depths of his gaze. "Since my visitations started, things have gone well enough. I'm trying to explain to her what's happening, who I am, how much I love her, but she still acts like I'm a stranger to her sometimes."

"Kids her age are often shy around adults. Give her time."

"I don't have time!" he grumbled under his breath. "The hearing on my custody suit comes up in a few weeks."

"She'll come around, Cal. Just don't push her."

A waitress arrived with their pizza, and Cal quickly replaced his scowl with a tight grin. "Thanks."

The waitress looked ready to swoon at Cal's feet. But Libby doubted the waitress saw what she did. The sparkle of his smile didn't reach his eyes. The tension in his cheeks gave the smile a false edge. Cal at full power, his megawatt grin and laserlike eyes, had enough force to stun, to leave permanent damage.

Turning her attention to the steaming pepperoni-and-cheese concoction, Libby used the spatula to serve a gooey slice onto a plate for Ally. She inhaled the spicy scent of oregano and tomato, and her stomach growled. "Wow, Ally, this looks great. I hope you brought your appetite."

Bright blue eyes, lit with eagerness, peered out from behind Mr. Bear and grew to the size of pepperoni slices when they landed on the pizza.

"Careful, kitten, it's hot," Cal warned as he slid the plate in front of Ally. The little girl cast her father a leery glance then looked longingly at the pizza.

Libby understood the girl's wariness more than she cared to. Sympathizing with Cal's daughter, she searched for a way to engage Cal's attention so that Ally would have the space she needed to eat without feeling in the spotlight.

"So…tell me more about the job you have now with the road crew."

Cal sent her a puzzled look. "Not much to tell. I help with whatever road construction or repair needs to be done."

When he turned his attention to Ally again, Libby caught his hand and gave her head a subtle shake. "Give her space," she mouthed. "Talk to me."

With a nod, he leaned forward, his gaze now riveted on her. Libby shifted in her seat, bearing the brunt of his piercing gaze for Ally's sake.

"All right, there is something I've been meaning to ask you. What can you tell me about David Ralston? What happened to him after I went to jail?"

It took a moment for the name to register. "Ralston? You mean the guy you—"

"Yeah, the same." The intensity of his gaze stirred a quiver in her veins. She recalled too well the same intensity burning in his eyes when he'd made love to her.

Libby, you and I both know I don't do anything half-cocked.

"Actually…I prosecuted his case."

His eyes widened. "*You* did?"

She nodded and cleared her throat before she went on. "As soon as he recovered from the injuries you inflicted, Ralston faced charges of his own. We got him for assaulting the woman whose honor you were defending."

Cal quirked a dark eyebrow. "I'll be damned."

Libby sneaked a peek toward Ally, mostly to escape the scrutiny of Cal's unsettling stare. Free from her father's surveillance, Ally plucked the pepperoni from her slice of pizza and jammed the pieces in her mouth as fast as she could. A fevered excitement glowed in her eyes, and tomato sauce circled her mouth. Warmth stirred in Libby's chest.

"Was he convicted? Did he do time?"

Libby snapped her gaze back to Cal. "Yes and no."

"Meaning?"

Libby picked up her own slice of pizza but found she no longer had an appetite. She set the food back down and met Cal's querying gaze. Bracing herself for his reaction, she said, "Yes, he was convicted. No, he didn't serve time. He got a hefty fine, parole and one thousand hours public service."

Cal rocked back in the booth as if from a physical blow. He gaped at Libby, a parade of emotions—shock, disbelief, horror, and finally fury—crossing his face. Through clenched teeth, he bit out a curse. Obviously realizing his mistake, he winced and shot a glance at Ally.

"I argued for a stiffer penalty, but Ralston's lawyer played up the guy's own abuse as a child. Ralston swore on the stand to seek counseling. Obviously, the jury felt he deserved a second chance." She sighed her own frustration with the verdict and turned to watch the family at the next table.

The father had his arm around his wife's shoulders, his fingers strumming the woman's arm in a loving caress. Libby jerked her gaze away when memories of Cal's hands roaming her skin flashed in her mind's eye. A tingle raced through her, and her mouth became dry. The hands she'd just envisioned stroking her body reached across the table and caught her wrists.

"Hey, what is it? You look like you just saw a ghost."

Pulling free from the tantalizing warmth of Cal's grasp, she tugged up a corner of her mouth in a failed grin. "I did." She sighed. "But I'm okay now."

Cal poked at his dinner, his somber mood reflected in the grim set of his mouth, the deep furrows in his brow. "Some justice system we have, huh?"

"It works most of the time."

He lifted a dubious glare. "Not that I can see."

When he sent his daughter a sideways glance, his eyebrows shot up, and the first real smile to grace his lips all night lit his face.

Libby took in Ally's empty plate and sauce-smeared face and had to grin herself.

"Hey, kitten. Looks like you're a member of the Clean Plate Club!" He leaned a little closer to dab a napkin at the mess on Ally's mouth and chin. "You know that means you get a lollipop for dessert, don't you?"

Ally arched an eyebrow in a manner so like her father, Libby's pulse stumbled. The little girl sat an inch or two closer to the table and eyed the remaining slices on the tray. "Is there more?"

"Sure, you can have more, sweetie." He reloaded her plate and backed off as Ally dived in, once again stripping off the pepperoni for consumption first.

Cal's relief was palpable. His shoulders relaxed, and the tension flowed out of his jaw, allowing the radiance of his smile to shine through. He turned his dazzling grin toward Libby, and a strange warmth expanded in her chest, stealing her breath.

She'd promised to play family with Cal for as long as it took for him to secure his rights to Ally. How would she ever survive months of marriage if just one night with him and his precious daughter had her emotions twisted in knots?

The only way she saw herself getting through the next several months with her heart intact was to set limits, lay out some ground rules, enforce some safeguards. She watched Cal tuck a wisp of hair behind Ally's ear and her own skin burned, longing for that tender touch. Libby chafed her arms and looked away.

Rule number one had to be no physical contact. Her relationship with Cal had to stay strictly hands-off.

Or she was a goner.

Chapter 4

"What can you tell me about a guy who calls himself Roach?" Libby tossed her purse in a bottom file drawer on Monday morning and gave Stan a pointed look as she scooted her chair up to her desk.

"Roach? Geez, where'd you run into him?" Stan settled in a chair across from her and bridged his fingers. When he propped one ankle on the opposite knee, his pressed khakis slid up to reveal a pair of green-blue-and-tan argyle socks.

"Long story. So you know the guy? Can you lay your hands on his file for me?"

Adjusting his wire-rimmed glasses, Stan leaned back in his seat. "Gonna tell me why you're interested in him?"

She shrugged. "Just curious. I have reasons to want to keep an eye on him."

"Mail call!" Libby's assistant, Helen, stepped into the office and dropped a pile of envelopes and magazines on Libby's desk. "'Morning, Stanley. Good weekend?"

Stan sat straighter and tugged at his tie. "Very good. And you?"

Libby caught the intimate grin Helen sent Stan and jerked her gaze to her colleague in time to see his returned wink. Helen and Stan? She covered her smile with a little cough and began shuffling through the stack of mail.

"Helen, would you be so good as to pull the file on Lawrence White? Look in the case files from about two years ago," Stan said.

Libby glanced up from sorting out the junk mail for the round file. "Lawrence White?"

"Roach's brother. You helped send him to Angola a couple years ago for dealing narcotics."

"Yeah, I remember the case."

"So what has little brother been up to?" Stan scrunched forward on his chair and propped an arm on her desk.

"I just ran into him this weekend. Seems little brother may have taken over the family business. I'd like a good reason to pin something on him that'll stick." She tossed the rest of her mail down with a huff and rubbed her temples.

Stan frowned. "Hey, you okay?"

"Uh-huh. Why wouldn't I be?"

"Well, besides that threatening letter you showed me last week, I heard that someone followed you to your car Thursday night."

Libby's stomach lurched. Cal's marriage proposal and Ally's plight may have offered a distraction from her own problems over the weekend, but something had to be done about her stalker. Soon.

"Did you call the cops like you promised? Have you told them what happened the other night on the stairs?"

Libby scowled at Stan. "Wait a minute. You were in court all day on Friday. Where did you hear about the guy following me?"

Besides the police, no one knew about that incident except Cal and…Helen.

Stan shrugged. "Just heard it…around."

Libby gave Helen a meaningful look.

Her assistant flushed and hurried for the next room. "I think I hear my phone."

Clearing his throat, Stan picked at the crease in his slacks.

"If Helen told you about Thursday night—" Stan's guilty grimace confirmed she was right "—I'm surprised she didn't mention I was up half the night giving the police my statement. I was a zombie most of the day Friday." She didn't bother to tell Stan the reason she'd lost so much sleep Thursday night had more to do with Cal and his marriage proposition.

"What did the police say?"

She dismissed him with a wave of her hand. "The usual questions, told me to report anything new. Yada yada."

"I don't think you should be so blasé about this."

She nearly laughed. Blasé? She hadn't had a decent night's sleep in weeks, and her stomach felt permanently tied in knots. The prospect of marrying Cal didn't help her state of mind, either.

"Do you think this Roach character is the guy who's hassling you? Sending those letters?"

Libby shook her head. "No. At least, I don't have any reason to think so."

She thought of the menacing voice in the stairwell Thursday night and shuddered.

"I want you to at least have someone walk out with you to your car until this creep is caught." Stan punctuated his demand by tapping her desk with his finger.

"You sound like a mother hen."

"I'm a concerned friend. And I'm just talking about using a little caution."

Libby raised her palms. "I know. You're right. It's just

that…" Even that tiny precaution felt like giving up a piece of her independence.

After years of taking care of herself, depending on anyone else seemed a step backward. She sighed. "I won't go out alone, Stan. I promise."

"Good." Stan paused and tipped his head in inquiry. "You seem…distracted. You sure you're telling me everything about this stalker?"

Libby sighed deeply. "I'm fine. I've just…got a full plate."

While she dug in her purse for an aspirin, Stan scooted aside a manila envelope with a pencil and tapped an incriminating blue one in her mail. "What have we here?"

Her breakfast threatened to come up. Slowly, she pulled in air, filling her lungs to loosen the tightness in her chest.

Deep breaths. Don't lose control.

"Wait, Libby, don't touch it. They might be able to lift some prints—"

But she was already ripping the letter open, scanning the familiar script. "You can run, but you can't hide. Next time, I will get you. I will have my revenge."

Tremors raced through her. *Revenge.* She hated to think what form that revenge might take. Would she have known this man's revenge if Cal hadn't been waiting in the garage on Thursday night?

I can protect you. His presence *had* protected her in the parking garage. Was it possible that marrying him would prove a sufficient deterrent to the creep trying to terrorize her?

She'd purposely downplayed her concerns about her stalker to Cal, knowing how he'd overreact. If Cal knew the full extent of the stalker's threats, he'd smother her, never leave her side, try to usurp control. Having him around the house at night for added protection was one thing. Letting Cal take over her life with his overprotectiveness was quite another.

But had she gone too far minimizing the situation with the

stalker? She was still worried about Ally, even if Cal felt he was all the protection the girl needed.

Stan grabbed her phone and started jabbing the keypad.

A chilling new thought slid through her mind as she listened to Stan report the new letter to the police. Marrying Cal might not deter her stalker.

It could provoke him.

"Act 894, huh?" Cal's parole officer flipped through the file on his desk and scribbled notes as he talked.

"That's right." Cal sat on the edge of the hard wooden chair opposite the officer and tried not to let the nerves dancing in his stomach show.

As he read, the heavyset parole officer stroked a bushy white mustache, which hid most of his mouth except when he smiled. Fortunately for Cal, Henry Boucheron seemed to smile often. The officer's good humor boded well for Cal's relationship with the man who'd play such a large part in his life for the next two years.

"Lucky guy." Boucheron rocked back in his seat and folded his hands over his barrel chest. "Not too many fellas who come through my office get the chance to erase their record, start fresh." He flashed Cal one of his ready smiles. "Keep your nose clean, toe the line for the next five years—" he waggled a finger at Cal "—and your record will be expunged."

Cal simply nodded, not bothering to tell the man his lawyer had already been over the details with him of what Act 894 entailed—a second chance to get his life on track, possibly even be reinstated at the fire department.

God, he wanted that clean record so badly he could taste it. It would be sweet, so sweet, to have his life back, his name cleared. "Yes, sir. I understand."

"The job with the road crew workin' out all right?"

Tamping the frustration that rolled through him, Cal nodded. "It's not firefighting, but it's a job. I'm grateful to have it."

His P.O. cocked his head and studied him through narrowed eyes. "I know a guy who volunteers for the Clairmont Fire Department just down the road. I believe they're a bit shorthanded."

Now the man had his full attention. Cal leaned forward. "A volunteer department?"

"Yep. No pay, but you'd still get your hands dirty every now and again."

Cal sighed. "Doubt they'd take me on with my conviction."

"I could pull some strings, put in a good word for you…."

A bubble of hope rose in Cal's chest. "And Clairmont is within this jurisdiction? I wouldn't be violating my parole if I got called over there for a fire?"

Boucheron shook his head. "Not at all. Since Clairmont is in our parish, you'd be within your legal jurisdiction. As long as a fire doesn't take you outside the parish, you *wouldn't* be jeopardizing your parole. Want the contact number?"

Cal grinned. "Absolutely."

His P.O. lifted the top sheet from the file and handed it to Cal. "Read this and make sure we have your current address correct, then sign the bottom. And I'd like to run a drug test today."

Cal swallowed a groan. "Yes, sir."

The humiliation of peeing in a cup was a small price to pay for his future. He'd fill a thousand jars if it meant being with Ally, seeing her grow up, having his freedom.

A second chance to get things right with Libby.

The tagalong thought startled Cal. Marrying Libby meant more to him than a means to an end. Reviving what they'd had would take a little effort and compromise. Okay, a *lot* of effort and compromise. But Libby was worth it.

Boucheron flipped the file closed, and his mustache lifted

as he smiled again. "That's about it. I'll see you again next month."

"Um, well—"

"Yes? Something else, Mr. Walters?"

"I'm getting married. I plan to move in with my wife later this week. I'm also…suing my ex for custody of our daughter."

His parole officer whistled through his teeth and slid the file back in front of him. "Busy guy." He jotted a few more notes. "I'll need that new address, and you'll need to let your new wife know that her home will be subject to searches if I deem it necessary. Any weapons she owns will have to be locked up where you have no access to them."

"She understands all that. Better than most. I'm marrying Libby Hopkins, from the D.A.'s office."

Boucheron hooted with laughter. "I'll be damned. Libby Hopkins? You are one lucky son-of-a-gun."

A sensation like warm honey seeped through Cal, and his mouth crooked in a grin. He *was* lucky to be marrying Libby. He'd asked her to be his wife because he didn't want anyone else. He'd never gotten Libby out of his system. Despite the prickly feelings still to be worked through, Libby was beautiful, intelligent, compassionate…and a wildcat in bed. Honey morphed to a tongue of fire licking his veins.

Okay, so she'd warned him away from her bed. But he wouldn't give up quite so easily.

"I believe you're gonna be one of my more interesting cases, Mr. Walters."

"Let's hope not," Cal mumbled.

"Well, give the lovely Ms. Libby my best, won't you?"

"I will." Cal signed the form Boucheron had given him and hurried for the door. Talking with his parole officer, even one as amiable as Boucheron, wasn't his idea of fun.

* * *

Talking to the police made Libby late for a deposition. Which made her late to meet Cal for lunch.

When she breezed into her office at twelve-thirteen, he gave her a disgruntled sigh. "I was beginning to think you'd stood me up."

"Don't start. You cannot imagine how bad this day has already been." She dumped a stack of files on her desk and dug her purse out of her bottom drawer.

"Yeah, your secretary said something about the police being here this morning. What was that about?"

"Don't let Helen hear you call her a secretary. She's got several semesters of law school under her belt and plans to take the bar next spring."

Cal raised his palms. "My mistake. Sorry. So why were the cops here?"

She snatched her coat out of the closet and jammed her arms in the sleeves, stalling. "I...had another note from the jerk who's pestering me."

Slinging her purse strap over her shoulder, she faced Cal. She'd spent most of the morning worrying about Ally. Worrying that her stalker posed a greater risk to the people around her than she'd wanted to admit. She refused to be responsible for anything happening to Cal or his daughter.

"Are you sure you wouldn't rather wait and get married after the cops find my creepy pen pal?"

"No, I don't want to wait. The custody hearing is only a few weeks away." He frowned. "You're not trying to back out of our deal, are you?"

Libby shook her head and threaded the fringe of her scarf through her fingers. "I just don't want Ally in any danger because of the guy stalking me."

Cal tugged up the corner of his mouth, and warmth filled his eyes. "I appreciate your concern for my daughter. Really.

But I won't feel Ally is truly safe until she's out of Renee's apartment. I'm perfectly capable of protecting my daughter from this bully who is harassing you. But I can't protect Ally from Renee's neglect and scummy friends unless I can win custody."

He stroked her cheek with a crooked finger, and heat spiraled to her core.

"Can we go get the license now?" he asked.

A marriage license.

Libby's stomach performed a forward roll, and she gave a jerky nod.

Placing a hand on her back, Cal ushered her out into the corridor. Through her thick winter coat, the weight of his hand stirred a flutter inside her.

Before Cal moved into her house, she had to find a way to control her body's carnal reaction to him or she'd go crazy in a matter of days.

"Ally asked about you this morning."

"Oh? How so?" she asked, latching on to the distraction from thoughts straying in the wrong direction.

"She wanted to know if you'd be with me when I picked her up next Saturday. I told her you would." Dark shadows dimmed the vibrant blue of his eyes. "She cried when I took her back to Renee's this morning."

Sharp claws raked her heart and squeezed her chest. The grim lines that hardened Cal's face told her how difficult that had been for him.

"Damn rat hole. I'd keep her at my place if not for the court orders that give Renee rights to her during the week. My lawyer, Jay Wright, warned me that if I ignore the court mandate, it will work against us in our custody suit."

"Mmm, I know Jay. He's the best."

"He'd better be. I need every ace I can find."

"And he's right. Following the letter of the law will show

the courts you can be trusted. That's key to your case, especially with a conviction on your record."

He glanced sideways at her. "I understand that. It's just damn hard taking her back to that cesspool."

He stopped in front of the elevator, jabbed the call button. Heat flickered in his eyes as he stepped forward and smoothed a hand along her cheek. "Have I thanked you yet for what you're doing to help me with Ally?"

A delicious shiver chased down her spine. From deep in her core, a pull like industrial-strength magnets beckoned her to lean into him, to reach out to him. Shaken by her gut-level response, she turned her face away from his touch.

Stepping back, she cleared her throat. "Must I remind you of my terms?"

He cocked his head. "Excuse me?"

"You promised to keep our relationship strictly hands-off. You've touched me twice today already."

"Hands-off?" Cal raked his fingers through his hair. "Geez. I agreed to take the guest room, but I never said anything about this no touching thing."

"Well, those are my terms." She squared her shoulders. "No touching, or the deal is off."

"And how do you plan to convince people we're happily married if I can't even touch you?"

A ding announced the arrival of the elevator. She marched into the car and crossed her arms across her chest as she faced him, her back stiff. "Rules are rules. If you're going to ignore my rules then we might as well forget this whole mess now and save ourselves a lot of trouble."

Cal slouched against the opposite wall of the elevator, and his blue eyes gleamed like twin lasers. His heated gaze stroked her more sensually than a physical caress. A warm tingle rippled through her, following the path of his slow perusal. "Rules were made to be broken."

She grunted. "Ah, yes. And there, in a nutshell, is the difference between you and me. If you spent half the energy following the rules that you do looking for loopholes, then your life could be so much simpler."

"Simple is boring." His lopsided smile needled her.

She drew a slow breath, searching for her composure. She knew he loved to provoke her, so why did she let him?

"Without laws," she said with a more steady tone, "we'd have chaos. No control over anything." She gave him a confident smile. Score one for the prosecution.

His expression softened. "And losing control scares the hell out of you, doesn't it? Because of your mom?"

Her smile faltered, her pulse stumbling. He was too close to the truth. With her mother, she'd survived all the chaos and uncertainty she could stomach in one lifetime. She gave him a warning scowl. "Don't go there, Cal. I mean it."

He gave her a disappointed and sympathetic look and poked the button for the lobby.

Libby shoved the sharp ache of her mother's legacy back into the box where she kept it locked. She didn't want Cal's sympathy. She dealt with her childhood just fine by keeping the memories out of sight and out of mind. Perhaps by helping Ally, she could even put some of her own demons permanently to rest.

"I'll follow your hands-off condition for now," Cal said, pulling her out of the past. "But don't box yourself in a corner you might want out of someday."

Libby shook herself from the hypnotic lure of his eyes and deep voice, fixing her attention on the lit numbers that marked the elevator's descent. She didn't fear boxing herself in nearly as much as leaving the safety of her corner for a foolish fling with Cal.

What would happen if she left her comfort zone, even once, then couldn't find her way back to that safe place? More frightening was the thought that she'd not *want* to go back.

* * *

"Do you, Calvin Walters, take this woman to be your law-fully wedded wife, to have and to hold…?"

Libby bit the inside of her cheek to keep her teeth from chattering. Despite her long-sleeved suit—a dark gray tailored silk she'd chosen for her appearance in court that morning—she couldn't vanquish the shivers that chased all the way to the bone.

"I do," Cal told Judge Mathison.

Sometime since she'd last seen Cal on Monday, he'd gotten a haircut. The navy suit he'd donned for the ceremony seemed tailored just for him. Beneath his coat, his shoulders looked impossibly broad, and the pale blue in his tie highlighted the sapphire gleam in his eyes. He looked divine.

Mother of Pete, was this really happening?

Since they'd gotten the marriage license on Monday, Libby had buried herself in her work, trying hard not to think about the drastic step she would take on Thursday. Now she couldn't avoid the truth any longer. For better or worse, she was marrying Cal.

Libby eyed Judge Mathison, followed the proceeding around her as if watching under water.

With Renee's consent, Cal had picked Ally up from day care early so his daughter could attend the hasty ceremony. The little girl sat on a tall wingback chair in the corner of the judge's chamber watching the wedding with a curious knit in her brow. In the massive chair, Ally looked especially tiny and vulnerable.

She's the reason I'm doing this. I can't let Ally endure what I did as a child.

If she was so certain of what she was doing, why did her head feel like a blender at top speed? Whirling. Churning. Roaring.

The funny buzz in Libby's ears nearly drowned out the judge as he asked, "Do you have the rings?"

Cal turned to his buddy from his years with the fire department, a good-looking blonde he'd introduced as Riley Sinclair. The best man handed Cal two gold rings.

Her groom had thought of everything. He'd arranged for the judge, the witnesses, the marriage license, the rings.

Tears choked her throat remembering how Cal had greeted her at the judge's chambers with a small bouquet of white roses to hold while they exchanged vows.

During the three months they'd dated, Cal had been full of thoughtful surprises and loving gestures. She still had the angel charm he'd given her for luck when she'd faced a particularly tough and important trial. And the *I'm A Badass* T-shirt he'd bought her when she won that case. Flowers on her birthday, a can of chicken soup when she caught a cold, foot massages after a long day in tight shoes…

Was it any wonder she'd gotten swept away? What woman wouldn't be charmed by a *GQ*-worthy man who pampered her at every turn?

Desperately, she fought down the swell of emotion.

Distance. Detachment. She had to keep her objectivity in this marriage if she was going to survive unscathed. Had to remember that this same man had abruptly ended their relationship for another woman. He'd already told her that when he secured his rights to Ally, they'd be free to get a divorce. A disposable marriage. Just as she'd been disposable to him five years ago.

The touch of a warm hand on hers shocked her out of her wandering thoughts. She raised a startled gaze when Cal lifted her hand to slip a gold band on her finger. He handed her the second ring, then held his hand out for her to reciprocate.

Deep breaths. Don't lose control.

Her fingers shook as she slid the band in place. When she tried to pull away, Cal caught her hand and held her cold, trembling fingers in the warm fold of his own. The heat and strength in his grasp were almost enough to drive away the doubts chilling her to the marrow. His grip felt safe. Steady. Solid.

But the last time she'd needed him to be there for her, he'd abandoned her. Shattered her faith. Broken her heart.

The judge pronounced them man and wife and turned to Cal with a grin. "You may kiss your bride."

Libby's stomach pitched.

No way.

Cal had accepted her terms. He'd agreed to keep things strictly hands-off. He'd promised. So he wouldn't…he couldn't…he…cupped her cheek in his palm and tipped her chin up.

Libby gawked at him, her heart thumping.

His piercing gaze zeroed in on her mouth like a heat-seeking missile. And ka-boom.

The light touch of his lips rocked her world but was over before her knees could even buckle. A simple graze of warmth against her mouth, a whisper of his minty breath against her skin. He backed away an inch or two, and Libby allowed herself to sigh her relief.

She remembered too well how devastating his kisses could be, and she was in no condition today to handle one of Cal's soul-searing lip-locks.

She tried to back away from him, but his hand slid to the base of her neck and tugged her close again. When she gasped her alarm, he seized his chance and went in for the kill.

Sealing his lips over hers, he wrapped steely arms around her and pulled her body flush with his. Heat radiated from the tight cords of muscle and man, melting her bones. His mouth scalded her, sent waves of pleasure coursing through her body.

Cal shaped her mouth, molded it with his until they were one, as surely as she'd just bound her life with his. When his tongue stroked her lips, she opened to him, her will to refuse him incinerated by his touch.

Every memory she'd suppressed of lying naked in this man's arms rushed to the surface. Her body remembered what was too painful for her heart to recall.

They'd made music together—their bodies in perfect sync, their souls in harmony. They fit.

But then he'd walked away.

The icy reminder jolted her back to the present, cooled her overheated blood in an instant. Libby tore her mouth from his and gave him a firm shove, glaring her disapproval. "What happened to our agreement?" she whispered under her breath. "Hands-off. You promised."

He gave her a lazy grin, his lips still moist and swollen from their kiss. "Hey, I was just following the judge's orders." His eyes darkened to the shade of sapphires. "What's your excuse?"

Temporary insanity.

She'd left herself vulnerable to him by remembering how good things had once been between them.

"I have to get back to court," she said in clipped tones. With a nod of thanks to Judge Mathison, she marched over to the chair where she'd dumped her coat.

What was she thinking, kissing Cal back? Letting him sneak under her radar and devastate her control like that? She could only blame herself if she let him past her defenses and allowed him to wreck her life a second time.

Shoving her arms in her coat, she crossed the room again to the tall wingback chair where Ally sat. She patted the little girl's knee and flashed a smile. "Your dad says you get to spend the weekend with us again. Maybe we can go to the zoo in Monroe. Do you like the zoo?"

Ally bobbed her head. Her eyes brightened—eyes so like her father's, it hurt to look at them. "I like the monkeys."

Libby grinned. "Yeah. Me, too. They're funny, huh?"

The child's face grew serious, too serious for a four-year-old. "Do I call you mommy now?"

All the air whooshed from Libby's lungs. Her chest contracted as if sucked tight by a vacuum. "If…if that's what you want. But you understand you still have your real mommy, right?"

"Daddy said you're my—" Ally scrunched her nose, thinking hard "—s-stepmother?"

Libby took a deep breath, rubbed Ally's knee. "That's right, honey."

"He said that's like a second mommy. Like in Cinderella, 'cept you're nice."

Libby chuckled. "Well, thank you." She lifted Ally's chin to meet her eyes. So far, Cal had done an admirable job of explaining each new circumstance to his daughter, but Libby wanted to be sure Ally understood all the changes and wasn't unduly frightened. "You know I'm not trying to replace your real mommy? You'll always have your real mommy, too, no matter what happens."

"Uh-huh." Ally bobbed her head, bouncing her dark curls, then buried her face on Libby's shoulder.

An unexpected warmth seeped into Libby's chilled bones.

A mother. She'd ruled out the possibility of having her own children years ago. Her demanding career and her lack of a love life had made marriage and family seem remote. What did she know about being a parent? Caring for someone small and helpless?

The idea of someone depending on her, needing her guidance when there were no guidelines, scared her spitless. It was too much like the life she'd left behind when her own mother finally drank herself to death.

Which was exactly why she had to do this for Ally. Stubborn determination burned deep in her core. She wouldn't let Ally face the kind of lonely, trying childhood she'd known.

"Hey, kitten, are you all right?"

Cal's buttery tone brought Ally's head up. Wiggling from Libby's grasp, she reached toward her father.

Libby brushed aside the sense of emptiness, the cold void inside when Ally left her arms. She shrugged deeper into the folds of her coat, struggling to reclaim her composure. Her emotions had taken a beating this morning, and she needed time to regroup, to bolster her defenses.

Draping her purse on her shoulder, she cast Cal a quick glance as she backed toward the door. But even in that heartbeat, she found a tenderness and gratitude in his eyes that burrowed through her protective armor.

She was in deep trouble.

"So, I've got all my stuff in my truck. I plan to move my things to your place this afternoon," Cal said.

Her throat felt too dry for her to speak. Instead, she gave him a curt nod. Before her quivering knees gave out, she turned.

And fled.

Chapter 5

That evening, Libby parked beside Cal's truck in her driveway and dragged her briefcase from the front seat of her Camry. Despite the January chill, she stood beside her car for a moment gathering the courage to face Cal again. Alone. In her home. As his wife.

The whole situation seemed custom-designed to taunt her with all the domestic fantasies she'd once harbored concerning Cal. His marriage to Renee had ripped the rug out from under her and sent her dreams of home and family crumbling around her. Now she had what she'd once craved so much. But it wasn't real.

Libby set her briefcase down and hugged herself against the damp wind that cut through her coat. She turned to survey the houses on her street, imagining the children who would play in the other front yards come spring. The husbands who greeted their wives with a kiss at the end of a long day.

The family bliss she'd never had growing up but had seen portrayed in ideal form on TV.

And how do you plan to convince people we're happily married if I can't even touch you?

Shaking her head, Libby pushed aside envious thoughts of her neighbors' happy families.

Quit stalling, she told herself as she bent to hoist her bulging briefcase again.

She'd only walked a few steps toward the door when a strange prickling sensation skittered down the back of her neck—the same odd feeling she'd experienced a week ago, before her stalker had chased her down the stairwell.

He was watching her again.

Heart thundering, Libby held her breath and listened. The winter wind rattled empty branches. Dead leaves, stirred by the icy breeze, scratched their way across her driveway. In the distance, a lone dog barked.

Slowly, she turned and scanned the street. None of the cars seemed out of place. No one lurked in the shadows. Still, the uneasy sense that she wasn't alone didn't fade.

"Hello?" Her breath formed a white cloud when she spoke.

No one was there. Maybe it was just the accumulated stress toying with her imagination. Or maybe she was becoming paranoid, playing into the fear her stalker wanted to build in her. She huffed and strode briskly to the door. Enough dawdling in the damp, cold air, conjuring boogeymen who weren't there. She had plenty to worry about inside.

She stopped in the foyer to hang up her coat and craned her neck, looking for Cal in the living room. Empty.

"I'm home," she called toward the kitchen.

"Me-row." Jewel trotted out of Libby's bedroom and wound around her ankles as she crammed her coat in the too-full closet.

"Hi, sweet girl. How are you?" she cooed to the cat, lifting the purring feline to her shoulder and scratching Jewel's head. "You're my girl, aren't you? Uh-huh."

A masculine chuckle rumbled from the kitchen door.

"Fickle female," Cal said with a grin. "She just told me she was *my* girl. 'Course, she could have just been saying that so I'd feed her."

He propped one shoulder on the wall and crossed his feet at the ankles. His bare feet.

Libby set Jewel back on the floor, feeling suddenly breathless. Something about Cal's walking around her house without shoes seemed incredibly…intimate.

"Um…hi." She dusted cat hair off her blouse and carried her briefcase into the living room.

Cal followed. "Hi, yourself."

She sought comfort from the familiarity of her favorite room, filled with handpicked pieces she'd bought on Antique Alley in West Monroe. Her mother had owned only cheap, mass-produced furniture which easily wore out or broke. Seeking durability and beauty for her own home, Libby had gravitated to solid, handmade antiques, finely upholstered chairs and tables of solid wood.

"I was wondering when you might drag in. I was waiting until you got home to eat. Thought maybe we'd go out someplace in honor of our wedding," Cal said.

Libby thought of their dinner at the pizza parlor with Ally. The familial atmosphere. The cozy booth. Cal's casual touches and penetrating gaze.

She shook her head. "I'm…not hungry."

"Mmm." He shrugged. "Okay."

She read disappointment in the quirk of his mouth and his darkening eyes. She winced, feeling like she'd kicked a friendly dog. "Thanks, anyway."

"Well, I think I'll fix myself a sandwich or something. I'm starved."

She nodded. "Help yourself to anything in the fridge. I think there's some ham in the hydrator."

He didn't move, only stared at her with his square jaw set, his blue eyes blazing and his arms crossed over his chest. His muscled chest. Clad in a formfitting black T-shirt that delineated every ridge of sinew and strength. *Dear God, the man was even more breathtaking now than he'd been five years ago.*

Her pulse fluttered in her neck, and her mouth went dry. She tore her gaze away. Heaven help her, she had to share a house with all that masculinity.

She forced her voice to work. "Did you, uh, get everything moved in okay?"

Giving the room a cursory glance, she didn't notice much more than a few boxes in one corner.

"There wasn't much to move. Renee got all the furniture in the divorce. What was I gonna do with it? I was in prison."

She gave him a little nod of acknowledgment. "So, what you're saying is you really married me for my sofa and lamps?"

He blinked and cocked his head, seemingly startled by her attempt at humor.

She half smiled and looked away, all the more awkward after her shot at levity fell flat.

"Actually, the table and chairs are what I'm after."

She faced him again, and his lopsided grin sent an arrow of bittersweet memory zinging to her soul. She'd missed this. Missed his lame jokes, his company, his sexy smile.

Emotion clogged her throat, and she spun away. "I'm going to…take a bath and read a few case files I brought home."

She had to remember the pain Cal had caused her, the starkness of her life when he'd abandoned her, rather than his charm. She had to keep her guard up, or he could so easily devastate her life again.

* * *

"Hey, are you with me?" Stan waved his hand in front of Libby's eyes and whistled through his teeth. "Earth to Libby."

Blinking Stan into focus, she gave him a sheepish grin. "Sorry, I've had trouble concentrating today. I…"

She pinched the bridge of her nose, shaking thoughts of yesterday's wedding—Cal's kiss, Ally's hug and her own abrupt departure—from her mind. "What were you saying about Mrs. Hendrick?"

"It's Kendrick, with a *K,* and we finished discussing her ten minutes ago."

Libby sighed and flopped back in her desk chair. Her wedding ring weighted her hand, a nagging reminder of all she'd committed herself to.

Marriage. Motherhood. Cohabiting with Cal.

She twisted the gold band nervously. Cal had spent his first night in her guest room last night. She'd thought she'd feel safer having Cal around, his presence an added protection from the stalker. But she couldn't help but wonder if Cal didn't pose a greater danger to her well-being.

"Hellooo. What is this?" Stan snagged her hand and examined the new addition. "A wedding ring? When did you start wearing this? Did the cops tell you to do this to put the stalker off?"

"No. My husband put it there to show the world we were married."

Stan laughed. "Come on, Lib. Really. What gives?"

She didn't smile. "Really. I—" she swallowed hard "—I got married yesterday at lunch."

Her colleague stared at her blankly, as if trying to decide if she were joking.

From the next room, Helen poked her head in the office. "You did what!"

Libby held her hand up for Helen to see the ring. "I got married."

"Holy smoke! But you…you're not even dating anyone. Who—?"

"An old flame. If circumstances had been a bit different the first time, we'd probably have gotten married years ago." She hesitated, wondering if that were true. Had Cal really cared for her as much as she'd cared for him? If he had, how could he have walked away so easily? She squashed the niggling doubt and squared her shoulders. "Anyway, he asked me to marry him, and I said yes. So…"

"Wait a minute. An ex? You don't mean Cal Walters, do you?" Helen scurried closer to examine the ring, her eyes wide.

Stan frowned and sputtered an obscenity that left no doubt what he thought of Cal. "Tell me it's not Walters. Please!"

Her phone rang, sparing her from answering Stan. She scooped up the receiver and turned her back to her colleague's expression of horror.

"Libby Hopkins."

"Hey, Lib. Listen, I need a favor."

The rich sound of Cal's voice puddled in her gut like melted chocolate. She chastised herself for her schoolgirl reaction and squeezed the phone tighter so her hand wouldn't shake. "I can't really talk now. I'm in a meeting—"

"Gary, Renee's boyfriend, busted his head somehow this morning. They're at the E.R."

"Cal, I—"

She heard Stan's groan, Helen's whispered "I knew it!"

"I'm not clear on the details," Cal said. "He tripped or something, banged his head on the corner of the cabinet when he fell."

"Stoned, no doubt," she added.

"No doubt. Anyway, Renee needs us to get Ally. She doesn't know how long they'll be tied up at the hospital. I could pick Ally up, but I can't bring her back here to the construction site."

"Are you asking *me* to watch her?" Panic shot through her veins. "Cal, I've got meetings all afternoon! What am I supposed to do with a four-year-old girl while I'm discussing the Oliver case with the D.A.?"

"Can't she sit in your office and color, or something?"

"I thought she went to day care."

"She does, three days a week. Today is one of her preschool days. She gets out at noon. Renee usually has her on Friday afternoons."

"Oh." She scribbled that tidbit on her desk calendar, knowing she'd need to learn Ally's schedule.

"I already called her day care about a drop-in today," Cal continued, "but they're full. Please, Lib. I need your help on this."

Helen waved her hand and pointed to her chest, mouthing, "I'll watch her."

Libby's head spun. How did other working mothers deal with crises like this? There had to be an obvious solution, but what did she know about motherhood?

Married one day, and already her life was getting turned upside down. Libby pressed her palm to her desk and concentrated on slowing her breathing. She could handle this. She'd worked her way through college, tackled law school alone and secured a coveted position in the D.A.'s office. Surely a woman of her capabilities could shuffle her schedule enough to babysit her stepdaughter for the afternoon.

"I…guess I can reschedule most of my appointments." She eyed Helen, sending her unspoken request.

"I'm on it," her assistant replied.

"And Helen says she'll watch Ally while I meet with the D.A."

"Great. I owe you one, honey."

Libby gripped the phone harder and turned her back to her audience. She pitched her voice lower. "Don't call me honey."

"It never bothered you when we were dating."

She could picture the devilish grin on his lips, the gleam in his damnably seductive blue eyes. She counted to ten, refusing to rise to his bait. "That was then, this is now. Things are different."

"That's right—you're my *wife* now, not my girlfriend."

She sighed. "You know what I mean."

"Yeah, I know."

Was that regret she heard in his voice? Could Cal want to reclaim the affection they once shared? Libby's pulse fluttered, and she tamped the irrational thought with a dose of cold reality. She reminded herself Cal had readily agreed to a celibate marriage. No more. That's all she could allow it to be.

"Do you know where Ally's preschool is?" he asked. "On Broad Street, by the post office?"

"I know the place."

"Thanks, Lib. I'll see you at home tomorrow morning when my shift ends."

"Tomorrow morning?"

"I told you I'd have to pull an occasional night shift, working on overpasses and highways while the traffic's low." He paused. "So I'll tell Renee to get in touch with you about Ally."

When she'd agreed to marry Cal, she'd accepted the responsibility of having a stepdaughter. She refused to shirk that duty. Heck, Ally's welfare was the reason she'd accepted Cal's proposal in the first place. She just hadn't counted on solo-testing her parenting skills quite so soon. After reassuring Cal she could handle Ally, she replaced the receiver and faced the weighted stares of her colleagues.

"Cal Walters." Stan's tone dripped disdain as he shook his head. "Have you forgotten what he did to you four years ago?"

"It was five years, and no, I haven't forgotten."

"Then you must have lost your mind. The man pleaded guilty to aggravated battery! You *know* what this man is capable of!"

Libby tensed. "Cal is not dangerous. I told you then, and I'll say it now—Cal Walters does not have a vicious bone in his body. He was defending a woman, because that is the kind of man he is. A protector. A defender. Not an ogre." She knew there was a reason Cal snapped that night, a reason the gentle man she knew would put another man in the hospital. And she knew he regretted his actions. She'd seen it in his face at his sentencing.

"Libby," Stan pressed. "He brutally assaulted a man. He crossed a line. Who's to say it won't happen again?"

Lifting her chin defiantly, Libby doused her demon doubts. "I say. I know him. Brutality is not in his blood. That night was a fluke. I know it was."

Someday she hoped he'd trust her enough to explain what *had* come over him that night in the bar. But until that day came, she knew deep in her heart Cal wasn't the violent type. Knew it with a certainty that gave her pause, made her heart feel warm and full.

But if she was right, Cal had been unfairly accused....

Guilt yanked a knot in her throat, strangling her. Before Cal's return, she'd been able to silence that murmur of doubt. He'd pleaded guilty, hadn't he?

Stan glared at her, clearly unconvinced. "Have you considered that *he* could be your stalker?"

Libby snorted. "Don't be ridiculous. Why would Cal want to stalk me?"

"Think about it." Stan stood and began to pace, jamming his hands in his pockets to rattle his keys as he lectured her. "Walters showed up again about the same time this maniac started harassing you. And you have history with him. You know better than to believe in coincidence."

Libby crossed her arms over her chest. "I know better than to believe wild speculation, too. And that's all you have. He asked me to marry him, for Pete's sake! Don't you think stalking me would be counterproductive? Cal has no reason to stalk me, Stan."

"Libby—"

She held up a trembling hand to cut him off. "Stan, don't. I appreciate your concern, but I know Cal. And I know what I'm doing."

I just needed time to sort everything out.

Libby rubbed the thrum of tension coiled at her temple. "Regardless of how you feel about him, he *is* my husband now, and I'll thank you to stay out of my personal business."

Stan's jaw grew rigid, his eyes dark. "Fine. Have it your way, *Counselor.*"

Snatching a file from her desk, Stan stalked toward the door. Regret for her waspishness lodged like a fist in her chest. He *did* have her best interests at heart.

"Stan, wait…I didn't mean—"

"Don't forget our meeting with Roger at three." With a tight-lipped nod to Helen, Stan stormed out.

Libby sank back in her chair with a groan.

"Well, *I* think it's romantic that you and Cal are getting a second chance." Helen picked up a stack of files in Libby's in-box and tapped them into order. "Anybody who saw you two together back then could see how much you were in love."

Libby peered up at Helen with a weary gaze. With her nerves already raw, the reminder of what she'd once had with Cal sliced especially deep.

"And I always did think he was pretty hot." Helen fanned herself with the file in her hand and gave Libby a coy grin. "What is it about firemen?"

Libby pictured Cal as he'd looked last night, his muscled

chest and bare feet. He oozed testosterone. Better to not go down that thorny path.

"I hate to disappoint you, but he's not a fireman anymore," she told Helen.

"Yeah, but I bet he's still a hottie." Helen wiggled her eyebrows.

Chuckling, Libby shoved away from her desk and gathered her briefcase and purse. "I have to go pick up Cal's daughter. Do what you can to reschedule my afternoon appointments for Monday, okay?"

Setting her briefcase on the floor long enough to don her coat, Libby sighed. "I'll be back at three for the meeting with Roger. You're sure you don't mind watching Ally for me?"

"Positive."

Libby gave Helen a grateful smile. "Thanks."

As she hustled out to her car, she glanced at her watch, noting she was already five minutes late. She told herself the time was the reason she hurried in the parking garage, and not any residual fear from the night she'd been followed. She didn't want to give the stalker any control over her life, give in to his manipulation.

Down the aisle, a car door slammed. Libby yelped, her heart slamming against her ribs. So much for her denials. Until her stalker was caught, she'd probably never draw a completely easy breath.

Libby made a mental note to call the police department and see if they'd lifted any prints from the latest letter. All the others had been clean. Nothing helpful. A handwriting expert was analyzing the letters, too. Perhaps they'd find a match with something on file.

She fought the lunch-hour traffic through town and entered Ally's preschool by twelve-fifteen. Ally's teacher had already taken her to the office to wait, and thankfully, Cal had phoned the school to notify them that Libby would be picking up his daughter. After showing her ID, Libby was allowed to take Ally home.

As they walked across the parking lot toward her car, she felt Ally's small fingers slip into her palm and cling. Libby's breath caught in her lungs for a moment as her gaze darted down to their joined hands. Ally's hand seemed so small next to hers. The blue-eyed gaze Cal's daughter raised, as if asking permission to hold her hand, was so heartbreakingly innocent.

Cold fear rolled through Libby's chest. Ally was depending on her to fill in the gaps that Renee's drug use had left. Ally needed a mother. Needed warmth and security and love.

But giving this precious girl what she deserved meant putting her own heart on the line. She could tell Cal their relationship would be strictly hands-off. But how could she deny Ally a hand to hold, hugs and kisses and warm snuggles at bedtime? And why would she want to deny *herself* those sweet indulgences with this raven-haired angel?

She couldn't.

Libby squeezed Ally's hand and flashed her a smile. "I bet you'd like a hamburger and french fries for lunch."

The light of excitement filled Ally's eyes, and she tipped a small grin at her stepmom.

Warmth unfurled inside Libby, filling her, expanding until her chest ached, chasing away the cold and doubt.

Libby's smile spread. "Good. Let's go. I'm hungry."

With Ally, at least, she knew she'd made the right choice.

After lunch, Libby took her laptop to the living room, hoping to get some work finished before heading back to the office for her meeting with the D.A.

She'd only gotten one page of a brief read before Ally appeared at her knee. "What is it, honey? Don't you want to watch Winnie the Pooh?"

Ally pouted and shook her head.

Libby's shoulders slumped. So much for getting some work done while Ally watched TV. "What *do* you want to do?"

"Draw. I have some paper, but I don't have a crayon."

Libby pushed off the couch and went in search of something the girl could use to draw. "Your daddy told me you like to color. Now where is the paper you found?"

Ally pointed across the room to a box of Cal's things waiting to be unpacked.

"Aha!" Libby rubbed her hands together and wiggled her eyebrows for Ally's amusement. "Maybe your dad has some crayons in there, too."

Libby knelt by a box that held a few office supplies and dug into it. She rifled through Cal's things, hoping Cal had bought some sort of art supplies for Ally, and finally came up with a box of markers. "Will these do?"

Ally nodded then grabbed out the paper she intended to color on.

A pad of blue stationery.

Libby gasped. "Ally…honey, can I see that paper, p-please?"

Cal's daughter passed the pad to her with a worried knit in her brow.

"It's okay, hon," Libby said, wanting to reassure Ally, but fearing the worst. The hamburger and fries she'd shared with Ally sat in her stomach like a rock. "I…I just need to look at it for a minute."

But she didn't need more than a quick assessment to recognize the blue paper. She'd seen it too often in the past few weeks.

She flashed Ally a tremulous smile, feeling the muscles in her cheeks twitch. "There's a…y-yellow note pad in my briefcase. Why don't you get it, okay?"

The little girl gave her an uncertain frown, then nodded and scurried off.

Libby stared at the pad, her mind whirling and her heart

staggering in disbelief. Stan's voice filled her head. *Have you considered that he could be your stalker?*

Angling the pad into the light, she noted the indentations left by the last use.

Hands trembling, she scrounged in Cal's box until she found a pencil. Gently, she rubbed the broad side of the lead across the page, highlighting the dented marks. Letters took form. Words.

Her heart in her throat, Libby tipped the pad to the light again and read.

run, but…hide jumped out at her first.

Bile burned her throat as she read on.

Next time…

…revenge.

Clapping a hand over her mouth, Libby bolted for the bathroom. She barely made it to the commode before she lost her lunch.

Chapter 6

Cal used his new key to Libby's house and let himself in early the next morning then relocked the door. Jewel rubbed against his legs in greeting, and he bent to scratch the cat on the head. With a loud meow, she trotted across the room to sit by her empty food bowl.

"Hold it down, cat. People are sleeping."

"Mrow!"

"Yeah, I'm hungry, too. Sit tight. I'll be right back."

Bushed didn't begin to describe how he felt. His muscles ached from wielding a jackhammer all night. His eyes burned from concrete dust, exhaust and lack of sleep. A gnawing hunger and pounding headache exacerbated his fatigue.

Food, a shower and some serious shut-eye were finally within reach. But first things first.

After draping his coat on the back of a kitchen chair, Cal crept quietly down the dark hallway to the guest room door and peeked in. In the watery gray light seeping through the blinds, he found Ally cuddling her scruffy teddy bear on the daybed. Just as he'd hoped.

A smile tugged at his lips, and a sweet ache filled his chest until he couldn't breathe. Sneaking closer, he pressed a tender kiss on Ally's brow, then silently backed out of the room.

And into a soft body.

Libby screamed.

Whirling around, Cal snaked an arm around her waist, steadying them both, and clapped a hand over her mouth. "Chill, Lib. It's me."

He felt the shudder that raced through Libby's body and instinctively tightened his hold. "Sorry to scare you like that. Guess I should have told you I was home first."

Libby grabbed his wrist and yanked his hand from her mouth. "Yeah. Guess so!"

He buried his nose in the cloud of silky hair at his cheek and inhaled deeply. After breathing exhaust fumes and construction dust all night, the floral scent of Libby's shampoo and the hint of musk from her perfume smelled heavenly.

"Honey, I'm home," he whispered in her ear. Her lush, womanly curves pillowed his sore muscles and stirred a different sort of ache near his groin. He had only a moment to savor the crush of her body against his before she wrenched herself free.

Scowling, she put an arm's length between them.

"You can let go now," she grumbled. Even in the dim hall, he could see the blaze in her eyes, the tension quivering through her muscles.

Oh, yeah—her no touching rule.

He scoffed and raised his palms. "Geez, taking your hands-off thing to the extreme, aren't you?"

Without answering, she stalked toward the kitchen and flipped on the light. He followed, bemused by her drastic reaction to their collision.

"Hey, come on, Lib. I said I was sorry for startling you."

Her back to him, she jabbed on the coffeemaker and yanked open the cabinet above her. "I'm fine."

Her stiff, jerky movements said otherwise. Cal pinched the bridge of his nose, too tired to get into a fight with her over something so trivial. So much for the lighthearted, albeit awkward, mood they'd enjoyed Thursday night.

He sighed. "Did the school give you any problems about picking Ally up?"

She took out a mug and thunked it onto the counter. "No."

"Did Ally give you trouble?"

"No." She marched to the refrigerator and snatched it open.

Noticing Jewel still waiting by her bowl, impatiently twitching her tail, Cal searched the cabinets for cat food. "Did Renee call? We're still keeping Ally this weekend, right?"

"No."

Cal gritted his teeth, determined to keep his tone even, calm. "No, Renee didn't call, or, no, we don't get to keep Ally today?"

Libby spun around and crossed her arms over her chest. "No, she didn't call. I assume, since she never arranged to get Ally from me yesterday, we're to keep her as planned. But why don't you call her and ask?"

He gaped at Libby, stunned by her snappy tone. "Fine."

"Fine."

He studied her flashing eyes and the flush of color in her cheeks. With her arms crossed, her breasts swelled against her thin nightgown as she drew deep, ragged breaths.

Damn, but she was beautiful when she got angry. His nerves hummed with an urge to channel her fury into a round of wild and passionate sex.

But he knew how his overtures would likely be received and knew his daughter was asleep in the next room. He'd have no satisfaction this morning for the desire pulsing through him in hot waves.

He ground his teeth until his jaw hurt. *Damn squared.*

He tore his eyes away from the tempting view, shoved his need back down and resumed his search for Jewel's food. "So where do you keep the cat's chow?"

Pushing him aside, Libby grabbed the box from the shelf and slapped it against his chest. "Here."

He sighed wearily and crossed the room to pour Jewel her breakfast. "Don't you think you're overreacting just a bit? I said I was sorry for startling you."

"That's *not* why I'm upset." Her tone could have cooled a chemical fire.

At that moment, he'd rather have faced a blazing ammunition factory than get into a heated argument with Libby. But his fatigue made his tongue work without thinking. "Then why *are* you mad?"

"I'm not mad."

He snorted. "Coulda fooled me."

She strode to the other end of the counter and swiped up a blue notepad. "What do you know about this?"

He arched an eyebrow, completely lost. "What about it?"

"Is it yours?"

He hesitated, knowing his answer mattered a great deal to Libby, but for the life of him not understanding why. Maybe she wasn't angry, but she was sure edgy as hell. "I, uh…don't think so."

Her eyebrows shot up. "Oh? It was in one of your boxes."

Okay, wrong answer. He tried again.

"Well, it could be, I guess. What's the big deal?" He crossed the kitchen to pour Jewel her breakfast.

"Then you don't deny it? You admit the paper is yours?"

He tensed and shot Libby a wary glance. How could he have forgotten he was dealing with a lawyer? He smelled a trap. "Care to tell me what it is I'm charged with here, *Counselor?*"

"Just answer my question."

"All right, no! No, it's *not* mine." He returned the cat food to the cabinet and met Libby's glare evenly. "I've never bought colored paper in my life. It's too...*feminine* for my tastes. Why does it matter?"

"I just had to know for sure." She took another step toward him, her body quivering. Emotion swirled in the depths of her mahogany eyes, making her look so...*vulnerable*—not a word he thought he'd ever use in connection with Libby.

Something definitely wasn't right here. Something he couldn't put his finger on. Libby seemed...scared.

A chill prickled his scalp. As a teenager, he'd seen that fear in his mother's eyes.

"But if you didn't put it in that box, then where did it come from?" Her voice trembled, and the first sparkle of tears glistened in her eyes, landing a sucker punch in his gut. *Damn.*

More than anything, he wanted to tell her what she wanted to hear, whatever would chase away the shadow of fear and sadness that stole over her. Why the hell did a stupid notepad warrant tears? He flexed and balled his hands at his sides, hating that he didn't know how to ease her worry. "I don't know, Libby, what's going on?"

The sheen of tears in her eyes grew brighter. Wrenching inside, he stepped toward her, wanting to draw her into his arms, comfort her. But she spun away.

Holding her back stiff, she tossed the notepad aside and raked her fingers through her sleep-tousled hair. "That's what I thought. It wasn't logical that you'd do something like this to antagonize me. You'd never do anything to hurt your case to get Ally. But...I had to be sure."

He watched her as she jammed a slice of bread in the toaster, her hands shaking. Hell, her whole body trembled. A cold dread knotted his stomach.

"I don't follow. Had to be sure about what, Libby?"

Finally, she turned, drawing a deep breath into her lungs. "Remember when I told you that I've been receiv—"

Her eyes darted to a spot over his shoulder, and she schooled her face, wiping it of emotion. "We'll talk later."

Puzzled, he turned and found Ally standing in the doorway and rubbing her eyes. When his daughter raised her head, a tiny smile flickered across her lips. "Daddy's here."

Ally's grin sent gooey warmth straight to his heart.

"Hey, kitten." He stepped over to scoop her into his arms and give her a bear hug. "D'you sleep okay in that big new bed?"

Ally bobbed her head and scanned the room. "Where's kitty?"

"Jewel is eating her breakfast, sweetie," Libby said, her tone now void of the anguish that had tangled him up moments ago. If he didn't know better, he'd think he'd imagined the tears in her eyes, the quaver in her voice.

The poised, detached prosecutor was back.

What would it take to penetrate those defensive walls and get her to open up to him? The physical intimacy they'd shared five years ago had shaken him to the core, but he wanted more. He wanted the spiritual connection he'd only seen glimpses of before he'd had to give her up. Before Libby, he'd never seen himself spending his life with one woman. After Libby, he'd couldn't imagine his life with anyone else.

Yet here they were, married, living under the same roof—but still miles apart. Cal grimaced. Somehow he had to win back Libby's trust, find the woman he'd fallen in love with before life had thrown him a curveball.

He turned his focus from his new wife to his daughter. "I bet you're ready for some breakfast, too. Huh, kitten?"

He stroked the rumpled curls away from her eyes and kissed her cheek. "What'll it be? Cereal? Toast? I bet Libby's got some eggs."

* * *

While Cal greeted Ally with a morning hug, Libby watched the father and daughter, her heart in her throat. She'd known that a man who was this gentle and loving with his little girl couldn't be sending her ugly, threatening letters. Not only was Cal not the type to terrorize a woman, but his stalking her would serve no purpose, would hurt his chances of winning custody of Ally.

Still, hearing Cal confirm her belief that the pad wasn't his did little to calm the icy fear that had kept her awake through the night. It left only two possibilities she could see.

Either her stalker was trying to frame Cal, or the creep was toying with her emotions, leaving proof that he'd breached the sanctity and safety of her home.

When Cal had moved his possessions to her house, his boxes had been outside, in the bed of his truck as he'd unloaded. While Cal carried a load into the house and unpacked, her stalker could have easily sneaked up to Cal's truck and slipped the notepad into an unguarded box. And he'd have had time to get away or hide before Cal came back out again. So simple. Too simple. Libby shuddered and swallowed the bile that rose in her throat.

"You smell funny," Ally told Cal, wrinkling her nose.

Cal chuckled. "Gee, thanks."

He ruffled Ally's hair then set her in a chair, which he scooted over to the open cabinet. "I stink because I haven't gotten a chance to shower since I got home from work. So tell me what you want for breakfast, and I'll go get cleaned up. Okay?"

Libby tried to quiet the anxious flutter in her gut, wanted to enjoy the relaxed rapport between Cal and his daughter, but she couldn't. The stalker's threat had invaded her safe haven, her home. The danger was that much closer to Cal and Ally.

She'd underestimated the stalker's potential, the lengths he'd go to. Or perhaps she'd just been in denial. Either way, she should have insisted they wait to get married.

As soon as Cal got Ally her breakfast, she'd talk to him, tell him about her chilling discovery.

Ally stood in the chair and studied the shelf's contents. After a moment she pointed and said, "Chips!"

"Potato chips?" Cal made a comical face of exasperation and buzzed his lips in dismissal. "Chips aren't for breakfast!"

Ally pouted and pointed again. "Chips!"

"Hey, Libby likes this stuff," he said taking down her box of bran cereal. "And this is what Jewel is having. Want some cat food?" He grinned, obviously thinking he was clever, but Libby could see the wheels start turning in the child's head, the gleam of challenge in her eyes.

Uh-oh.

"Cat food!" Ally grabbed the box and hugged it to her chest.

Cal rolled his eyes and grimaced. "Uh, honey, daddy was just kidding. Little girls don't eat cat chow."

"No!" Ally wailed when he tried to pry the box from her hands. "Cat food!"

Libby almost felt sorry for him. Almost. Let him learn the hard way what happens when you offer a young child too many choices, wrong choices. Life was simply easier within the framework of basic guidelines. Limited decisions between black-and-white options. Structure. Reason.

"How about a piece of toast?" Cal asked over his daughter's howl of protest as he put the cat food back on the shelf.

The girl's cries did little for Libby's jittery mood. She gulped her coffee, needing the caffeine reinforcement.

Cal pinched the bridge of his nose and groaned. "Will you handle this? I'm going to get my shower."

Her coffee went down the wrong pipe, and she sputtered. "Me handle it? But you—"

"I'm sorry. But I'm too tired to think straight, much less appease a screaming four-year-old."

She gaped in disbelief as he backed toward the door

with an apologetic smile. "Wait! You can't leave me to deal with this."

"Please, Lib. Will you just…make her some cereal or something?" Cal turned his back and walked out of the kitchen, already tugging off his shirt.

His retreat chafed already raw emotions, scraped old wounds that had hovered close to the surface in recent days.

Libby, I'm sorry, but I have to marry Renee. It's over between us.

Resurrected pain and resentment swept through her veins with a blindsiding force. Shoving away from the counter, she marched into the hall, trailing him.

"I should have known it would be like this," she growled. "When things get tough, you walk away." The sharp edge in her voice surprised even her.

Cal stopped. Turned. His dark brows furrowed in consternation. "Excuse me?"

"I know how it feels to have you walk out, and I know that your daughter deserves better than that. She needs to know she can depend on you to be there for her!"

He scowled and raised a hand. "Hey, hold it down. I don't want Ally to hear us and think we're fighting."

Guilt pinched her. She didn't want to argue in front of his daughter, either. She kicked herself mentally for letting Cal rile her, for letting him under her skin. For letting him make her *feel* enough to lose control.

In a calmer voice, she said, "I'm sorry. I didn't mean to shout. But did it occur to you that Ally was testing you? Your daughter needs someone she can count on for the rough times, for the long haul. When are you going to realize that when you balk, when you shirk your responsibility, people get hurt?"

"Hell." He dragged a hand over his face then rubbed the scar on his chin with his thumb. "You know that's what this marriage is about. I fully intend to be there for Ally."

For Ally. But what about for her?

Libby shoved that thought aside. She didn't need Cal. She'd taken care of herself for too long to rely on anyone else now.

Cal closed the distance between them, a troubled gaze narrowed on her. "Is this really about Ally, or is it about whatever had you upset earlier?"

"Yes. I mean, it's both. I—" His proximity rattled her concentration. Waves of body heat shimmered off him, spurring an answering warmth that wound through her blood. The subtle musk of man and sweat mingled with the remnants of his aftershave, scents she remembered from their lovemaking.

With effort, she reined in her errant thoughts for more immediate concerns. "I need to talk to you. Something's happened you should know about."

His taut, bare chest filled her line of sight, and she tried to ignore the play of muscle and sinew when he rolled his shoulders in fatigue and sighed. "Something to do with Ally?"

"Not exactly."

"Then will it keep?"

Pain sliced through her. Dismissed. Again.

Ally rated his attention, but her concerns didn't. She'd never been a priority. Not for Cal. Not for her mother. She battled the suffocating pressure squeezing her lungs. "Guess it'll have to."

His eyes darkened, and he brushed a finger along her jaw. "Look, I want to talk. I want to understand why you're so upset, but…I really need a shower and a few hours of shut-eye first."

Libby backed away from his touch. "Ally's waiting for her breakfast."

Cal hesitated, studying her with his damnably perceptive gaze. She wished she could believe that the concern in his eyes meant he really cared, but she knew better than to harbor false hopes with Cal.

Finally, with a tight nod, he disappeared into the bedroom.

Libby sighed and steeled herself to face the four-year-old challenge he'd left her. She'd lost her temper too easily with Cal, and she prayed Ally hadn't overheard. Cal's daughter deserved better. She needed security, not fighting.

Besides, letting Cal stir up her emotions was dangerous to her own peace of mind. Better to keep the old hurts locked away in the same box where she'd shoved her more tender feelings for him.

"Ally, honey, I think I'm going to have a scrambled egg." Her stomach revolted at the thought of food, but for Ally, she'd force down a little breakfast. "Will you eat an egg with m—"

Libby came to an abrupt halt and scanned the empty kitchen. "Ally?"

Panic fluttered to life in her chest as she checked under the table and behind the door. Nothing.

Ally was gone.

Chapter 7

"Ally?" Libby called as she hurried into the living room. "Ally, where are you?"

Jewel sat on a windowsill, licking her paw and grooming after her meal. But no Ally.

Don't lose control.

Exhaling a bit of the breath she held, Libby checked the front and back doors and assured herself they were locked. At least Ally hadn't left the house.

She heard the shower start down the hall and considered getting Cal to help search for his daughter. An image of him, naked, with soap and water streaming down the hard planes and angles of his body, popped into her mind. Along with a more scintillating picture of an encounter in a shower she'd shared with Cal before…

She groaned.

Deep breaths. She filled her lungs slowly, clearing her mind. She couldn't face Cal naked. No way.

What would she say, anyway?

Excuse me, Cal, but I, um, lost your daughter. Libby winced. Guilt and regret were not a palatable morning brew.

Think like a frightened four-year-old. Libby gritted her teeth, and her stomach pitched. She'd vowed long ago to leave the past and all its troubles and uncertainties firmly behind her, yet Ally's plight had resurrected all the skeletons she'd thought were securely locked in her closet.

In her closet…

A rustle from the front hall confirmed her suspicion. Relief rushed through her, left her muscles weak and shaky.

"Ally." She rapped lightly on the closet door. "Come out of there, sweetie. It's okay."

"No!" the child wailed. "Stop yelling!"

Libby's chest tightened. "Sweetie, I'm so sorry about yelling in front of you. I'm not mad at you."

A muffled sniff was her only reply.

Libby knelt at the closet door and pulled it open. She could see the little girl sitting in the back corner, just out of arm's reach. "Everything's okay now, Ally. You can come out."

Ally shook her head and scrunched farther away from Libby's outstretched hands.

She would have to go into the closet to get the child out. An icy ball of fear settled in Libby's gut. As much as she identified with Cal's daughter, her opinion of closets differed greatly. Ally ran *to* the tiny, dark space to feel safe. Libby took one look into the narrow, shadowed interior and wanted only to run. Far and fast. A cold sweat beaded on her lip.

"Please, Ally, c—"

Something soft brushed her arm, and Libby gasped.

"Mrow."

Heart thundering, Libby scooped Jewel into her arms and hugged the warm body close, seeking solace in the cat's rumbling purr.

"Me."

Libby peeked into the closet. Ally had crawled forward, her gaze locked on Jewel.

"You want to hold kitty?"

Ally bobbed her head, her dark curls springing around her tear-streaked face.

"You can. Come on out here. You can hold her on the sofa while I fix us some breakfast. Okay?"

Biting her bottom lip and giving Libby a wary appraisal, Ally finally scooted out of the closet and wrapped her arms around the cat. Libby pulled both child and feline into her embrace.

Thank you, Jewel!

"Honey, you're safe here. Okay? Even if I mess up and shout at your daddy. You don't have to be scared."

Ally tipped her chin up and blinked damp eyes at Libby. "Did I make you mad at my daddy?"

Libby's breath hitched. "I'm not mad at your daddy, hon. Really." *Just hurt. Disappointed.* "I know a lot of things are different for you right now, having your dad back and all. Things are different for all of us. We're learning to deal with the changes. It will take all of us, even you, working to-gether. Will you help your daddy and me make these changes work out?"

Cal's daughter seemed to consider her offer to make peace, then leaned into Libby's chest, snuggling closer.

Touched by the trust she'd somehow earned, Libby had to clear her throat before she could speak. "I'm making myself an egg for breakfast. Will you eat an egg and toast with me?"

No multiple choice questions. One valid option to accept or decline. Keep it as basic and clear-cut as possible. Black-and-white. Yes or no.

Ally nodded and sniffed. "Okay."

If only her relationship with Cal could be that simple.

* * *

How had things gotten so complicated?

Cal braced a hand on the shower wall and clenched his teeth, hearing the pain and resentment in Libby's voice echo in his mind. *When are you going to realize that when you balk, when you shirk your responsibility, people get hurt?*

Remorse needled him. He had hurt a lot of people in his life, let them down—some failures bigger and more costly than others. His mom. Ally.

And Libby. Libby's pain ran deep. Because of him. Maybe marrying Libby had been a mistake. He didn't want to cause her any more pain.

Damn it, didn't good intentions count for anything? He tried to do the honorable thing. Tried to take care of the people he loved.

But it wasn't enough. Had never been enough. Not when his mom had needed protection. Not when he'd defended the woman at the bar. Not when Ally needed a father in her life.

Self-reproach lashed him with biting licks to his soul, hardening his resolve not to fail again. He'd prove to Libby he could be counted on. He'd prove it to himself.

Cal tipped his face into the stinging, frigid spray and groaned.

Despite the chilled water, his blood still ran hot. He couldn't erase the image of Libby standing in the kitchen, rumpled and sleepy and sexy as hell.

Her thin nightgown left nothing about her seductive curves a secret. The way she pursed her mouth in frustration, the sweet scent of her hair, had tempted him. Almost beyond endurance. He'd come so close to silencing her arguments with a reminder of what they could have together, what they had once shared.

But the vulnerability he'd glimpsed in her eyes had stopped him. Cold. Vulnerability was not a trait he associated with

Libby. Strength and resilience, yes. The scrappy fighter who'd overcome so much to work her way through college and law school, the passionate woman who took on the toughest challenges and won—that was the Libby he knew. What the hell had frightened her so badly? Whatever it was, he'd move heaven and earth to protect her. He'd never again make the mistakes he had with his mother.

He rubbed the scar on his chin, remembering, and berating himself for his blindness, for his gullibility.

I know how it feels to have you walk out. He'd heard a load of hurt in Libby's voice as she'd chastised him for delegating his fussy daughter to her. So many regrets. He couldn't undo the past, but maybe they could still have a future.

If he could remind Libby of the times when nothing had come between them but a condom and passion-generated sweat, they might have a chance of making their marriage of convenience real. Making it last.

Cal caught his breath. When had he decided he wanted a real marriage? He'd promised her a divorce once the court secured his rights to Ally.

Maybe he'd been fooling himself all along. He knew for a fact he'd never gotten Libby out of his system.

The way she'd responded to his kiss at their wedding told him she still had some feelings left for him. The heat in her eyes said she wanted him, even if she denied the truth to herself. The brief glimpse she'd shared of her sense of humor Thursday night showed him that the warm, vibrant woman he'd known lurked just beneath the cool reserve she presented. Maybe he'd lied to himself by thinking he just wanted the old Libby back for Ally. He wanted to recapture what he'd shared with Libby for *himself.*

Giving Libby up had left an emptiness inside him. An ache. A need.

Sighing, he squirted a small daub of shampoo in his hair.

He worked his frustration out scrubbing grit from his scalp with a vengeance. Too late, he smelled the dainty, floral scent and realized he'd used Libby's shampoo.

Hell. Now, on top of the erotic images of her body silhouetted by the kitchen lights, he'd have the sexy aroma of her hair teasing his senses all day. Already the scent of—he read the label—*mountain heather* had his body taut and humming, his groin aching.

Why had he ever agreed to her hands-off mandate? Every minute that he was around Libby he grew more certain he wanted more from this marriage than just a safe and happy home for Ally. He wanted Libby back. For good.

He had his work cut out for him. He had to find a way past Libby's defenses. The passion, the camaraderie—*the love*—they'd had five years ago deserved a second chance.

As he rinsed the heather-scented soap from his hair, Cal formed a plan, a no-holds-barred course of action designed to seduce his wife.

Seduction proved a tricky feat while Cal had a four-year-old chaperone. In addition, Libby seemed distant, and the shadows he'd seen that morning continued to lurk in her eyes. He hadn't forgotten her request to discuss something of importance, but with Ally around, there never seemed a good time.

Late in the afternoon, he finally suggested a trip to Ally's favorite park, hoping that while Ally played they'd finally have a minute or two alone. Time for him to work on his seduction plans and time for Libby to share what was bothering her.

Once at the city park, Cal watched Libby help Ally on a swing, marveling at the rapport the two had developed. He sensed a new level of trust and understanding between his wife and daughter that warmed him.

Libby gave Ally a push to start the swing then joined him

on the bench where he sat with his body leaning forward, his arms on his knees.

"This morning, I promised you a chance to talk."

She glanced over, her eyes reflecting a certain surprise that he'd remembered his promise.

He turned his palms up. "Now seems like the best chance we'll get. So, what was it that was bothering you this morning?"

Libby turned her attention back to Ally. She pulled her coat more tightly around her, but Cal suspected her shudder had more to do with his choice of conversation than with the cool air.

"Remember the notepad I showed you?" she asked, her gaze fixed on something in the distance.

"You wanted to know where it came from. Why?"

"It's the same one my stalker used to send his letters."

Cal frowned and let her words sink in. "You mean, the same kind of paper?"

She shook her head. "It was *that pad.* I rubbed a pencil on the top sheet and found impressions that matched the latest letter."

"But you said you found it in my things. One of my boxes."

She turned her face to him, and the haunted look in her eyes chilled him. "I did."

"How—" He paused, his heart beating double time. "Wait a minute. You thought that I—"

"No. Not really. I just—" She raised a hand to her mouth, and her eyes teared up. "I had to be sure. Cal, he got in my house. He had to have broken in at some point to put that pad in with your things."

Cal sat up straight, the hairs on his neck bristling. "What?"

Libby released a ragged sigh and looked away. "I told the police about it yesterday while Ally took a nap. They couldn't find any sign of forced entry. Since I couldn't prove the notepad wasn't yours, they had no real evidence that a break-in had occurred. They promised to do drive-bys and watch the house."

He stared at her, slack-jawed for a moment, absorbing the shock. "You told me this guy wasn't dangerous. That he was just an annoyance."

Her shoulders slumped, and she hugged herself. "I didn't want to believe he was more than that. I'd hoped he was just trying to scare me."

Cal muttered an oath under his breath. Grabbing her elbow, he turned her to face him. He met her startled eyes with a no-nonsense look. "When we get home, I'm calling a locksmith to change all the locks."

She scowled and lifted her chin. "I've already set it up for Monday morning. And I've called about putting in a security system." Her frown deepened, and she balled her hands into fists. "I hate rearranging my life because of that creep. I'm in a safe neighborhood. I shouldn't have to have my house wired against break-ins."

He pulled her into his arms, though she held her body stiff and unyielding. "Taking precautions doesn't mean you're selling out, Lib. It's just good sense."

"I'm sorry about Ally," she whispered.

Tensing, he pushed her to arm's length and met the dark look in her eyes. "What about Ally?"

"I didn't want her in any more danger. I thought I was doing what was best for her when I married you. But I was wrong. Marrying you was wrong."

"No!"

"Cal, I've put both of you at risk."

His hands tightened on her arms. "I still believe we made the right choice. Ally is safest when she is with me, where I can protect her. From Renee's bad habits and from your stalker. I won't let anything happen to her. Or to you. That guy will have to come through new locks, a security system and me to hurt either of you. Understand?"

Libby wrenched free of his grasp, her eyes flashing with

stubborn self-assurance. "You just take care of Ally. I can protect myself."

She drew a deep breath and glanced out at the swing where Ally played. "We should probably leave soon. It's getting dark," she said in the cool, professional voice he could imagine her using in court. Even her tone said *Keep away.*

Frustration plucked at him as he scooped Ally's scarf off the bench and strolled to his daughter's swing. Wrapping the scarf around Ally's neck, he tied a loose knot under her chin. "Time to head home for dinner."

Libby waited by the bench, turning her back as she pulled her hat lower over her ears. Cal tried to focus on his daughter rather than Libby's remoteness. Why did she insist on dealing with this creep following her alone? Well, she'd have his help, his protection, whether she wanted it or not. He'd listened to his mother's reassurances and excuses and had regretted it ever since.

"Libby says I can have macaroni for dinner," Ally chirped.

He gave his daughter an enthusiastic grin. "Mmm, that sounds like what I want, too. With lots of cheese?"

Ally nodded and hopped out of the swing. He took her hand and started for the car, glancing back over his shoulder. "Coming, Lib?"

With a wave of her hand, she signaled that he should lead the way. "Right behind you."

Behind. Not beside. He shot her a disgruntled scowl, took Ally's hand and headed toward the parking lot. What would it take to bridge this gap between them? Their mutual concern for Ally was a start, but he needed to recapture the magnetic connection they'd had when they first dated.

Hoping Libby would catch up, Cal kept his pace slow. So slow that Ally peered up at him with a puzzled frown and tugged on his arm to urge him to go faster. But Libby kept her distance.

Cal wouldn't be so easily denied. He was determined, despite the new concerns he had regarding Libby's stalker, that he wouldn't let anything interfere with creating the warm home environment he wanted for Ally. The last thing his daughter needed was another reason to be scared. His home would be filled with hugs and laughter, warmth and security. He was confident he could be Ally's fun and loving father without compromising his role as vigilant defender.

He turned and walked backward, calling to Libby, "Ally tells me you're a pretty fair Twister player. I challenge you two to a match tonight after dinner."

Ally bounced on her toes. "Yeah!"

"I…I don't know," Libby said. "I have some work I need to look over before Monday."

Ally's crestfallen face was priceless. He couldn't have bought a better accomplice for his cause.

"Please, Libby," his daughter begged, her blue eyes puppy-dog sweet and beseeching. He made a mental note to give Ally an extra scoop of ice cream for dessert.

"Come on, work will keep until Ally's gone to bed."

"Cal, I—"

"Please…" Ally repeated.

Libby's brow creased, and her shoulders drooped in defeat. "Well…maybe for a little while."

Ally smiled triumphantly, and Cal gave Libby his own grin of appreciation, savoring the small victory. He faced forward once more and picked up his pace, anticipating the opportunity to twine his limbs with Libby's, even if only in the name of family entertainment.

Ally skipped beside him, showing as much childlike exuberance as he'd seen from her all weekend. He dreaded Monday morning, when he'd have to take Ally back to Renee's. In the past couple visits, he and Libby had chipped away the flat, lifeless look in his daughter's eyes. He hated to think that returning Ally to Renee's could undo the progress they'd made, break the fragile trust they'd earned.

Damn it, if it weren't so important to stay within the letter of the law, to meet the terms of his parole, to have a shot at winning custody and eventually having his record wiped clean, he'd—

Ally came to an abrupt halt, jerking his arm to stop him.

Yanked from his thoughts, he glanced down at her with a curious frown. "What's the matter, kitten?"

She huddled close to his leg, ducking behind him with a whimper.

"Ally?" He pried her off his leg then squatted down to eye level with her. "What's wrong?"

She sidled closer, her eyes round and dancing with fright. "I don't like him."

"Who? Who don't you like?"

She cut her gaze quickly to the parking lot and shivered. "That man. He scares me."

Cal twisted to scan the parking lot. He saw nothing at first, but finally spotted a man in a dark trench coat, smoking a cigarette as he leaned against the hood of an old-model sedan. A line of Bradford pear trees partially obscured Cal's view. In the fading daylight, he couldn't make out many facial features, but the man seemed familiar.

"He talks loud, and when he comes over, Mommy acts funny," Ally whispered, pressing closer to his side.

Cal swallowed the bile and the vicious curse that rose in his throat. How much illicitness had Ally been exposed to? He hated to think.

Libby caught up and crouched beside Ally. "What happened?"

He nodded toward the parking lot. "The guy that was at Renee's last week. Roach?"

Libby cut her eyes to the man in question, and her face set

in hard lines. She dug in her purse and flipped open her cell phone. "You go on and take Ally home. I want to stay and monitor our friend. If I can catch him in the act—"

"Not a chance. I'm not leaving you here alone. Especially not with that creep hanging around." Cal stood, lifting Ally into his arms. He glanced back toward the sedan in time to see Roach push away and approach a couple of teens standing in the shadows of a large live oak.

"This is Libby Hopkins from the D.A.'s office," she said quietly, speaking into her cell phone. "I need you to send a patrol car to Loumeaux Park, ASAP. I think we've got a drug deal going down."

Cal shifted Ally to one hip and seized Libby by the arm. He tried to lead his wife toward the far end of the parking lot, where they'd left his truck, but she shook off his grip.

"Tell the responding officers that the suspect is known on the streets as Roach. I don't want this guy getting away. Be sure the arrest is clean." She flipped the phone closed and faced him with her eyes snapping. "Take Ally home. I'll be fine."

"Libby, this isn't a courtroom. You don't have an armed bailiff standing by for protection while you go head-to-head with this scum." He nailed a no-nonsense look on her that she dismissed, rolling her eyes.

Again he took her arm and nudged her toward safety. "You've called it in. Now come home with us."

"No. I have to stay, keep an eye on him until the cops come." Even as she spoke, she followed Roach's movement as he crossed the playground with the two teens. "If something goes down, I want to be here, I want to see it myself so we can throw the book at this guy once and for all."

He noted the spark of determination that lit Libby's gaze, and his gut twisted. Didn't she realize the danger she was putting herself in?

It occurred to him that her job put her on the adversarial end of dangerous criminals every day.

And now one of those jerks was stalking her. The knot inside him yanked a notch tighter.

If not for Ally, he would stay with Libby, gladly help her catch the guy in incriminating circumstances. Hell, he'd take Roach on himself if it would mean ridding his daughter's life of one more threat to her security.

But he had Ally to think of. He had a responsibility to get her out of harm's way before anything volatile could happen. Damn Libby's stubborn hide!

When she took several quick steps in Roach's direction, he grabbed her coat before she got away. "For God's sake, at least stay out of sight. Don't go confronting him. He could have a weapon."

"Let go! I'll lose track of him if I don't follow him." She shook free and took off across the grass, tailing her suspect.

Cal clenched his teeth and debated going after her versus getting Ally to safety. The crunch of gravel in the parking lot called his attention to the arriving police car. Relief swam through him, and he hurried to meet the officers.

"They went that way," he told the police, pointing in the direction Roach and the teens had disappeared. "Libby Hopkins, from the district attorney's office, is following them. Make sure nothing happens to her."

"We'll do our best," the older of the two men told him as they took off in pursuit.

Cal hustled Ally back to his truck and buckled her safely in the back seat. He drummed the steering wheel, feeling useless and frustrated by his inability to go after his wife himself. If he didn't need to stay with his daughter, he'd be across that playground in a flash, hauling Libby and her risk-taking hide back to his truck by force if needed.

A cold sweat popped out on his brow as one interminable

minute stretched into the next. He wouldn't leave without her, without knowing she was all right.

Where was she? Damn it, when the cops arrived, she should have turned it over to them. She should be back by now.

He shoved a restless hand through his hair and sighed.

Cal, he got in my house.

A chill snaked through him. What did her stalker want? Just what sort of threat did the bastard pose? And how did Cal keep his wife safe when she was so determined to fight her own battles and charge headlong into the fray?

"Where's Libby?" Ally asked. "Isn't she going home with us?"

Schooling his expression, he turned and gave Ally a grin. "She's coming. She's just taking care of something first. She'll—"

Out the side window, he saw a flash of color, a movement in the distance. Darkness had stolen over the city, and he could see little on the unlit playground. Cal squinted, bringing the distant figures into sharper relief.

Sure enough, the movement proved to be the two policemen escorting an uncooperative Roach back toward the patrol car.

Libby marched alongside them, her head high and her steps clipped.

"Kitten, you stay right here. I'll be back in a jiffy." Locking Ally in the truck, Cal hurried to them, prepared to bodily drag Libby away if necessary.

"I'll get you for this, bitch! You saw nothin'! You got nothin' to hold me on!" Roach spat at her, the venom in his tone sending chills down Cal's spine.

"I advise you not to say any more until you've spoken with an attorney," she responded calmly.

Roach lunged toward her, but the officers restrained him.

Every fireman knew there was a point when a fire became

too involved, when the risk to firefighters' lives outweighed any gain in saving property and you got out of the burning building. Yet Libby still charged into the inferno.

Cal wasted no time snagging Libby's arm and dragging her toward the truck. "Finished saving the world, Counselor?"

She glared at him. "I have a job to do. I'm sorry if you have a problem with that."

"Watch your back, bitch!" Roach taunted as the officers jammed him into the black-and-white.

If he didn't have his hand on her arm, guiding her away from the scene, he would have missed the shudder that shimmied through her. So, she wasn't as immune to the creep's threats as she'd like everyone to think.

Libby pulled a notebook from her pocket and dashed a few words on the page. "Threatening an officer of the court. So noted."

He tightened his grip on her arm and pushed her to a faster pace. "Just another day at the office for you, huh?"

"I had to do something. Don't you want that guy off the street? I have no doubt he's the one supplying Renee drugs."

"Of course I want him caught. But that was a stupid, dangerous thing you just did."

She whirled to face him, snatching her arm from his grasp. "Someone's got to do it. It may be easier to turn a blind eye, but I swore to uphold the law. Even when it's not the easy thing to do. Responsibility means looking a difficult situation in the eye, not hiding from it."

He met the challenge in her gaze head-on. "You could have been hurt, Libby. Do you have any idea the hell you put me through just now? I didn't know what was happening to you, and I couldn't leave Ally. If anything had happened to you, I'd—"

He blew out a harsh breath, dragged a hand over his mouth and jaw. Just the thought of Libby getting shot or stabbed made him sick, made his breath back up in his lungs. He rejected the notion, unwilling to consider anything that horrible.

"You'd what?"

He snapped his gaze back to hers. She studied him with a bewildered, distrusting scrutiny. Even in the darkness, her keen eyes cut into him, exposing vulnerabilities he didn't want to examine.

He'd lost her once before, and the pain had been almost more than he could stand. He knew now that the only thing that had pulled him through their years apart was the dim hope that someday he'd have her back again. That somehow they'd find a way past all the stumbling blocks and hazards fate had wedged between them.

Yet looking into her eyes now, that future seemed farther away than ever. He felt his second chance with Libby slipping through his hands. Because all he saw staring back at him were her doubts and her distance. The suspicion in her eyes flayed his heart, sliced him to the marrow. Libby just couldn't see beyond the cold facts of their past. She limited her view to strict right-or-wrong parameters. Feelings, circumstances and motives be damned.

"You'd what, Cal?" she repeated, her eyes gleaming with challenge. "Tell me what you'd think, what you'd do, if something happened to me."

If he'd seen even a shred of warmth or open-mindedness in her gaze, he might have tried to give her the truth, tell her how deep his feelings for her still ran.

Instead he found only cold dispassion and rigid skepticism.

Frustration and regret arrowed though him. "Forget it. You wouldn't believe me anyway."

Chapter 8

"You're not going to believe this," Stan said as he strolled into Libby's office Monday night after-hours.

"Try me. I'll believe about anything these days." Grateful for the excuse to take a break, Libby stretched her arms over her head, flexing work-weary muscles in her shoulders.

Stan helped himself to the chair opposite her. "I just got off the phone with Richard Hampton's lawyer. They're ready to plead to manslaughter. They want a guarantee that he'll serve no more than five years, though."

"Ha! Not a chance." She dropped her hands back onto her desk. "Murder two and a minimum of twenty years."

"That's what I told him. He's discussing it with—"

A knock on her door interrupted Stan. Cal stood in the doorway, his damp hair suggesting he'd recently showered. He'd shaved, as well, and in his crisp white button-down shirt and navy slacks, he looked good enough to eat. "Sorry. Uh, am I interrupting something?"

She knew the minute Stan recognized Cal. Her colleague's face darkened, and his nostrils flared. "Yeah, you are."

Cal gave Stan a who-the-hell-are-you? look then turned to her. "Lib?"

"It's okay, Stan. This will just take a minute." She studied Cal's attire, trying to ignore how his clothes accentuated his muscled shoulders and great butt, and mentally reviewed her planner. "Did we have an appointment?"

Cal arched a dark eyebrow and shot her his most charming grin. "Your husband needs an appointment to have dinner with you?"

She pressed her palms together, hoping to steady the flutter in her pulse. Why did the man have to be so doggone appealing?

"I'm not having dinner tonight. I've got work to finish up before tomorrow."

Still wielding his devastating grin, Cal scoffed. "Come on, Lib. You gotta eat. We can grab a sandwich at the deli across the street." Growing more serious, he added, "And I don't like the idea of you working late, being alone in your office when there's a—"

"She's not alone. I'm here." Stan pushed out of his seat. "She said she was busy. Now scram."

Libby blinked, stunned by her colleague's interference and hostility. "Stan—"

Cal swung a hard glare on the other man. "Stay out of this, pal. It's none of your business."

"Oh? Well, I'm making it my business. I don't know what your scam is, Walters, but I'm going to be watching you. Closely. You hurt Libby once, but there's no way I'll let you hurt her again."

Cal shoved his hands in his pockets and gave Stan a scornful glare. "I'm sorry, who did you say you were?"

Stan returned a tight, smug smile that was anything but

friendly. "Stan Moore, assistant district attorney for the state of Louisiana."

Libby sighed. "He was the lead prosecutor on your case. I think he had a beard at the time, which may be why you didn't recognize him."

Her husband's face reflected surprise then hardened with contempt. "Of course. I remember."

"Great. Now that we're through with this walk down memory lane, you can leave. We've got work to do." Stan turned his back on Cal and returned to his chair.

"I wasn't asking you. I came to take my *wife* to dinner."

Feeling a bit like the bone at a dogfight, Libby groaned and divided a scowl between the men. "*Boys,* if you two are ready to put away the testosterone, I think I can decide for myself what I want to do."

Cal drew a deep breath, obviously struggling to calm his temper. She gave him points for that. Maybe dinner with him would be all right. She *was* hungry. Her stomach growled, as if to say, *Make that starved!*

But she also didn't want Cal to think he could show up at her office whenever he liked, looking like something out of her dreams, and rearrange her schedule just like that.

Libby picked up her pen, flipped open a file on her desk and scribbled some notes in the margin of a case report. She glanced up at Cal. "I can leave in about an hour or ninety minutes. Why don't you come back then?"

Stan grunted and shook his head.

Cal clenched his jaw, making the muscles in his jaw twitch. "All right. I'll see you then."

With one last narrow-eyed glance at Stan, Cal stalked out.

Libby tossed down her pen and drilled her colleague with a hard look. "What was that?"

"What?"

"Don't play dumb. That he-man, beating-your-chest thing

you just pulled on Cal? What right do you have to interfere in my life?"

"I'm just trying to look out for your—"

"Don't! I can look out for myself. I remember well enough how things ended last time, and I went into this marriage with my eyes open."

"I don't trust the guy. Something about this whole thing doesn't add up. Why you?" Stan leaned forward, his face red, and jabbed his finger on her desk to emphasize his point. "Why did he come straight back to you the minute he's released from prison?"

"Have you considered that he might have feelings for me? Isn't that why most people get married?" She'd intended the question to be rhetorical, but her stomach flip-flopped. Could Cal have feelings for her?

Do you have any idea the hell you put me through just now?

"This whole thing smacks of a setup," Stan grumbled. "He's out to hurt you. You work for the same people that sent him to jail, Libby. A guy doesn't just forget a thing like that!"

She clamped her hands to the sides of her face and massaged her temples. "Stan—" Blowing out a harsh breath, she collected her composure before she went on. "I appreciate your concern. Truly I do. But you've overstepped your bounds. My marriage is my business, and I'll thank you not to mind it for me. Now…"

Stan grunted and pinched his nose under the rim of his wire glasses.

Libby flipped a page in the open file and pointed to a highlighted section with her pen. "We have Mr. Hampton on record at his arrest saying, quote, 'She's had it coming for a long time. I just gave her what she was asking for.' I'd say this could be construed as premeditation. Murder two is a gift. Tell him, take it or leave it."

He gave her a tense, penetrating stare, arguing his distrust of Cal without saying a word. "You got it. Murder two." Stan slapped a file on his leg as he stood and stalked toward her door. "Just…watch your back, okay?"

Libby shivered, hearing Roach's similar warning from Saturday night replay in her head. She had ticked off more than her share of people of late. *As if her stalker weren't enough for her to worry about.*

She stared at the work spread on her desk, doubting herself for the first time since her early days at the D.A.'s office. Was she only fooling herself about her ability to make a difference? About the security in a job where laws guided you? How could she be doing everything right, following the rules, and still feel like the whole world was against her?

And why did thinking about dinner with Cal start a tickle of excitement deep inside her?

She thought about his troubled expression, the earnest concern darkening his face when she'd helped bring Roach in Saturday night. For him to truly be that worried about her would mean…he cared.

And he didn't care. Not about her. He'd proven how little he cared when he'd discarded her like last week's newspaper in order to marry Renee. Circumstances be damned. If he'd loved her as he claimed, he'd have found another solution, some way to save their relationship and still be Ally's father.

Like now.

Libby shifted uncomfortably in her chair and ignored the prickle of ill ease. It was too late for second chances. Cal was using her for his own purposes, nothing more. This marriage was about protecting Ally from Renee's neglect.

Another barbed prick of conscience stung her.

Libby shuffled through the stack of files on her desk, determined to get something accomplished, needing to distract herself from the disturbing track her thoughts had wandered down regarding Cal.

Forget it. You wouldn't believe me anyway.

Libby sucked in a sharp breath but couldn't quell the pain that sliced through her chest. The defeat and misery in Cal's tone taunted and tortured her. She wasn't supposed to care this much about what Cal thought. Sentiments were not supposed to be a part of this marriage. She'd put her feelings for Cal behind her long ago. It was the only way she could have survived losing him.

When Libby read the same paragraph for the fifth time and still had no idea what the brief was talking about, she slapped the file closed. Miffed with herself, she shoved away from her desk and rose to pace. Since she couldn't concentrate, she might as well get ready to meet Cal for dinner.

Swiping her purse from her desk drawer, she headed into the ladies' room down the hall. The click of her heels on the marble bathroom floors reverberated with a hollowness in the high-ceilinged bathroom. Other than a couple of secretaries and legal assistants, she was the only woman on this floor of the seventy-year-old municipal building. The old-style amenities held a certain charm for Libby. The sink might be rust-stained and the mirror cracked, but the fact that the facilities had weathered so many years spoke of a quality and workmanship that was absent in too many modern products. Dependability, in any form, was heartening to her.

She poked at the strands of hair that had worked free from the knot at the back of her head, but the more she tried to fix the damage, the more she destroyed what was left of her bun. Growling her frustration, Libby finally pulled the pins out and let her hair fall loose. She whipped a brush through the mussed strands and touched up lipstick. She surveyed her work then paused, frowned. She was *not* primping for Cal. Her pulse tripped guiltily.

After tucking the lipstick tube back in her purse, she checked her watch. Cal had left an hour ago. Maybe she could still get a few things filed away before he arrived to get her for dinner.

She tugged open the heavy wooden door to the restroom, and headed back to her office. The sound of heated male voices brought her up short. She cast a glance around to determine which direction the noise came from and realized the arguing was coming from *her* office. Puzzled and a tad wary, she approached her door quietly, listening carefully.

Stan's voice was easily identifiable. He had practice raising his voice with an authoritative air to carry across a courtroom. "Two years is a long time. A long time to think, a long time to plan."

"Wasn't that the point? Lock me up so I could think about what a horrid mistake I'd made, the debt I owed society?"

Cal. His tone dripped sarcasm and bitterness.

Libby gritted her teeth. She didn't have the energy to referee a confrontation between those two. She slumped against the wall outside her office and let her purse drop to the floor.

"And did you? Did you do a lot of thinking in prison, Walters?" Stan's taunting tone grated along her nerves. The man sure could be condescending when he wanted. She scowled.

"What's your point, Moore?" Cal asked.

Libby wondered the same thing.

"Well, I know if I was sent to prison, and I thought I'd been wronged by the judicial system, a lot of my thinking would center on how to right the wrong done to me."

"Are you admitting the plea bargain you offered me was out of line? Too harsh considering the circumstances?" She heard an eager excitement in Cal's voice, as if he were close to some long-awaited payoff.

"I'm saying no such thing. But obviously *you* felt we gave you a raw deal. Am I right, Walters? Did you feel like you'd been railroaded?"

"Your words. Not mine."

Stan pushed, his tone growing more hostile and more provoking. "Did you wonder if Libby played a part in the hard line the prosecution took? Wonder why, considering your history together, she hadn't tried to defend you to her colleagues?"

Cal's silence spoke volumes.

Libby swallowed hard and leaned closer to the door to hear.

"A woman you'd once slept with. Trusted. How could she turn her back on you? Let you be hung out to dry the way she did?"

Stan knew she'd had nothing to do with Cal's prosecution. What was he up to?

Nausea twisted inside Libby. She waited to hear Cal deny the ugly accusations Stan was flaunting.

"Back off," Cal warned.

"You hated the idea she might have influenced the prosecution's approach to your case. Maybe she'd supported the prosecution's hard line to punish you for dumping her. Is that what you thought?"

Stan's assumptions churned in her stomach, Cal's silence adding an acid bite. How could Stan suggest such things? He knew better than anyone she'd stayed far away from Cal's prosecution. Ethically, she'd had to. Why would Stan plant suspicions to the contrary in Cal?

"Libby swears she had nothing to do with my case, and I believe her," Cal said.

"But you didn't know that then. You had plenty of time in prison to stew over it. To wonder. To get good and mad."

She thought of the night he'd proposed his marriage plan. *You owe me.*

Her stomach revolted, and Libby pressed a hand to her mouth, keeping herself in check by sheer force of will.

"You thought she'd sought revenge on you by allowing you to go to prison when she could have prevented it. Didn't you?"

"You don't know what you're talking about."

She heard the shuffle of feet, furniture being jostled.

Libby moved into the doorway and took in the scene before her. Stan had her husband backed against her filing cabinet, his nose in Cal's face, clearly trying to provoke a fight.

Cal squared his shoulders and returned a taut, even stare. "I know what you're doing, pal, but I won't take your bait. I have too much to lose to get into a schoolyard brawl with you."

Her colleague's face grew red as he ranted. "Admit it. You believed Libby betrayed you. And you hated her for that. Didn't you?"

"Yes!" Cal growled. "Yes, damn it!"

Libby gasped. Both men turned.

She studied Cal's face, searched for understanding. The hard anger and resentment quickly melted to something like guilt or shame. He swiped a hand over his face and bit out a curse. "Libby, I…"

To her horror, tears burned in her eyes and knotted her throat. She shook her head, snatched her briefcase from the chair by the door then spun away, racing down the corridor.

"Libby, wait! It's not like that!" Cal caught up and kept pace with her, stride for angry stride, as she hurried to the elevator and jabbed the down button.

"I know what I heard. You think I betrayed you. You hate me."

He huffed and raked his fingers through his hair. "No. Stan was putting words in my mouth. Needling me. Damn it, he was trying to get me to punch him. Testing me or something. But I wouldn't."

"Why did you marry me if you hate me?" She heard the tremor in her voice. Her hands shook.

"I don't hate you. Those were *his* words. I admit that after my sentencing, I was angry for a while. I thought you might have had something to do with my stiff sentence."

"How could you think I'd betray you?" She heard her tone becoming shrill but didn't care.

He growled and slapped the flat of his hand on the wall. "Damn it, Lib. Listen to me!"

Libby squeezed the handle of her briefcase so hard it bit into her palm. "I am listening."

"Then hear this. I was hurt and angry when I went to prison. Angry with myself, with your office and, yes, angry with you. I did feel betrayed. By you. By Renee. By fate. I hated the thought of losing Ally. I hated losing my job with the fire department. But I could never hate you."

A jab of pain prodded her below the breastbone. "Why did you marry me if you thought I betrayed you?"

"You know why. I have to get custody of Ally. She is my priority." Cal's words reverberated off the marble floor, down the empty corridor. And in the cold, vacant places in her heart.

Why couldn't someone want her, love her, enough to make *her* their priority?

Okay, Ally had to come first for Cal. She was his child. But just once, Libby wanted to be someone's most important person. Someone cherished above all else and not shuffled off when a new boyfriend came to live with them, as her mother used to do. Not the girlfriend tossed aside when an old lover needed a father for her baby.

The elevator bell dinged as the doors slid open. Libby stepped inside with clipped strides, her briefcase slapping at her legs.

Cal followed her into the empty car and stood right in front of her, crowding her. His warm, masculine scent surrounded her, making it difficult to breathe. Reminding her of the searing brand of his lips on hers just a few days earlier at their wedding.

"I understand now that you couldn't have had anything to do with my case. Because of our history. But at the time, with everything that was crashing down on me, I assumed the worst. I'm sorry." He loomed over her, his gaze probing hers. "Considering the circumstances—"

"Circumstances shouldn't matter. You should have known. After what we'd had together, you should have *known*." She paused, her chest aching. "But then, maybe I misunderstood what we'd had. You sure found it easy enough to walk away when the time came."

He dropped his chin to his chest and mumbled an expletive.

Libby reached around Cal to jab the lobby button, careful not to touch him in the process. Avoiding him was difficult considering the expanse of his chest and the way he'd wedged himself right up against her.

Her arm brushed the soft cotton of his shirt and the solid wall of muscle beneath. The heady rush the simple contact created irritated her immeasurably. How could she be so hurt and still want him as much as her next breath?

The elevator lurched into motion, rattling slowly down while Cal's hard stare gave her the sensation of falling into a bottomless, icy-blue pool.

With a quick twist, he turned and slapped the stop button. The elevator jerked to a halt. "Libby, you know leaving you wasn't easy for me. It was something I felt I had to do. For Ally. But I hated hurting you."

She pulled herself to her full height and returned a steady glare. "I know nothing of the sort. Our breakup was abrupt and clinical. You cut me out of your life like I was a diseased growth and left me with nothing. Not even a decent goodbye."

"Because I was dying inside. If I didn't made the break clean and quick, I didn't think I'd be able to do it at all," he said, his voice pitched low.

Her breath backed up in her lungs, and the discomfiting sense of being trapped closed around her. She reached for the button panel to send the elevator back on its way down, but he snagged her arm with a callused hand. His fingers circled her wrist, scorching her with his touch.

So many nights she'd dreamed of having that hand on her skin again. Stroking. Soothing.

Arousing.

"Libby, I—"

A loud, metallic screech interrupted Cal as the elevator car tipped to one side. The movement threw them both off balance.

Libby stumbled backward and ended up sandwiched between Cal and the wall.

He whistled between his teeth. "That didn't sound good."

Pushing him away, Libby edged toward the control panel and the emergency phone. "Master of the understatement. This stupid elevator gets stuck on a regular basis, and I don't cherish the thought of spending the night in here."

The lit number over the door said they were at the second floor. She jabbed the door-open button, praying the doors would move with the car at the awkward tilt.

Nothing.

Trying the phone next, she scowled at Cal. "The phone's dead. Just had to stop the car, didn't you?"

"Hey, you're with a firefighter, remember? I'll get us out of h—"

The elevator shifted again, and Libby grabbed Cal's arm with a gasp.

The shriek of grinding metal rent the small compartment.

And the elevator started to free-fall.

Chapter 9

A scream ripped from Libby's throat. She grabbed wildly for something solid to hold on to. And found Cal.

She just had time to throw her arms around his thick chest when the car crashed in the basement with a bone-jarring jolt. Together they sprawled on the floor, Cal somehow managing to twist under her enough to cushion her fall.

The air whooshed from her lungs with the impact. The lights flickered out with a static crackle and pop.

Stunned and breathless, Libby lay paralyzed, trying to orient herself in the darkness.

Then silent blackness enveloped them. Like a tomb.

Like her mother's closet.

A frisson of panic skittered through her like a mouse, scratching, gnawing.

Below her, Cal muttered a curse. His hands slid over her slowly. Carefully. "Talk to me, Lib. Are you all right?"

"I—I think so. I—" She tried to scoot off him, and her muscles protested. "Ooh," she moaned before she could catch herself.

"What? Are you hurt?" Worry laced Cal's voice, and she blinked back the tears that even that much concern from him brought to her eyes.

She backed gingerly away from his hold, testing her arms and legs, her head. "I'm fine. Just…sore. How 'bout you?"

She heard him sigh his relief. Heard him move, though the darkness hid him.

"I'm good. At least, as good as you can be after plummeting a couple floors."

A chill chased down her spine when she thought of what could have happened to them. She hugged herself and moaned. "Oh, God, I always knew this elevator was unreliable, but…I never dreamed it could be dangerous. I use it every day. I…"

Cal stirred again, and when he spoke his voice came from farther above her, indicating he'd stood. "So if you know a good lawyer, I suppose you could sue the manufacturer."

She frowned at him, even though she knew he'd not see it. "You're not funny. Besides, this elevator is original equipment. The building's, like, seventy years old."

His only response came in the form of muffled grunts and the slight rumble of metal. The elevator shuddered slightly, and Libby gasped. "What are you doing!"

"Trying to pry the doors open. But they're jammed."

Libby swallowed hard, forcing down the ill ease that shimmied through her. "Do you mean we're…trapped?"

"It's looking more likely every second."

In an instant, the darkness shrank in around her, and the floor seemed to tilt under her. A hollow rushing sound filled her ears as blood whooshed through her head, leaving her dizzy.

Cal grunted again, obviously giving the doors another shot. "So do you have a cell phone or a flashlight or set of tools in that briefcase? Anything that will help us get out of here?"

"M-my cell phone." Her hopes rose then sank just as quickly. "But I can't get a s-signal in the elevator. I've t-tried before."

He grunted. "Anything else?"

"A p-protein bar that was…supposed to have been my lunch."

Deep breaths. Don't lose control.

In the suffocating blackness, Cal huffed and moved again, this time shifting nearer to her, patting the walls.

"Think you can boost me high enough to reach the emergency door on the ceiling?"

And you can stay in there until you can learn some respect!

Libby twitched, hearing the voice from her past. It sounded so real, so close.

"Lib? Think you can give me a hand up?"

"I—"

A creak filtered through the blackness. A quiet sound. But it reverberated in Libby's ears like a shout.

Like the snick of a closet door lock.

"No!" She scrambled across the floor, groping along the wall. *Not again. Not again!* Hand over hand, she felt her way up the smooth door, searching for an opening, the doorknob, escape. But found nothing.

"No! Let me out!" A sob hitched in her throat, a bubble of hysteria rising to choke her. "Please don't! Let me out!"

The darkness pressed in on her. The air grew too dense to breathe. She struggled to draw oxygen into her lungs, terrified she'd die before her mother found her.

"Libby?"

A large hand closed over her shoulder, and she flinched.

"Whoa, easy there, Counselor. Calm down." The rich, honeyed voice slid over her like a familiar blanket, warming, soothing.

"Cal?" She barely recognized the wobbling voice as her own.

"Yeah, I'm right here." A second hand touched her face, smoothed her hair then drew her against a wide chest. "How about you? Where'd you go just then?"

Trembling with the memories that still seemed too near, she nestled closer to the warmth and strength of his body. "Locked in. Don't like it…in here. I can't…breathe."

"Hey, Lib, don't hyperventilate on me. Try to breathe slowly. Deep breaths."

Deep breaths. Don't lose control.

She tried to calm the ragged gulps, but the blackness clawed at her, crushed her. Her lungs ached. Her head throbbed. A violent tremor raced through her body.

"C-can't breathe…c-can't…scared. So scared."

Cal's arms wrapped tighter around her, pulled her to sit on the floor. "Geez, Louise. Are you claustrophobic?"

"Only…when t-trapped."

"Ah, Libby. We won't be in here for long. I bet there are people working to get us out right now." He chafed his hands up and down the goosebumps on her arms. "Come on. Slow, deep breaths for me."

She tried. Really tried. But the dark walls hissed to her, *You can rot in there for all I care!*

A door slammed, and then not even his yelling answered her cries for help.

"No," she moaned into the soft shirt at her cheek. "He left me. Now I'll never get out." A sinking dismay tangled with the icy fear that sliced to her soul.

"Who left you? What are you talking about, Lib?"

"I'm going to die in here."

The hands holding her shook her gently. "No! Nobody is going to die. Trust me to take care of you, okay?"

Tears filled her eyes and spilled, warm and wet, onto her face. "Hold me," she squeaked. "Just hold me."

Cal eased her back until she was reclining against the muscled bed of his chest. His arms surrounded her while his hands stroked—her hair, her nape, her arms.

"Close your eyes, Libby."

She did.

"Now, think of…an open field. Think about the meadow we found that day we went driving into Arkansas. Remember? It was spring, and little blue and yellow flowers were blooming everywhere."

She knew the field he meant and conjured it in her mind. The fragrant scent of clover and honeysuckle had perfumed the air. She'd lain down in the tall grass to watch the clouds, and before long he'd joined her, holding her and nibbling her neck.

She drew a deep, if shaky, breath, wanting to smell those blossoms again. Needing to recapture the peace and joy she'd known that day.

"We stayed until the sun set," she whispered, her heart giving a bittersweet pinch.

"Yeah, we did." Cal shifted until he fully cradled her body with his own. "Missed our reservation for dinner in Little Rock. But the colors, the beauty of the little meadow was so great, we didn't care. It was a little piece of paradise." He smoothed his hands down her spine, rubbed her back. "You told me that was the first time you'd ever made love outside."

He slid a callused hand under the neck of her blouse, and the gentle scrape of his work-toughened hands against her skin, kneading her shoulders, stirred a heady pleasure in her blood. A prickle of apprehension tickled her brain, but the drugging balm of his hands clouded her thoughts. There was something here she should beware of, but when Cal strummed her body with his caress, all other thoughts fled.

A purr rumbled from her throat, and he answered with a low growl of his own.

"That's it. Relax. You're safe."

She sank deeper into the lull of his voice and clung to the

sweet escape he offered. Slowly, he eased the tension from her body with hypnotic strokes, murmured reassurances.

When she shifted her weight, wanting to crawl further into the blissful calm he offered, she encountered a bulge. The hard ridge rubbed the juncture of her thighs when she angled her hips toward him. The friction of her body's softest spot against his hardness jarred her system, put all her nerve endings on red alert. Libby strained forward again, not thinking of anything but the beguiling thrill of his body grazing hers.

The hot, moist pressure of his mouth suckled her throat, intoxicating her senses, and she arched her neck to receive more.

Cal worked his kisses along the line of her jaw then captured her mouth. She drew as eagerly on his lips as he did on hers, both feasting like starving peasants on the bounty of each other's kiss. The tender assault of his mouth felt like a homecoming. She'd missed this, missed him, so much. Their lovemaking had always been more about bonding, about a union of bodies and souls, than about sex. She refused to acknowledge the nagging voice that said this time it was all wrong.

Cal skimmed a hand up to unclasp her bra, and when her breasts were freed, she moved across his chest, savoring the rasp of his shirt on her nipples.

Quickly, her clothing was pushed aside, and he closed his mouth over the sensitive peak, tweaking the tight bud with his tongue, his teeth. The rush of sensation, the pulse-pounding ecstasy that rocketed through her as he nipped her breasts left her gasping for air.

"Cal…"

He seized her by the hips and ground his steely length along her cleft. Stroking. Exciting. Building the sweet torment inside her. "That's it, Libby. That's it." He swept his tongue inside her mouth and groaned. "Waited so long…for this."

She grew impatient. Her body wept for him, needed him

inside her. With clumsy hands, she grappled with his jeans, fighting the button, while he inhaled her with his kiss. Desperation became a pounding in her brain, her whole body pulsing and clamoring for completion.

Bam, bam, bam.

"Dammit! Not now!" he growled through his teeth.

Bam, bam, bam!

"Please, Cal! Please now!"

He grabbed her hands, pushing them away. "Libby, stop. Listen! We have to stop. They're here."

Her desire-muddled mind couldn't make sense of anything except that Cal was pushing her away. He turned, denying her the climax her body craved, the moment when her soul and his united in sweet release.

Pain arrowed through her, lodging in her chest. "Why?"

His flurry of movement beside her stilled, and he scraped a finger down her cheek, a gesture wholly at odds with the cruelty of his abrupt dismissal of her.

"Later, honey. I promise," he murmured and kissed her nose. "We'll finish this at home. Right now, we have company."

Only then did she recognize the pounding above them as someone banging from the other side of the elevator doors.

"Hello?" a deep voice called. "Anyone in there?"

Cal tweaked her chin. "I believe the cavalry has arrived."

With a mighty screech of protesting metal, the firefighter pried the doors open enough to shine a flashlight into the darkened elevator cab. "Hey! Is anyone hurt in there?"

Cal recognized the voice and stifled a groan. Peabody. Biggest gossip in the department. Worse than any woman he'd ever met. By morning, every firehouse in the city would know one of their former colleagues had been trapped in an elevator at the courthouse.

And how he'd filled his time waiting for the rescue squad.

Surely there was no mistaking the reason for their rumpled clothes, flushed faces and swollen lips.

Irritation mixed with the ache of unfulfilled desire, wrenching inside Cal like the crowbar Peabody used to jimmy open the doors. "No serious injuries. Nice of you guys to show up, Peabody. What took so long?"

The beam of the flashlight swung right into his eyes, blinding him. Cal squinted and raised an arm to shield his eyes. "Hey! Watch it, man!"

"Cal? Cal Walters? Is that you?" Humor infused Peabody's tone. "Leave it to you to get into a mess like this!"

Peabody chuckled, and Cal gritted his teeth. "How 'bout less talking and more muscle on that door, huh? My wife is pretty freaked out by small, dark spaces."

The flashlight beam swung over to Libby. "We'll have you out of there in a jiffy, ma'am. Hang on."

Libby cleared her throat. "Thank you."

Even with the extra measures to steady her voice, Libby sounded shaky to Cal. Flustered.

Hell. He couldn't blame her. If not for Peabody's rotten timing, he'd be buried deep in Libby's sweet body right now. The heat they'd created, the urgency vibrating in Libby's body, had rocked him to the core. If he'd had any doubts before whether Libby still wanted him, he didn't now.

Her hands-off rule was nothing more than a shield, something to hide behind. Another attempt to control him and their relationship. But having seen her my-way-or-the-highway dictate for what it was, he had every intention of turning things around on her. They would finish what they had started today. And when they did, Libby would want it as much as he did.

Cal finger-combed his hair and moved to add his muscle to the effort of prying open the stuck door. Soon he and Peabody had created an opening wide enough for Libby and himself to slip through. In addition to Peabody, Riley Sinclair and a couple other men he didn't know clustered around, ready to assist.

"Cal Walters. I should have known," chuckled Riley, who'd completed the firefighting academy with him and served as Cal's best man—for both weddings. "Man, trouble just follows you!"

Cal kept a steadying hand on Libby's arm until he was sure she had her balance and composure back.

"Stupid elevator," Libby grumbled, casting a scathing glance back at the wreckage. "It's been giving us problems for months. Someone gets stuck on a regular basis." She shook her head and dusted invisible dirt off her skirt. "Figures I'd be the one in it when it finally gave way."

"Ma'am?" Peabody, squatting in front of a long toolbox, lifted his head. "You're saying this elevator's done this before?"

"No, it's never fallen before. Usually it just stops between floors. It's old and unreliable, but I never thought it would—" She waved a hand toward the jimmied doors and shivered.

"It shouldn't have crashed." Cal glanced to Riley for confirmation.

"All elevators are equipped with a braking system in case something goes wrong with the lifting mechanism." His academy pal guided Libby to a chair in the lobby and had her sit. Kneeling in front of her, Riley lifted Libby's wrist to check her pulse.

"So what happened to the brakes?" Her tone was understandably high-pitched and tinged with frustration.

"I'd like to know the same thing," Cal said, turning to Peabody. "I know I'm not in the department anymore, but I'd like to go with you guys when you check out the operational system."

Peabody shrugged. "No skin off my nose. We're headed up with the rest of the squad as soon as we check you for injuries."

"I'm good. Just bruised," he told Peabody, waving him off.

The door to the stairs flew open, and Stan Moore strode out. He scanned the lobby and, finding Libby, hurried to her. "Dear God, Libby. What happened? Someone said the elevator crashed. Are you okay?"

"I'm fine. Just shaken." She shook off Riley's hands when he tried to check her pupils. "I'm fine!"

Cal placed his hands on Libby's shoulders, and she tensed beneath his touch. "Will you be all right for a few minutes if I go with these guys?"

"Of course. Don't be silly."

"I'll keep an eye on her," Stan said.

Cal sent Stan a wary glower then looked into Libby's eyes, assuring himself she wasn't hiding any lingering ill effects of their accident.

Libby cocked her head to a defiant angle, and sparks lit her eyes. "I'm fine. Go!"

Before she could pull away, he thumbed her chin up and brushed a kiss over her mouth. "I'll be right back."

With the taste of Libby on his lips, Cal followed the other firemen to the top of the building, to the penthouse area where the main elevator mechanisms were located. The cops were there already, along with the maintenance supervisor for the building.

Cal introduced himself to the other men and peered over a police officer's shoulder while the seventy-year-old steel elevator cables were examined and the safety setting scrutinized.

"We just inspected the system a few weeks ago," the maintenance man, wearing overalls with a name patch that read Howard Grimes, told the policeman. "The system is old, but it wasn't unsafe."

"You have paperwork on that inspection?" the officer asked.

Grimes nodded. "In my office. I'll get it in a minute. But…I don't think you'll find answers to tonight's system failure in the inspection papers. Look here." He held one of the cables out. "This baby is made up of dozens of steel cords. *Steel.* They don't just break."

Cal shifted forward for a better look at the cable, the maintenance worker confirming his suspicions. An uneasy prickle started at the nape of his neck.

"Look at these ends," Grimes continued. "The breaks didn't come at random places. It's a clean break, all the cords cut clear through at the same place. Except right here." He pointed to one side, where a small part of the steel showed signs of distress and a jagged end. "Furthermore, there's no rust or discoloration on the ends indicating this damage is old. The other four are just like this."

"What are you saying?" the policeman asked, though his expression said he knew the answer but needed confirmation.

"I'm saying, someone did this. Someone took a good hacksaw, most likely, and purposely cut the cables down to this last couple cords. Weakened the cable to where the weight of passengers made the cab fall."

"Sabotage?" Peabody asked, his tone stunned.

"The evidence is right here." Grimes waved the blunt end of the elevator cable.

Cal stiffened. "What about the braking mechanism? Why'd it fail?"

"I don't know that it did fail."

"Then why did we crash?" Cal pressed.

"It takes a few floors for the cab to reach a speed that will trigger the safety setting. I'm guessing you were already at about the lobby before the last cables broke. Am I right?" Grimes asked.

Cal thought back. "We were at about the second floor."

Grimes lifted a hand. "There you have it. Y'all hit the basement before the safety could set."

The policeman flipped his notepad closed. "That's all for

now, Mr. Grimes, but I'll need you to be available for questions in this matter later."

Grimes wiped grease from his hands and nodded. "You got it."

Riley grunted and shook his head. "Long and short of it is…someone set out to make that elevator fall."

His best man gave voice to what Cal wanted to deny but couldn't in the face of the evidence. A chill crawled through him, and he suppressed a shudder.

Peabody whistled through his teeth. "I guess that leaves only one question—beside who did this. Was this creep lashing out at the occupants of this building in general, or did he have a specific target?"

Cal's gut twisted with a horrible suspicion the saboteur had gotten exactly whom he'd targeted. The only questions that remained were *why?* And how did he protect Libby from another insidious strike?

Chapter 10

Libby glanced across the dark front seat of Cal's truck and studied the rugged lines of his face. The dim glow from the dashboard lights made the cut of his jaw seem harsher and the shadows around his eyes more pronounced. He'd been grim and silent since returning from his scouting expedition with the other firefighters. His somber mood didn't do much for her own rattled nerves.

She chafed her arms, trying to rub out the chill that seeped to her bones despite the truck's heater blowing full blast at her feet. Ugly images of their brush with disaster replayed in her head, and she trembled all over again. The horrifying screech of metal. The sensation of falling. The numbing jolt when they'd crashed.

She cast a longing look toward Cal's hands, wrapped around the steering wheel and tight with tension. She recalled the dizzying effects, the lulling tranquility of his gentling strokes. Being back in his arms had been sweeter than she remembered.

Dang it! She gave herself a mental thunk between the eyes for her lapse of willpower, for losing control and giving in to her fears. She'd ignored the costs, ignored the fact that he'd shattered her life once before, and she'd crawled right back into Cal's embrace at the first sign of weakness.

Libby groaned.

"What'd you say?" Cal asked.

Darn his hide for looking at her with such concern and compassion. She stood a chance of keeping her distance when he was stubborn and cocky, but she didn't have a prayer when he turned on his charm, his kindness, his warmth.

"Nothing. I was just…thinking." She faced the side window, avoiding the penetrating intensity of his eyes. "You never said what you found when you looked at the elevator controls. Could you tell what happened?"

She heard him sigh deeply. "Yeah. 'Fraid so."

"What does that mean?"

"Sabotage. Blatant, malicious sabotage made that elevator fall."

Libby jerked her head around to face Cal, her heart rate kicking up. "Excuse me?"

He cut a quick, sharp glance across the front seat. "The cables were cut."

Libby's mouth went dry. "My stalker?"

A muscle in his jaw twitched. "That's what I'm thinking."

The last of her tattered composure disintegrated. Violent shivers seized her. She squeezed her eyes shut, wishing she could make the past several hours, the past several weeks, the threat of her stalker just disappear. Though she kept her eyes closed, she felt Cal's worried gaze.

"Seems too big of a coincidence for anything else," he said, his tone tight and rough. He pulled the car onto the shoulder and shifted into park.

A sour churning swirled in her gut. Tonight, the madman

who'd been following her had drawn Cal into his web of evil. If the elevator had fallen more than the couple floors it did, Cal could have been hurt. Or worse.

The idea of something happening to Cal stole her breath, made her want to weep from the depths of her soul.

Beside her, Cal remained ominously still, deathly quiet.

In the distance, a siren wailed.

"Libby…" Cal's jaw tensed, and he rubbed his thumb along the scar on his chin. "This cretin could have *killed* you tonight. I know you think you can handle this on your own, but this is no time to let your willfulness override common sense. I know you've told the police about him, but…what have you done to protect yourself?"

Libby twisted a button on the front of her blouse, her fingers still unsteady. "I'm being careful. The locksmith changed the locks at the house today and—"

"Locked doors? That was fine when we thought he was just some Peeping Tom type. You said he was just playing mind games and trying to scare you. But he's tried to hurt you now. This is much more serious than you let me believe." Cal blew a deep breath through his teeth. "You have to do more. Much more."

She huffed and twisted harder on the button. "I hate the idea of rearranging my life because this creep took a notion to terrorize me. I won't let him control and manipulate me out of fear." She sliced the air with her hand for emphasis.

Cal dragged a hand over his face and muttered an obscenity Libby was just as glad she couldn't make out.

He took her chin in a firm grasp and raised her head.

"Do you own a gun?" he asked, his voice low and lethal. And disturbingly sexy. The deep rumble slid over her and coiled low in her belly.

Libby attacked the button again with a vengeance, fumbling, twisting, trying not to think about how Cal's soothing tones had relaxed and seduced her in the dark elevator. How warm his hand felt on her skin even now.

"Yes. I have a gun, and I know how to use it."

He snatched her pocketbook off the floor and began rifling through it.

"Hey!" She grabbed the purse back.

"Where? Where's the gun? What kind?"

"It's not in there. I keep a .22-caliber locked in a box in my nightstand."

"Hell of a lot of good it's doin' you there!"

"I bought it for home security. I never intended to carry it with me. It has to stay locked up because of Ally. And because of your parole. I had a chat with your P.O., Mr. Boucheron, last week. He warned me to keep all firearms locked up to be in compliance with your parole terms."

"My parole," Cal grumbled and rubbed his eyes with two fingers. "Damn it!"

"But I don't want to carry a gun, anyway."

"Libby—"

"No, Cal! I won't cave to his scare tactics. I will not live my life looking over my shoulder. I spent most of my childhood being afraid of something. The temper of my mother's newest boyfriend or the landlord kicking us out for unpaid rent. I was scared of roaches and rats and creditors. But I learned to live with my fears because the roaches and rats and creditors weren't going to go away. You deal with problems and move on."

Cal's brows knit over eyes full of compassion. "Was it that bad? I thought you told me—"

She held up a hand to hush him. "The point is, I got out of there. I put my childhood behind me, and I don't ever want to live my life ruled by fear and intimidation again. As long as I don't give in to his terror tactics, I am in control. Not that creep."

He continued to stare at her with an odd, discomfiting expression. His look said he could read her mind, see clear to her soul. "What did your mom's boyfriend do?"

Her pulse tapped a wild, restless cadence.

"Excuse me?" she asked, pretending not to know exactly what he was asking.

He stroked the side of her face with his knuckles, and the tenderness of his caress nearly made her cry.

"Your mother's boyfriend. Why were you scared of him? What did he do to you?"

She pulled away from his touch even though her every instinct clamored for her to climb over the truck's center console and into his lap, into his arms. It would be so easy to lose herself in his sweet embrace and block out the ugliness haunting her.

"It doesn't matter now. It's over. It's in the past, and I don't want to talk ab—"

"It does matter." He caught her chin in his fingers again and brought her head around.

The care and concern in his laser-blue gaze blasted her defenses. The warm, soap-and-woods scent of him made her head spin, her heart hurt.

Damn it. Tonight she was too tired, too shaken, too vulnerable, to fight his assault on her senses, his pull on her emotions.

"I was a complication he didn't want to deal with." The words slipped free before she could stop them. God, she didn't want to relive those memories. Yet with Cal beside her, his strong but tender hands cradling her face, she felt safe. Safe enough to face the ghosts, purge her soul. "His way of dealing with me was…to lock me in…the closet."

Cal winced, but his eyes held steady with hers, probing, comforting.

"He'd leave me in there for hours. Days. Until my mother came home and found me."

"Came home? Where would she be?"

She shrugged. "I never really knew. A friend's house, at work, off somewhere getting drunk, or maybe in jail drying out."

"How old were you? Where was your father?"

"Ten, and I don't know who my father is. He was a one-night stand."

"Aw, hell, Libby. I—"

"One time, Jimmy disappeared for several days." She plowed on. Numbly, she sorted through the events that had frightened her for so long, offering Cal a part of herself she'd never shared with anyone. "He left me in the closet for…four days…or so. Alone. In the dark."

Cal closed his eyes and cursed.

"A neighbor finally heard me banging on the walls and investigated. I was dehydrated and weak from starvation, so they sent me to the hospital for a few days."

"Why didn't they send you to a foster home after that, for God's sake!"

The anger in his voice reached deep inside her, wrapping around her heart. No one had been outraged for her when it happened. She'd been something to be pitied, another sad statistic. But no one had cared enough to fight for her, to protect and defend her. Yet Cal was outraged on her behalf….

"Because my mother didn't do it. Jimmy left then. He never came back. Besides, I couldn't leave my mother. She needed me to take care of her, to help manage things when she couldn't. Paying the bills and buying the food and—"

"Geez, Libby, do you hear yourself? You were a child! It's not your job to take care of your mother. She was the parent. Where was she when you needed her?"

Tears burned her throat, crept into her eyes. "Not everyone is lucky enough to have the picket-fence childhood you had, Cal."

He flinched, and the lines of his face deepened. "I may

have had a picket fence, but my childhood was hardly ideal."
He paused, and pain flickered in his eyes.

What old wounds did he harbor from his youth? Sympathy plucked at her. She felt a new connection to Cal. Maybe they had more in common than she thought.

He gave his head a brisk shake. "I'm not the issue here. You are. And what happened to you."

She pulled away from him. "I don't see how rehashing my history is going to change anything. I made it out of that roach-infested closet, and I worked two jobs to put myself through college and law school." She poked her chest for emphasis. "I survived because I didn't let my fears win. I took control of my life and made something of that little girl who was left in a closet to die."

Tears spilled onto her cheeks, and when she wiped her eyes to clear her vision, she found moisture clouding Cal's eyes, as well. The sight of tears puddling in his azure gaze hit her with the force of a kick in the chest.

"Damn right you did. My Libby's a fighter." His smile had a bittersweet edge. "It's one of the things I admire most about you."

He admired her? While she reeled from the words he'd tossed out so casually, he pulled her close and sucked the moisture from her cheek with a kiss. Her body vibrated with the landslide of sweet sensations that rushed through her. She angled her head and found his mouth with hers, needing him, wanting him so much it was a physical ache. He soothed her with the hot press of his lips before backing away and resting his forehead on hers.

"Guess I understand now what happened in the elevator. Why you wigged out on me. Understandable, considering."

She shook her head. "I shouldn't have lost it. I should be past it by now. I—"

He silenced her with another deep, shattering kiss. She

knew she should stop him. She needed to pull away before the magic of his stroking lips drew her completely into his spell, made her forget all the reasons why falling for Cal again would be a mistake. But the gentle caress of his mouth scattered rational thought. She wanted to sink into the sweet oblivion he offered. Just for a little while.

Tunneling her fingers into his thick hair, she pulled him closer, canted forward and angled her chin to better receive the heady ministrations of his lips.

A satisfied growl rumbled from his throat. He smoothed a hand over her hair, and she winced when he found a sore spot on her skull. "Ow."

Putting her own hand up, she explored the sensitive area. "Guess I bumped my head when we crashed."

"Maybe we should see a doctor, after all."

"No. Just…please, just take me home."

"With pleasure." He stared into her eyes for another heartbeat then lifted her chin. He sealed his lips over hers, and she reveled in the heat and comfort of Cal's kiss. Cal, who could always make her forget. Who could melt her with a look, a touch.

Cal, who had abandoned her to marry another woman.

She drew a sharp breath and pulled away. "Stop. You…you promised not to…"

He groaned and rocked back into the driver's seat. He planted his hands on the steering wheel and squeezed. "Damn it, Libby. We both know your hands-off rule is for the birds. You want this—" he waved a hand between them "—you *need* this as much as I do."

He dragged his finger across her lip, and she knocked his hand away.

"What I need is some sleep and to put this night, this whole day, behind me. Take me home, Cal."

He blew a slow breath through his teeth while he rolled his shoulders. "Don't pretend that anything is settled between us,

Libby." He sent her a no-nonsense look that drilled to her core. "We *will* make love again. It's just a matter of time."

She hugged herself as a fresh shiver raced through her. Once again, she knew he was right. Too much energy sparked around them, too many memories of the heat and electricity they'd shared lay between them to be ignored.

So why did she fight it?

"And we aren't through talking about your stalker. I want to know everything. I want to see the letters. I want to know what you've told the police." He put the truck in gear and pulled back onto the road. "I'm your husband, Lib. I have to know *exactly* what we're up against if I'm going to protect you from this maniac. No more soft-selling this situation to me."

She didn't answer. She couldn't. Her mind, her heart, had snagged on the word *husband.* A bittersweet wish that he could truly be her husband, in every way the term implied, nestled deep in her heart. But their marriage wasn't real. Not in the way that mattered. Tonight they'd crossed a line in their relationship, touched raw emotions and forged an intimacy deeper than sex alone could ever build. Having a glimpse of that soul-deep connection, a peek at that communion of kindred spirits, filled her with a lonely ache. This pain, this longing, was exactly what she had to guard against, or she'd end up devastated when her usefulness to Cal ended.

Cal might protect her from her stalker, but how did she protect herself from Cal?

How the hell was he supposed to protect Libby from her stalker?

Sitting on the edge of Libby's sofa, Cal yanked off a boot and let it drop to the floor. As he stripped down to his boxers, he listened to the sounds from the bathroom, where Libby was getting ready for bed. The water running, the tap of her toothbrush on the sink. The thunk and rattle of mysterious jars of cold cream and other sweet-smelling ointments that had teased his senses during their heart-stopping kiss in his truck.

His body tightened another painful degree. He'd been in a perpetual state of arousal, well beyond wanting her, since the moment their lips touched. He ached.

And not just physically, although his bodily discomfort had reached new levels in the past few hours. He ached mentally, spiritually. He *needed* her. She challenged and completed him in a way no other woman ever had.

He grabbed a throw pillow from the couch and squeezed, wishing he could get his hands on her stalker instead. Knowing that some goon wanted to kill her was driving him crazy. Why had he accepted Libby's evaluation of the stalker's threat? He should have taken the situation far more seriously from the beginning, taken more drastic steps to safeguard his wife. And his daughter.

Hell. Maybe Libby had tried to impress upon him the danger they could be in and he'd refused to listen, hadn't been able to see beyond his desperate desire to get Ally out of the immediate dangers at Renee's.

Hadn't he learned anything from his failure with his mom? Guilt raked through him with sharp tines. If anything happened to Libby because he'd dropped the ball again, he'd never forgive himself.

The light in the hall flicked on, and he listened to the whisper of silky fabric as Libby walked into the kitchen. Shoving up from the couch, he met her by the cabinet, where she was fixing Jewel a midnight snack. He allowed himself to drink in the sight of her satiny pink robe, savoring the way it molded to every feminine curve and hugged the body he'd explored in the dark elevator.

She angled a glance in his direction, and he heard her breath snag when she took in his dishabille. He remembered that sexy hitch in her breath from their stolen time on the el-

evator, from days long gone when no rescue squad had interrupted. From nights when he'd made her moan and call his
name. Desire hummed through his veins like the buzz of the
florescent light over the sink.

Her tired sigh prodded him from his sensual perusal.

"You all right?"

The vulnerability shadowing her bedroom-brown eyes
punched him in the gut. "I'm fine."

But when had Libby ever admitted she needed anyone
else? Damn her stubborn independence.

She crossed the kitchen to set Jewel's bowl on the floor.
When she bent over, her robe gaped open, and he glimpsed
the curve of her breast.

Gritting his teeth, Cal opened the refrigerator and stood in
the sobering chill of the cold air. After a moment, he grabbed
a bottle of beer. He needed *something* to steady his jumping
nerves and cool his overheated blood. Twisting off the cap,
he sucked down a large gulp while he watched her. "Your
head's okay?"

"Nothing a few aspirin didn't handle." She crouched and
stroked Jewel's sleek fur while the feline ate. Libby's chestnut hair shimmered with gold and red highlights, and his fingers itched to plow through the silky veil the same way she
ran her hand over her cat.

"Did you want something?" she asked without looking up.

"Nah, I'm good."

Liar. What he *wanted* was to bury himself in Libby's body
and stake his claim to her. He wanted to slay the dragons that
haunted her, defend her from the invisible enemy that threatened her life and her happiness. Given the chance, he'd gladly
rip out Jimmy-the-boyfriend's lungs with his bare hands for
having locked a young Libby in the closet.

She wouldn't appreciate his caveman mentality, but he
couldn't help the possessive, protective instincts that flared to

life when he was around her. If his failure to protect his mother had taught him nothing else, he'd learned to guard those he loved from danger, no matter the cost.

He'd do anything, *anything,* to protect Libby from her stalker. The very idea that someone could harm her filled him with cold terror, blazing fury.

But who was this creep? Where was the threat coming from? And how did he fight an invisible enemy?

"I want to see the letters. The ones from your stalker." He took another swig of beer to cool the bite of acid gnawing inside him.

"I don't have them anymore. I gave them to the police." She looked up now, and her gaze went to the bottle in his hand. "Isn't alcohol a violation of your parole?"

"I—" Her question caught him off guard, and he hesitated. Huffed. "Yeah, I guess it is."

"Rules are rules, Cal." She stood and marched over to him. "No alcohol." She took the bottle from his hand and carried it to the sink. With a flip of her wrist, she dumped the contents down the drain.

He groaned and rubbed his thumb along the scar on his chin. "I didn't even think about it. I needed a drink tonight and—"

"Well, you'd better think next time. You could go back to prison for violating parole."

He tensed.

Cal studied her through narrowed eyes while the kitchen clock ticked like the kicking of his heart. "Who's gonna know? Are you going to turn me in, Libby? For one beer?"

Even as he taunted her with what should have been a ludicrous proposition, a chill snaked through him. He wasn't sure he wanted to know the answer to his question.

Cal's thoughts spun, his emotions tangling, and he drew a steadying breath. "You know the kind of night we've had. I figure I'm entitled to at least one beer."

She chucked the empty bottle in the recycling bin and faced him with a scowl. "Entitled? What, you don't think the law applies to you? That you're somehow above it?"

"I didn't say that." He fought down the swell of frustration squeezing his chest. "Geez, I don't want to argue with you tonight."

Yanking open the refrigerator, he grabbed the rest of her six-pack from the shelf. "Here. Pour them all out if you don't trust me." He shoved them toward her. "Yeah, I forgot the rules tonight, because I'm not used to answering to anyone else when I want a beer. But I have no intention of going back to jail, so…here. Be my guest."

When she didn't move, he thumped them down on the counter.

Libby's chin trembled, and her eyes softened. "I don't want to argue, either."

When she bit her bottom lip, the desire to nibble her lush mouth himself slammed into him. He fisted his hands to keep from reaching for her and devouring her.

Sighing, she plucked the first of the bottles from the carton and twisted off the cap. "You have to be more careful, Cal. If you break your parole…" She emptied the beer into the sink and shook her head. "I'm an officer of the court. I swore an oath to uphold the law. The *letter* of the law."

An uneasy quiver started in his gut as he watched her pour out another beer. Every bottle she emptied cut deeper into his soul. She *didn't* trust him. Nothing had changed. Not for Libby, at least.

But everything had changed for him. His priorities. His goals. His understanding of what Libby meant to his future.

He wanted Libby in his life. Permanently. But how could he build a future with a woman who didn't trust him?

A woman *he* couldn't trust not to put her devotion to rules over her own husband.

He watched her uncap another bottle, and his frustration boiled over. Grabbing the beer from her hand, he growled, "Damn it, Libby! Stop! Aren't you listening? Don't you get it?"

Her eyes blazed, challenging him. "Get what?"

"*Nothing* is more important to me than meeting the terms of my parole." He seized her shoulders and drilled her with a hard gaze. "I *have* to stay out of prison, and I *have* to clear my name, because I *have* to be there for Ally." The desperateness of Ally's situation, of his own situation, rolled through him, stringing him tighter. "I want to see my daughter grow up. I want her to feel safe and be happy. I will *not* do anything to throw away my chance to make that happen." The taste of beer in his mouth grew bitter. How could he have been so careless? He had too much at stake to blow this chance....

He sucked in a deep, calming breath. "Believe whatever else you want to about me, but don't doubt that much."

Emotions swirled in her dark eyes, but her gaze didn't falter. "I do believe you."

He relaxed his grip and nudged her forward. She came willingly, leaning against his chest and stirring his protective instincts anew. "Then also believe this—I want to be there for you, too. We had something special once, and I want it back. I want you beside me at night. I want to hold you and make love to you and know that you are safe."

He felt her tremble, and he squeezed her tighter.

"Cal, I—" She hesitated then sighed, her breath a warm caress against his bare skin.

His body vibrated with need.

Flattening her palms on his chest, she pushed away, stepped back. "I can't. I—" When her voice cracked, she wrapped her arms around herself and took a deep breath. "There's too much history between us. I can't do it again. I can't let myself…"

Shaking her head, she spun away and hurried toward the hall.

Disappointment sliced through him. "Libby, wait! You can't let yourself do what?"

She didn't answer immediately, but when she did, the raw honesty in her eyes shook him to the core. "Love you."

Cal rocked back on his heels, caught the edge of the counter for support.

"I loved you once," she whispered, her voice hoarse, choked with emotion. "With my whole heart. And you threw it away." She paused, glanced down at her hands, where she twisted her wedding ring. "Looking back, I realize I probably loved you too much. I let my love for you rule everything I thought and did. I gave up so much control, putting my heart in your hands, and I paid the price. I got hurt. Deeply. But I learned a valuable lesson, and I won't let myself get hurt again."

He stepped toward her, needing to close the distance between them any way he could. "You mean you won't let yourself love again."

"Aren't they the same thing?"

A fist of regret clutched his throat. How had something as right as the love they'd had gone so horribly wrong?

He took another step, stretched his hand toward her. "Even the legal system was willing to parole me, give me a second chance. Why can't you?"

The pain in her eyes coalesced in a fat tear that dripped onto her cheek. She dashed at it with an angry swipe before she bolted from the kitchen.

Her lack of response spoke volumes. But so did that one tear, a tear that said she did care, whether she wanted to or not. A tear that gave him a flicker of hope.

One way or another, he'd kick down the walls she'd built and find the embers of the love he knew she harbored somewhere deep inside.

* * *

The next night in her kickboxing class, Libby bumped her gloved hands together and danced a boxer's shuffle, brimming with energy and ready to let loose.

"Talk about a stress reliever!" The class instructor bounced on her toes as she addressed the class. "Picture the face of that *someone* who has really been getting on your nerves this week, and let 'em have it!"

Though her muscles were still rather sore from the elevator crash, Libby needed the physical outlet for her pent-up frustrations more than ever. She'd spent the whole day at the office seeing the desire that had burned in Cal's eyes when he'd kissed her in his truck. She heard the sexy rasp of his voice echo in her mind and felt his gentle touch in the subtlest breeze. Just when her body was quivering with sexual tension, a different memory of Cal would zing through her mind.

Even the legal system was willing to parole me, give me a second chance. Why can't you? The raw emotion in his voice. The tender appeal in his eyes. The way he'd reached for her...

She shook her head to clear her thoughts. Her senses were on overload, ready for meltdown. She had to get a grip on her runaway emotions before she found herself in deep trouble. Before she embarrassed herself at work. Before she did something foolish at home. Like go to bed with Cal.

Fast-paced music blared into the exercise room, and Libby pushed away images of burning calories with Cal in sweaty, frenetic sex. She stared at the punching bag in front of her and tried to picture Cal's face, one of his smug, self-satisfied grins.

She jabbed at the mental image a few times, but it didn't feel right. She wasn't mad at Cal. He might be the source of a great deal of her stress, but she didn't want to punch him.

And *that* was her problem. She wanted to touch him with the same loving caresses he'd shown her last night. In the elevator. In his truck. She wanted to strip him naked and feel the hard planes and sinewy strength of his body moving against hers.

A throbbing pulse sparked low in her abdomen, and Libby swung harder at the bag.

She wanted the fiery heat of Cal's lips clashing with hers, tugging her nipples and nibbling the sensitive spot behind her ear.

Libby swallowed a moan and lashed out at her imaginary opponent with a roundhouse kick and a series of uppercuts. Still her body vibrated with repressed need and erotic urges.

Dropping her arms to her sides and shaking out the tension in her muscles, Libby refocused her thoughts, her energy. So if she didn't want to punch Cal, who did she want to hit?

Her stalker sprang immediately to mind. The creep who'd put her life in a tailspin. The jerk who'd tried to kill her yesterday by sabotaging the elevator and who could have hurt Cal in the process. A spike of fury rolled through her, and she swung again at the punching bag. *Pow!*

What if her stalker went after Cal as a means to terrorize her? A foreboding chill slithered through her, and she unleashed a flurry of jabs. *Pow, pow, pow!*

What would she do if something happened to Cal because of her? Her gut knotted, and she channeled the surge of fear into a fierce right hook. *Ka-pow!*

Adrenaline fueled her assault as she battered the bag with a jab and an uppercut, followed by a swift snap kick. Sweat streamed down her cheeks and trickled between her breasts as she poured her fears and frustrations, her anger and agitation, into her workout.

Picture the face of that someone who has really been getting on your nerves this week. But she had no face to go with her stalker. Only the disembodied hiss of warning—*I'm going to get you, bitch!*—and the threatening blue notes.

Right, left, right. The impact of her blows radiated up her arms and reverberated through her body. With a shuffling bounce on her toes, Libby glared at the center of her punching bag, remembering the notepad that had been planted in Cal's moving box. *Pow, pow, pow!*

Her stalker didn't care who else he snared in his trap, may have even targeted Cal for suspicion, for elimination.

A pain that had nothing to do with sore muscles twisted inside her. She'd only just gotten Cal back in her life. How could she survive losing him again? And how did she live with herself if she lost him because of her own doing, because she'd brought the stalker's menace into his life?

The chilling thought stilled her workout. She stared sightlessly into the mirror on the exercise room wall. Panic swelled in her chest, working its way up to her throat. She wrapped her arms around herself, her gloved hands clumsily chafing the cold that prickled her skin. Closing her eyes, she let herself step into Cal's welcoming embrace. She burrowed deep into the pine-and-sex scent that clung to his skin and took refuge in his encompassing warmth.

You mean you won't let yourself love again.

With a sigh of defeat, she unlaced her gloves and shucked them off. Kickboxing couldn't relieve the stress winding her tight, the fear scrambling inside her. Exercise couldn't ease the achy need thrumming through her veins.

Her shoulders slumped, and she blinked back tears. She wanted Cal, needed his comfort and strength. Realizing that Cal had found a way back into her heart frightened her more than the psycho stalking her.

Maybe she'd never truly gotten Cal out of her system. Maybe that's why being around him hurt so much.

Either way, she was in more danger than being stalked. Every minute she was near Cal chipped away her ability to resist his lure. She had to get away. She needed time to think, room to breathe, distance from the temptation of falling into bed with her husband.

Her temporary husband. Her in-name-only husband. Her broke-her-heart-before husband.

Gulping oxygen into her tightening lungs, Libby jammed her boxing gloves in her gym bag and hurried out of class.

Stan had a cabin near Lake D'Arbonne. He'd told her where he stashed a spare key and issued a blanket invitation for whenever she needed to get away.

That time had come. She'd call Cal from the road, explain to him she needed to sort things out. She wasn't hiding, wasn't running from her troubles. She wasn't.

Her conscience needled her. *At least be honest with yourself.*

She tossed her gym bag on the back seat of her Camry and slammed the door.

Okay, you want honest? I'm honestly running scared. Scared of the lunatic who knows my every move. Scared of falling in love with a man who'll have no use for me after he gets custody of his daughter. Scared I've lost all control over my life, and I'm headed for disaster.

Libby left the parking lot and headed toward the rural highway that led to Stan's cabin. In the cool night, a dense fog had settled on the landscape, obscuring her view of the road.

What was she supposed to do? Where were the rules to guide her? *There is no black-and-white anymore.*

She squinted into the blanket of mist shrouding her path. Gray. Libby's palms grew damp, and she struggled for a breath.

My whole life has turned gray.

Chapter 11

The next morning, a gray mist swirled over the surface of Lake D'Arbonne while a great blue heron waded along the edge of the murky water, hunting his breakfast. Sitting on a homemade pine bench, Libby tucked her knees into her chest and leaned against the splintered wood rail of Stan's boat dock. The cold, damp air made her nose run and goosebumps pop up on her arms, but the tranquil scenery held Libby in thrall. Unable to sleep on the cabin's lumpy bed, thoughts of Cal tumbling through her head, Libby had rolled out from under the covers before dawn. She'd grabbed her coat and her cell phone and made it to her waterside post just as the sun peeked over the trees on the opposite shore.

Now, two hours later, the splash of fish gulping bugs on the water's surface and the peep of waking birds renewed a calm deep inside her. She inhaled the clean air and replayed her conversation with Cal from last night, when she'd told him where she was going.

"Are you out of you mind?" he'd railed. "You have a maniac trying to kill you and you take off for the boonies alone?"

"Only you and Stan know I'm here. I'll be fine. And I'll be back by tomorrow night. I just need…to think."

Cal grunted. "And you can't think somewhere in town? Somewhere I can keep an eye on you?"

"I don't need your protection."

"You've got it, anyway. I won't sit back and let this guy hurt you." His frustration crackled through the phone line. "I'm coming out there. Where is this cabin?"

"You can't. It's outside your parole jurisdiction. Besides, Stan knows how to get here if there's a need. Okay?"

Cal cursed. "No, it's not okay. I want you here. I want you safe."

Libby thought of the dangers waiting at home. Cal's hypnotic eyes, his fiery kiss, his soothing touch. "I'm safe here." *Far away from you, away from temptation.* "I promise to keep my cell phone close by. All right?"

As if on cue, her phone trilled, ending last night's conversation in her mind and startling a cardinal from the dock railing. Digging in her coat pocket, she answered the call.

"We have Ally today," Cal said without preamble. "Her preschool's closed for some kind of teacher in-service, and her day care said the drop-in slots for today are all full."

The sound of his voice swept through her, stirring a sweet vibration in her blood. Libby lowered her feet from the bench and stretched a kink in her back. "I don't remember any mention of this before."

"Because there was none. Renee forgot to tell me. Drugs will foul up your memory. Probably forgot about it herself until she got to school and was turned away." A deep grumble filled the airwaves. "I'm supposed to be at work in two hours. What am I supposed to do with Ally?"

Libby stood and dusted the seat of her sweatpants. "You're sure this isn't a ploy to get me home earlier?"

"It's no ploy, Lib. But if it brings you home sooner, fine."

She headed up the dock to the leaf-strewn path back to the cabin. A cup of hot coffee sounded good now that she'd greeted the sunrise. "What if I weren't taking the day off? I can't always drop things to baby-sit like I did last week. We need to have a contingency plan for situations like this. Now's as good a time as any to find an alternate solution."

"Such as?"

Libby shuffled the damp leaves with her feet as she strolled up the path through the woods. She inhaled deeply the refreshing, earthy scents of decaying foliage, dew and clean air. "Find another day care that allows drop-ins. Or call Mrs. Russell next door. Her number's written on the front of the phone book. She might watch Ally for a while. And the people across the street, the Everetts, have a daughter in high school who could come in the afternoon."

"Everett. Got it." Cal paused, pitched his voice low. "I still want you home, though. I didn't sleep a wink last night worrying about you."

She imagined the intensity that came into his eyes when he used that tone. Deep-sea blue. Piercing. So alluring.

She considered telling him that thoughts of him had kept her up, too. But worry hadn't been the cause of her lost sleep. The achy, pulsing restlessness hummed to life inside her again. Damn it, just talking to him, hearing his voice, made her body thrum.

She picked up her pace back to the cabin. She needed that caffeine. Now. "Melissa."

"What?"

She cleared her throat and stepped over a fallen tree in her path. "The Everett's daughter is Melissa. I think she's sixteen. She doesn't get home from school until about two, so she's not the best choice. I'd try Mrs. Rus—"

Something moved in her peripheral vision. She stopped, heart thumping, and scanned the woods.

"Lib, you there?"

"Yeah, I…thought I saw something. I—"

The rhythmic snapping of twigs and crunching of leaves filtered through the morning silence. Footsteps. Her mouth grew arid.

"Someone's out there," she murmured. She stood, rooted with fear, while the sense of being watched crawled up her spine.

Her skin flashed cold then hot then icy as the rustle of leaves and crack of branches echoed around her. Turning slowly, she tried to pinpoint the source. Shadows shifted as trees swayed in the murmuring breeze.

"Cal?" she whispered, her throat dry.

"I'm still here. Libby, what is it? What's wrong?"

"I…don't think I'm alone."

His response singed the airwaves. "Get out of there. Now!"

Legs shaking, she stumbled to a run. Her scrambling steps over the uneven earth jarred the breath from her lungs.

A flash of blue through the winter-bare branches caught her eye, brought her up short. "Who's there?"

No reply.

"This is private property, and you're trespassing!" she called, hoping the intruder was just a kid, a hunter, a trick of her imagination. If only Cal were here rather than on her phone. If only she'd listened when he'd told her to carry her gun with her. If only—

"Damn it, Libby, get the hell out of there!" Cal shouted over the phone.

Suiting his words to action, she bolted toward the cabin. She slipped in the dry leaves and pine needles that littered the ground. Her breathing ragged, she flew up the sagging wood steps to the porch. She burst through the front door, eager to gather her few possessions and be gone. Still clutching her cell phone, clinging to that small contact with Cal, she snatched her gym bag from the floor, tossed it on the bed.

And screamed.

A voodoo doll lay on her pillow, a penknife through the heart. Crimson stains covered the crude likeness of a woman, the sort sold as souvenirs to tourists in New Orleans voodoo shops. Beside the doll, a blue envelope poked out from under her gym bag. The cell phone slipped from her trembling hand, clattered to the floor.

"Libby! Libby, answer me!"

She heard Cal's voice as if through a tunnel.

Backing from the bed, gasping for oxygen, she stared at the gruesome warning. She didn't need to read the note. The message was clear.

Her stalker had followed her. Found her. Watched her.

She groped blindly on the table by the door for her keys.

"Libby!"

Cal's panicked voice shook her from her trance. Swiping the phone from the floor, she raised it to her ear. "He left a message. Oh, God, he followed me here! How else could he have known where…?"

But if he'd followed her, why not strike last night? Why wait until morning?

Numbly, she lifted her purse strap to her shoulder and edged out the front door. She fled the cabin, racing for her car. Abandoning her gym bag. Wanting only to get away before her stalker returned to make good his threat.

"Hang up…call 9-1-1," Cal said, the tremble of anxiety ringing in his voice. "Get the cops out there. If he's still nearby, maybe they can track him."

"No, don't go!" she cried. "I need you now." *Even if only the reassurance of your voice.* "I'm leaving. I'll call the cops once I'm out of here." Libby jogged around the corner of the cabin to the drive where she'd parked her car. "Right now, I need to hear you. I need—"

With a gasp, she skidded to a halt. "Oh, no!"

"Judas priest, Libby! I'm going crazy here!" Cal's voice rasped over the line. "What's happened? Are you all right?"

Libby gripped the phone tighter, her lifeline to Cal. She forced air through her constricted throat and crept back toward the safety of the cabin. Her body shook, and icy prickles nipped her skin. Her gaze darted about, and she scanned the line of trees surrounding her. "I'm o-okay, but—"

As she edged backward, she stumbled on a root and landed hard on her bottom.

"But what? Libby, talk to me!"

She dragged in a shuddering breath. "I can't leave. My tires are slashed."

Cal paced the living room, wearing a path on Libby's Persian rug, and waited. Waited for the sound of Libby pulling in the front drive. Waited for another call, another chance to hear Libby's voice. Waited for the opportunity to hold her and reassure himself she was all right.

Something. Anything. But if the waiting wasn't enough, the sense of helplessness, his complete inability to do anything to help her, sucked outright. As soon as he'd heard Libby's tires had been slashed, he'd been on the phone to the police, hating that he couldn't go to her himself. His parole terms chafed like a pair of too-tight manacles.

He hadn't found anyone to watch Ally yet. He was going to be late for work, possibly get fired. And he had an ulcer the size of Louisiana gnawing inside him from worry.

But none of that mattered. Only Libby mattered at that moment. Her safety. Having her back in his arms. Even though she'd called to check in with him an hour ago from the car mechanic's shop where they were replacing her tires, he was still insane with worry. She'd insisted she was all right, for him not to worry, but he wouldn't be satisfied until he could touch her, see her, hold her.

"Look, Daddy. I made a picture of Jewel." Ally held up the paper she'd been coloring on and grinned.

He gave his daughter the best smile he could, but it felt brittle, tense. "That's great, kitten. You're a real artist."

Ally clambered off the floor where she worked and flopped onto the sofa, next to the sleeping cat. She stroked Jewel's fur and grinned brighter. "She's purring. I think she likes me."

The phone rang, jangling his taut nerves, and he pounced on the receiver like Jewel jumping on a mouse. "Libby? Is that you? Where are you?"

"Uh…no, sorry," said the man on the phone. "This is Reyn Erikson of the Clairmont volunteer fire department. You'd left a message earlier about being on call for us?"

Disappointment zinged through Cal even though he'd normally be thrilled to talk about getting on the roster with the volunteer firefighters. "Oh, right. I did."

"Great. I understand you've got ten years' experience? That's awesome. I've talked to your parole officer and cleared your hire with the town council. We're a bit shorthanded and still battling drought conditions in the region. So I'll put you on the call list and get you a pager as soon as we can. Let me make sure I've got your contact info correct and—"

"I…listen, can I call you later today? I need to keep this line free."

Cal watched Ally pop up from the couch and cross to the front window, where she peered out.

"Oh, sure. You've still got my number?" Reyn asked.

"Yeah, I've got it. And thanks. It'll be good to get back to firefighting." He heard the rumble of a car engine as he hung up.

"Libby's home!" Ally bounced on her toes and clapped.

Cal crossed the room in three strides and tossed the curtain back to see for himself. When Libby stepped out of her Camry, relief crashed through him. His kinked muscles loosened so suddenly, his knees nearly buckled. He met Libby at the door and swept her into his arms the second she walked in the house.

He crushed her to his chest, and she clung just as tightly to him, shaking all over and gulping shallow breaths.

"Oh, God! I was so scared," she whispered.

He sank his fingers deep into her thick hair and buried his face in the silky veil. "Not half as scared as I was, not knowing what was happening to you."

Her fingers dug into his back, and she canted even closer, her soft curves molding to his hard lines. The press of her body reassured him she was alive, calmed the raging panic that clawed him. And set his blood on fire.

He needed her with a possessive ache, wanted her so much he hurt. But the deepest pain wasn't rooted in his groin. His heart felt like the Grinch's, suddenly growing too large to fit his chest. He'd believed himself in love with her years ago, but she'd never been so ingrained in his heart and mind that he feared a part of himself would die if he lost her.

Framing her face with his hands, he angled her head and claimed her lips. His kiss was not gentle. Not patient. He slaked the remnants of hours on the edge of sanity, waiting for news, praying she was safe. Teeth clashed, tongues dueled, passions rose. And Libby kissed him in equal measure, greedily devouring what he offered.

"Hey, Libby, look at the picture I made. You can have it if you want." Ally's voice filtered through the carnal haze that swallowed him.

Libby pulled away abruptly, panting and bleary-eyed. Blinking twice, she pivoted to face his daughter and clearly struggled to focus on the paper Ally held.

"Um, it's lovely, sweetie." She cleared the husky timbre from her throat and gave Ally a strained smile.

"It's Jewel. See?" Ally held the picture next to the cat curled on the couch.

Libby gave a hiccupping laugh, her eyes bright with a sheen of moisture. "I see. Very good."

Her hand fluttered to her chest and searched for buttons that weren't there to twist. Sliding his hands up the dip of her waist, Cal caught her wrists to still them and pressed a kiss to her palms.

She met his eyes, and the message telegraphed in her heated gaze was clear—the fire burning inside them would have to wait. They couldn't make sizzling love to each other with Ally playing in the next room. Impatience and frustration torqued his nerves like a guitar string wound too tight. Something had to give, or he'd break.

He rested his forehead against Libby's and sighed. "I haven't called Mrs. Russell yet. I wanted to keep the phone free in case you called."

She nodded, shuddered. "The police didn't get him. He must have heard me on the phone and run, knowing the cops were coming. They took the voodoo doll as evidence and were dusting the cabin for prints when the tow truck came. A deputy drove me to the tire place to wait for my car. The slashed tires are evidence, too." She closed her eyes and rubbed the back of her neck.

Drawing her back into his arms, Cal pressed his lips to her temple and growled, "Damn it, Libby. Don't ever do something so foolish again. If you'd been killed…"

She trembled, and he didn't finish the thought, didn't want to see that horror to an end.

Libby tugged free of his hold and walked over to the sofa, where she sank next to Jewel with a sigh. "Hadn't you better get to work before you're fired?"

"I can call in sick, stay here with you if—"

"I'm all right now. Really."

Ally sidled up to Libby and flopped against her for a hug. Libby pulled the little girl in tight and closed her eyes.

"I don't want to leave you if you think…" He rubbed his hands on his jeans. Who was he kidding? He wanted to stay for himself. Because he wanted to hold Libby and never let go.

But clearly she didn't need him as much as he needed her. A bad place to be. If leaving her had hurt him before, having her push him away now would be agony. Better to rein himself in. Put on the brakes before he crashed.

"I'll be back about eight. Will you take care of finding a babysitter?"

Libby shot him a look that said, *I am in control. I'll handle it.* Cool, efficient Libby. So fiercely independent and capable. So what did she need him for?

A spasm of regret twisted inside Cal.

Truth was—she didn't need him.

Chapter 12

That night, Cal looked straight into Renee's eyes and scowled. "Do you need me to drive you home?"

Libby was in the spare bedroom, helping Ally gather all her drawings to take home, while he waited with his ex in the front hall. When Renee didn't show up at dinnertime as expected, Libby had put Ally to bed rather than keep her awake indefinitely, waiting for a mother who might not show.

Now, at almost ten o'clock, Renee shot him a withering look, like a petulant teenager, and dangled her keys in front of him. "Hello? I have my own car. That's how I got here."

"That's not what I mean, and you know it."

"Why don't you just say what you mean? You think I'm stoned, don't you? Well, I'm not!"

"When's the last time you got high?" he pressed, although her eyes did appear clearer than in recent days and her speech wasn't slurred.

Renee set her jaw defiantly and narrowed her eyes. "None of your business."

"It's my business if you put my daughter in your car."

"She's my daughter, too. I'd never do anything to hurt her!"

Cal almost choked. "What! Every time you shoot up, you hurt her! Your lifestyle, your gross neglect, hurts her every day. Your apartment is a disgrace. It's dirty and smelly and full of bugs, and—"

"Not everyone can afford to live like your swanky new wife." Renee sneered as she cast an eye around Libby's house. "I do the best I can!"

"Your best would mean staying sober. For our daughter's well-being, if not your own."

She crossed her arms over her chest. "What do you care about my well-being?"

Cal swallowed the angry retort that sprang to his tongue, startled by the pain he saw in Renee's eyes. "I...I care plenty about what happens to you, Nee. We were married once. We made a little girl together. I care about you and what you're doing to yourself."

"Fine way you have of showing it. Trying to take away the only good thing I ever did with my life."

He exhaled with a whoosh. "I told you I'm not fighting for custody to hurt you, Renee. I'm doing it to protect Ally."

"Protect her?" Renee dropped her arms to her sides, her expression stunned, affronted. "From me? I love her! I'd never—" His ex wife's eyes darted past him down the hall, and she pasted on a stiff smile. "Hey, sugar! Ready to go home?"

Cal turned and watched Libby nudge Ally closer, his daughter's hair still rumpled from her pillow.

"I wanna stay with Daddy," Ally whined.

Renee shot him a glare full of resentment and laced with pain. Libby knelt beside Ally and brushed the flyaway curls behind the sleepy girl's ear. "We'll see you again this weekend, sweetie. But you need to go home with your mom now. Okay?"

Ally hesitated, gave Renee a wary sideways glance. "Can Jewel go with me?"

"Who's Jewel?" Renee asked.

"The cat." Cal scooped his daughter into his arms and gave her a fierce hug. "Jewel lives here, kitten. But you can come see her again in a few days." He kissed Ally's cheek, inhaled the sweet scent of baby bath and innocence, and his throat tightened. Sending Ally back to the cesspool and neglect at Renee's apartment ripped him apart. But obeying the letter of the law to win custody was so important. And he had to keep his nose clean for his parole and the conditions of Act 894 so his record could be expunged, so he could get his firefighting job, *his life,* back.

He peeled Ally from his neck and handed her to her mother. "If you love her, then prove it," he growled to his ex. "Put her first. Clean up your act and get straight."

Renee frowned and whirled toward the door. "By the way," she said and turned to shoot daggers at Libby. "I know you were responsible for having Roach hauled in." She flashed a haughty grin. "Nice try, but he made bail. Thought you might like to know."

Libby squared her shoulders. "The guy is trouble, Renee. You'd do well to stay away from him."

Cal's ex looked at him then back at Libby. "So would you."

Cal gave Ally one last kiss on the forehead as Renee swept out the door and headed down the sidewalk. He stood in the open door and watched until Renee's taillights disappeared around the block.

"You're letting bugs in the house," Libby called from the couch, where she'd propped up her feet. "Jewel thanks you for the toys, but I'd rather not have mosquitoes buzzing in my ear while I sleep."

Cal batted a moth away as he shut the door and faced his wife. "Roach."

"Hmm. What about him?" Libby flipped the page on the magazine she'd picked up.

Plucking the *Southern Living* from her hands, he tossed the magazine on the coffee table. "It was him out at the lake. I'd bet money."

"Based on what? Where's the evidence?"

"No proof, just a gut feeling." He sat on the edge of the sofa beside her, his hip bumping hers. Even that casual contact raised his blood pressure, teased his imagination. It would be so easy to push her back in the sofa cushions and cover her with his body, lose himself inside her. He stroked her thigh, starting at her knee and moving up her satiny skin. Under her cotton gown. Higher.

She caught his wrist and pushed his hand away. "I don't deal in feelings. Only facts."

I won't let myself get hurt again.

A bruising weight settled in his chest.

Somehow he had to make her see she could trust him not to leave, not to hurt her. Or to let her get hurt. He refused to repeat the mistakes he'd made as a teenager when his mom had needed him. With so many things working against him, he had a real fight on his hands. But Libby was worth the fight.

"Roach threatened you when you had him arrested the other day. The man had pure venom in his voice, in his eyes. He wanted to kill you."

He tried again to touch her, smoothing a hand over her shoulder and down her toned arm. Whatever she did at that kickboxing class worked. She had great muscle definition in her slender arms, sleek legs. He could almost feel those legs wrapped around his waist....

She rolled to an upright position and rose from the couch, moving away from him. Again. Distance. Always the gulf between them. The desire humming through him hardened into frustration.

For a few sweet moments, she'd relaxed her guard when she'd returned home from her ordeal at Lake D'Arbonne. She'd held on to him, let herself need him for a minute.

And then withdrawn, determined to fight her own battles.

Libby marched across the same Persian rug he'd worn out earlier in the day, then spun to face him. "It's not Roach."

"How do you know?"

"There was another note with the voodoo doll. I didn't read the note, but it was on the same blue paper that the other threats from the stalker came on." She raked her hair back with her fingers. "I started receiving the letters from the stalker well before I saw Roach at Renee's, and before I saw him at the park and called in the police."

"You're sure?"

She nodded, shuddered. "I hate this."

"I know. I do, too." He stepped closer and drew her into his arms. Though her back was stiff, she didn't resist. Small progress.

"I swear to you, Libby, we will find this guy, and we will have our lives back. We'll have the future fate stole from us before—"

"Fate?" She backed out of his arms, her eyes dark and stormy. "Fate didn't break us up. You did. Your choices did. You chose Renee over me. That is why we lost everything we had."

He let a breath hiss through his teeth. "No, I chose my child, being a father. And not because I didn't want you. How many times do I have to explain this?"

She sent him a pained look. "I don't need anything explained to me. I lived it."

Compunction pounded him. "I never meant to hurt you, Lib. Never. Lord knows, I hated giving you up. It ripped me apart. I felt like a vital piece of my soul had been torn out."

He saw her tense, and she stared at him, confusion and disbelief filling her eyes. "What?"

He studied her shocked expression through narrowed eyes, the thud of his pulse keeping time with her mantel clock. "Didn't you understand that? Libby, I wanted to marry *you*, not Renee."

She stumbled back a step, shaking her head. Her mocha eyes misted, and she hugged herself. "But you were so matter-of-fact, so blunt, when you told me it was over, when you walked out."

"I was numb, Lib. I was struggling to accept the cruel twist fate had tossed in my path. I was trying to do the right thing for my baby, but I was hemorrhaging inside."

"You never told me how you felt. How could I have known?" Tears welled in her eyes. "Your leaving, your stoicism the day you walked out, told me you didn't care. I felt used and discarded. No more than the inconvenience I'd been to my mother and her boyfr—"

Her hiccuping sob hit him like a fist in the gut. She lifted a hand to her mouth and turned her back to him. He moved up behind her and circled her with his arms.

Kissing the crown of her head, he murmured, "I thought you knew. I thought I'd said it in every kiss, every look, every minute we spent together. Whether we were practicing your closing argument for some big case or catching crawfish in Bayou Laterre."

She gave a short, soft laugh. More a burst of air, really. Angling her head, she glanced back at him. "I still have mud in my pores from that fiasco."

He squeezed her tighter. "But you had fun. Admit it."

She pivoted in his grasp and wrapped her arms around his waist. "I always had fun with you. I missed that when you left."

He lowered his head, pulled her nearer, until his lips were a breath away from hers. "We can have fun again. We have a second chance to make this work."

He closed the distance between their mouths, and he felt the tremor that shook her. Or maybe he was the one who trembled. The sensation of her lips moving against his and the minty taste of her toothpaste as her tongue mated with his rocketed through his system, shaking the ground beneath him. With his kiss, he tried to say all the things he'd never had the courage to say before. The tangled web of emotions that had never died for him, only rooted themselves deeper in his heart.

Only one shadow still lurked in the path of the bright future he wanted with Libby—someone wanted to kill her.

He broke their kiss, a cold sweat popping out on his brow and a sense of urgency drumming a war beat in his head.

"We have to find this guy. Your stalker." He held her at arm's length, regretting the flicker of fear that obliterated the hazy desire in her eyes. "We can't wait on the police. We have to figure out who he is and stop him before he gets to you."

She licked her kiss-swollen lips, and he determinedly squashed the surge of heat. *Later.* Encouraged that this time there would be a later, Cal shoved his libido aside for more pressing concerns. Like Libby's life.

"It could be anyone, Cal. In my line of work, enemies are more common than friends. My conviction list is long and varied. Who knows what set this guy off?"

Gripping her hand, he led her back to the antique couch. He pulled her down beside him, trying not to think about the sexual fantasy he'd indulged in moments ago regarding a quick tumble with Libby on this same sofa. "Okay, you want to deal in facts, let's look at the facts as we know them."

"Facts. Okay." Libby nodded and pushed back up from the couch.

"Where are you going?"

"I need paper and a pen. I think better when I can write things out, look at them, draw charts and so forth."

Cal had to smile at that. So logical, so orderly.

He watched her cotton gown swish around her legs as she left the room and admired the way the cloth slid over her curves. *Steady, boy.*

"Meet me in the kitchen. We can work at the table," he said. He rubbed his hands on his face and decided a shot of caffeine was called for.

Libby entered the kitchen while he stood staring into the refrigerator. He glanced up, met her curious eyes, saw the distrust that drifted through her gaze.

And he saw her stop the suspicious thought, watched her push the concern aside and give him a small smile. An olive branch?

"I'll have one, too, please." She settled at the end of the table, uncapped her fountain pen.

"One what?" He squeezed the refrigerator door handle, praying he was right about what he'd just seen.

"Whatever you're having. Make mine diet."

Relief spilled from him in a slow exhale while hope swelled in his chest. Maybe they *could* build on the fragile foundations of trust and faith they'd forged tonight.

Maybe…

"All right. I got my first letter—" she opened her calendar and ran a finger across the page "—on the third of last month. I didn't keep it because it really wasn't threatening. Didn't ring any warning bells other than it seemed strange."

Cal took two diet colas from the shelf and closed the refrigerator. He popped the tabs on both and set one beside her.

She glanced up from her note making, lifted the can to her lips, then hesitated when her gaze collided with his. For a heartbeat, she just stared. Five years of waiting and wishing and regrets passed between them in that moment.

Maybe…

Jewel trotted into the kitchen and announced with a loud meow that she was ready for a midnight snack. And the spell was broken.

Averting her eyes, Libby finished sipping. "Thanks," she mumbled, indicating her drink with a little lift of the can before she set it on the table.

"No problem." He put the cat's food bowl on the floor before he sat down. "What did the first letter say?"

With that, they launched into an itemized rehashing of the past weeks. The mounting menace in the stalker's letters. The creep's uncanny ability to know where she was and what she was wearing. His pursuit of her in the courthouse stairwell. The sabotaged elevator. The warning at Stan's cabin.

"You said you told Stan you would be at the lake? Right?" Cal rubbed his thumb along the scar on his chin, thinking aloud.

"Besides needing to let him know I'd not be at work, I figured it was the decent thing to do since it's *his* cabin."

"And we know he was in the building the night you were followed on the stairs and the night the elevator crashed."

Libby groaned and shook her head. "Don't even go there. Stan and I have been friends for years. He has no reason to want to hurt me."

Cal sat forward in his chair and braced his arms on the table. "You sure about that? What about professional jealousy? Do you think he's trying to scare you into leaving the D.A.'s office? The comment in one letter about you staying at home where a woman belongs could point toward—"

"No! It's not Stan."

He tipped his head from side to side, stretching the tired muscles in his neck. "No one else knew you'd be at the lake."

"I could have been followed."

"Were you? Did you see anyone behind you driving up to the cabin?"

"No." She sighed. "But that doesn't mean—"

Cal circled Stan's name on the paper he'd taken from Libby's notebook. "He's still a lead suspect in my book."

Growling her disagreement, Libby pushed her chair back and took her soda can to the sink to rinse.

Cal drummed his fingers on the table and studied the notes they'd made. "So, the cops found no fingerprints on the notes or the notepad. The guy is smart enough not to leave evidence. What about the envelope seal? Can't they get DNA from the glue if he licked the seal?"

"They tried that." She slid back into her chair and finger-combed her hair. "Apparently he used a sponge or rag to wet the glue. The handwriting analysis points toward an individual living under a great deal of stress or pressure, but these days, who isn't? And stalking an A.D.A. must be a stressful preoccupation." Sarcasm tinged her tone, and he reached for her hand.

"We'll find him, Lib. Okay? I won't rest until I know this guy is caught."

"It's not your job. It's mine and the police's."

He drilled her with a firm gaze. "It *is* my job to make sure you're safe. I'm your husband."

Libby caught her breath, jolting at his reminder of their marital status. He caught wistfulness, a flicker of something warm and promising in her chocolate eyes, before she visibly reined in her emotions and slipped her hand out of his.

Taking up her pen again, she scribbled a note on the paper in front of her. "I think we're overlooking something rather obvious. Maybe I haven't given it much credence before now because the reality was too frightening, but…"

The fear that sparked to life in her eyes racheted his pulse up a notch. "What, Lib?"

"He planted that notebook in your things. He's been in this house. He could live near here and be watching us through a telephoto lens or…"

The idea of someone spying on Libby, someone breaking into her house, raised the hair on the back of Cal's neck.

Not knowing the who, the where, the when of this scum's threat roiled inside him. Not since he'd learned the truth about his mother's frequent "accidents" had he felt such a sense of helplessness and protective rage.

"Libby, maybe you should leave town. Get away from h—"

The phone trilled. Libby flinched, gasped.

He looked at his watch. It was after midnight. A call this late could only mean trouble.

Ally.

If something was wrong…

Libby started to rise, but he waved her back down. "Let me get it."

He snatched the receiver from the cradle on the third ring. "H'lo?"

"Is this Cal Walters?" the male voice asked.

"Who's asking?"

"This is Reyn Erikson again. We talked earlier about you volunteering for the Clairmont VFD."

Cal could hear a commotion in the background. He knew what was coming, and adrenaline spiked in his blood.

"We've got a pretty massive blaze going down here. Someone camping in the woods started a forest fire that took off in the dry brush, and—"

"I'm on my way. Where should I meet you?"

Reyn gave directions, and Cal took mental notes. Even after the small-town fire chief had hung up, Cal stood with the phone in his hand, his heart thumping. A fire. This dragon-slayer was back in business.

"Cal?"

He faced Libby and blew out a sharp breath. "I've been called to a blaze. The volunteer department in Clairmont is battling a forest fire." He recradled the receiver of her 1970s-era phone and narrowed a worried gaze on Libby. "I have to go out for a while. Will you be okay alone until—"

She grunted and crossed her arms over her chest. "Buddy, I've spent most of my life alone. I'll be fine."

But most of her life she hadn't had a pervert stalking her. "Keep the doors locked."

She gave him an indulgent smile. "Of course."

"Don't hesitate to call the cops if you hear or see anything—"

"Cal, go. A forest is burning with your name on it."

He sucked in a deep breath, his blood singing with energy and anticipation. He took no more than two steps away from the phone before he stopped. Turned. Lifted the receiver again.

On a hunch, he unscrewed the cap on the mouthpiece and tipped the phone up.

"What are you—"

Libby halted midsentence when a tiny device like a watch battery rolled out into his palm.

Their gazes clashed. Terror danced in her eyes.

"A bug?" she rasped.

He bounced the incriminating device in his hand and scowled. "I think we just discovered how your stalker knew you'd be at Stan's cabin."

Chapter 13

A police-conducted sweep of her house hadn't yielded any more bugs. Still, lying in her bed later that night, Libby had the sensation of a different kind of bug crawling on her skin.

Every time she'd picked up her phone, her stalker had been listening. If he'd bugged her home phone, chances were good he'd bugged her office phone, as well. No wonder he'd seemed to be right on her heels wherever she went. Even a step ahead, as he had been when the elevator crashed. The invasion of her privacy galled her, left her nauseated.

She shook off her jitters, reminding herself that the cops had posted someone on the street to watch her house tonight. Police surveillance was Cal's second choice to staying himself, and he'd been unrelenting in his demand that someone be around to safeguard her.

"I'm blowing off this fire call. Telling them I can't come. I should stay with you," Cal had said, even before the police had arrived. But she'd insisted he go.

She could see what the opportunity to be back in action, battling fires, meant to him. He thrived on the excitement, the adrenaline rush, the pride of knowing he was helping save property and protect lives. Yet despite his love of firefighting, he'd been prepared to stay with her. To protect *her* tonight instead. And she lost another tiny piece of her heart to him. Because he'd been willing to sacrifice something he loved for her. Tonight, for just a moment, she'd been his priority.

And it felt good.

Snuggling under her covers, Libby tried to focus on the warmth Cal stirred deep in her soul with his concern for her, rather than the clammy grip of fear that lingered from that morning. The chilling images of the bloody voodoo doll lurked in her mind. Knowing how close her stalker was getting with his escalating threats shot ice through her veins.

When Jewel jumped up on the bed and curled next to her, Libby stroked the cat's soft fur. Jewel purred, and the lulling rumble settled around Libby like a comforting blanket.

So what if she was alone? For as long as she could remember she'd had only herself to depend on. She'd faced the unknown of the new boyfriends her mother brought home and survived the isolation and starvation Jimmy had doled out by locking her in the closet. One night without Cal should be cake. She'd survived much worse. By herself.

She had a policeman close by, keeping tabs on her house. She'd be fine.

But…

She missed Cal. More than his protection, she missed his soothing touch, his deep, sexy voice, his reassuring smile. In the short time they'd been married, sharing her home, she'd taken for granted having him in the guest room, a few steps away. Ready. Willing. More than able.

She trembled, her nerves crackling and her pulse jumping with an edgy need. Was it Cal's protection she wanted tonight or was it the man himself? She shifted restlessly in her wide, lonely bed. Her breasts tingled and ached, and the sheets proved a poor substitute for Cal's fingers caressing her skin.

She rolled over and blinked at the glowing numbers on her clock. Two thirty-six. How long would Cal be at the fire scene? If he got home before she had to leave for the office, what would she do with that time? Her body answered by pulsing a wave of shimmery sparks through her bloodstream.

She curled her fingers into Jewel's fur and sighed. Another night with no sleep. She stared into the darkness, waiting for morning and wondering what Cal faced at the fire scene.

Jewel stopped purring abruptly. The cat's head popped up, eyes alert and blinking. Jewel's ears perked, and her fur bristled.

A chill skated down Libby's spine. She strained to listen. Heard nothing but the thud of her heart in her ears. "What is it, Jules?" she whispered. "What'd you hear?"

With a strange, growling meow, Jewel slunk off the bed. Libby bit her cheek as the cat scurried in a crouch out the bedroom door. Libby wanted to believe Jewel had merely heard a dog in the neighbor's trash. But a sense of foreboding scraped over her skin.

She eased open the nightstand drawer. Hands trembling, she lifted the storage box where she kept her gun, unlocked it and removed the pistol. She set the weapon on the bed and swung her legs to the floor. Gulping shallow breaths, she fumbled in the drawer's clutter for rounds for the .22.

Apprehension strangled her. She loaded her handgun, ears tuned to the slightest noise. Maybe during one of the drive-bys, a conscientious cop had stopped and cased the house, checking the bushes.

The rumble of Jewel's growl drifted down the hall again, hiking her blood pressure another click. Clamping the weapon in one shaky hand, her flashlight in the other, Libby tiptoed to the hall. Toward the living room. Creeping. Eyes scanning the darkness. Breath lodged in her lungs.

Jewel yowled and lunged at the window. Startled by the howl, Libby shrieked, as well. She swung the nose of the gun where Jewel had pounced. Aiming her flashlight in the same direction, she encountered a glowing pair of eyes.

And yellow fur. Mr. Johnson's randy tomcat.

Weak with relief, mad at herself for her panic, Libby lowered the gun and flicked the safety on. She sagged against the wall and glared at her cat, who still thumped her tail with agitation over the trespassing tom. "Damn it, Jewel. You scared me to death! Tell your boyfriends not to visit in the middle of the night."

"Mrow!" Jewel hopped off the windowsill and trotted into the kitchen.

"No, you can't have a snack as long as we're up. I'm mad at you." Libby stumbled to the sofa and sank onto the cushions. No way would she get to sleep now. Not with her head throbbing, her heart racing, her imagination running wild.

Lifting the TV remote, Libby flipped on the television. Maybe the old-movie channel was playing *Twelve Angry Men* again. She needed a distraction.

As she clicked past the local news channel, the image of a wildfire caught her attention. Near Clairmont, the bottom of the screen read.

"Firefighters have been battling the blaze since before midnight, hoping to contain the fire before it reaches nearby farms," a reporter's voice-over said. "Recent drought conditions have left the forests around Clairmont dry and vulnerable to wildfires, and this blaze has roared out of control."

Libby sat forward, her attention riveted to the hellish images flashing across the screen. Walls of fire consumed towering pines while firemen blasted the flames with powerful hoses. Yet even the water spray seemed ineffective. The men appeared dwarfed by the flames shooting into the night sky. Like David and Goliath.

"Fire departments from as far away as Monroe have been called to assist in fighting the runaway blaze," the report continued.

Libby hugged a sofa pillow to her chest, squeezing it as tension coiled in her gut. Cal was there, somewhere, battling this giant.

"Tragically, one fireman was killed earlier, and two others were taken to the Clairmont Hospital to be treated for injuries when shifting winds caused a burning tree to fall."

Libby's heartbeat slowed, a paralyzing dread spinning through her. *One fireman was killed.*

"A dozen others have been pulled back from the front line, suffering exhaustion and heat-related symptoms. Those men are expected to return to the fire lines soon and continue their efforts to contain the fire before any more homes are lost."

The reporter came on the screen, and an older man stood with him. Libby stared at the TV numbly while the older gentleman described the shock and grief of losing his home to the forest fire. She didn't hear a word of it.

One fireman was dead. Two more hospitalized. The first flutter of panic beat its wings in her chest.

Even when Cal had walked out of her life five years ago, she hadn't experienced the level of pain that wrenched inside her now. The mere idea that he could be dead…

Libby blinked back bitter tears, swallowed the bile that rose in her throat. She wouldn't, *couldn't,* even consider the notion.

But denial didn't erase the real possibility that Cal could be injured.

Or worse.

Pain ripped through her. Clawing. Plundering.

Not Cal. Please, God, not Cal!

* * *

"Lib?" Cal crouched by the sofa where his wife slept and ran the back of his hand along Libby's cheek. Her skin felt slightly sticky, looked blotchy, and her nose was red. She'd been crying.

A knot of self-censure twisted inside him. He should never have left her alone last night. He'd seen how rattled she was by the bug they found in the phone, and he knew she'd suffered a lot more with her ordeal at Stan's cabin than she wanted to admit. Imagining her alone, crying, frightened, turned him inside out.

He slid the remote control from her limp hand and turned off the TV. Morning cartoons faded to black. He set the remote on the coffee table. And froze.

Libby's pistol sat on the coffee table. Why had she felt the need to get it out? Had something happened last night while he was gone?

He'd have to remind her to lock the gun back up. His parole officer had stipulated that Libby's gun had to stay locked away, where Cal had no access to it.

He twisted back to face her, searching her with a closer scrutiny to assure himself she was unharmed. Pushing her hair back from her face, he kissed her forehead.

Libby jolted. Sat up with a gasp.

And cracked her head against his with a whomp. He groaned and clapped a hand to the offended part of his skull. The throb of exhaustion and inhaled smoke ricocheted around in his head with the new assault. Libby also nursed her head with a rub.

"Ow," she mumbled, sleepily turning her gaze on him. Suddenly, her eyes flew open wide, and she launched herself into his arms. "Cal! You're home! Oh, thank God you're all right!"

He caught her and barely managed not to topple backward as she wrapped herself around him and clung.

"Yeah, I'm okay. Stinky with sweat and smoke and tired as hell, but okay. What about you? Are you all right?"

"Uh-huh. I am now that I know you're safe."

He tried to pry her off, even though having her pressed against him this tightly felt heavenly. "You're getting soot on you. I need to shower before—"

Libby grabbed his face and sealed her mouth over his. He didn't question the fervor of her welcome home, only savored it. In an instant, the taste of her lips renewed his energy. Sexual urgency hummed through his veins. Libby moved closer with a sensuous slide of her body along his. The less-than-subtle way she rocked her hips forward and circled him with her legs left no secret where she wanted this steamy greeting to go.

An electric pulse of desire sizzled through his tired muscles, his aching limbs. Her eagerness both stunned and encouraged him. Still, he was painfully aware of the grime and smoke that saturated his pores. As much as he wanted to lay Libby back on the couch and fulfill the promises she made in her hungry kiss, he didn't want to consummate his marriage in the grungy condition he was in. She deserved better.

Tearing himself away took every fiber of his willpower and strength. His body shuddered and ached with need. "Hold that thought," he murmured against her lips, "for five minutes while I grab a shower."

When he pulled away, she protested with a raspy mewl from her throat that rippled through him, straight to his groin.

He kissed the tip of her nose. "Just five minutes. Promise."

"Four," she countered. "Any longer, and I'm coming in after you."

Damn! She was killing him. He wasn't sure what had changed while he'd been gone tonight. But he wasn't arguing.

Libby wilted back on the sofa, lack of sleep and the relief of knowing Cal was safe sapping her strength. She touched her lips, which were still tingling from his ardent kiss, then sucked in a deep breath and released it slowly.

Who was she kidding? *She'd* kissed *him*. She'd jumped him. She'd been so happy to see him and know he was alive, she'd pounced like Mr. Johnson's randy tomcat.

Her reaction to Cal had been instinctive, automatic. She hadn't stopped to think about rules or repercussions.

Down the hall, the shower came on. *Five minutes.*

Glorious sensations zinged through her. She felt the imprint of his hard body on hers, the hewn muscle, the proof of his desire.

And last night, she could have lost it all. Some poor woman had lost her husband, or son, or brother. An arrow of grief for that woman pierced her heart. She clamped her lips tight to keep them from trembling.

I felt like a vital piece of my soul had been torn out.

Cal's words echoed in her head, in her heart. She understood that feeling, had survived it once, but didn't know how she could handle the loss if something happened to Cal now.

The sincerity and pain that had shone in his cerulean eyes had shattered everything she'd believed about their breakup years ago. He'd hurt as much as she had. He'd loved her.

Lying to herself about her true feelings was fruitless. Knowing the danger he'd faced tonight, battling the raging fire outside town, denials shriveled. Brutal honesty hammered home. Despite the risks to her heart, she was falling in love with him. Again.

A few days ago, he'd asked for a second chance. She'd already lost five years with Cal. Suddenly, even five wasted minutes seemed too long. An eternity.

With a surge of energy and anticipation, Libby shoved off the sofa and whipped her nightgown over her head. She discarded her panties in the hall and made a beeline for the shower.

Five years ago, she'd fallen in love with a gentle, compassionate man. A sometimes cocky and stubborn man. A man who made her body sing, her bones melt.

Having seen Cal interact with his daughter, witnessing his dedication to Ally and experiencing his protectiveness toward women, made her admire him more. His obvious concern about her stalker, his comfort and strength, his determination to work through the clues to the stalker's identity, touched her. How could she have believed him cold and selfish? Irresponsible? Unfeeling?

She'd been so wrong.

When she opened the bathroom door, steam enveloped her. Her pulse stuttered an eager rhythm as she padded across the cold tile floor.

Through the glass of the shower wall, she enjoyed the distorted view of Cal's tall, lean frame and wide shoulders. The catch on the shower door snicked as she opened it and stepped into the stall. "I got impatient. Hope you don't mind."

Cal twisted at the waist to look over his shoulder, surprise evident in his wide eyes. His gaze drifted down slowly then back up, and her nerve endings vibrated in the wake of his thorough perusal. His pupils dilated. His Adam's apple bobbed when he swallowed. "Have mercy."

She quirked a lopsided grin and stepped closer, into the warm water spray. "I'll take that to mean you don't mind."

With a lusty growl, he turned to face her more fully, and she savored her own chance to study him head to toe. Water dripped from his scarred chin. Soapy rivulets trickled down his broad chest and wove through the coarse, dark hair that thickened and narrowed in a path down his abdomen. Her gaze skimmed down powerful, muscled legs to his narrow feet. Heaven help her, he even had handsome feet.

"Come here, you," he said with a provocative gleam in his eyes, a smug hitch to his lips.

She reached for him, smoothing a hand over his soap-slickened shoulder and around his neck. She nipped at his lips, his cheek, the stubble-roughened line of his jaw. He tasted dark and sensual, dangerous. The remnants of smoke and salty perspiration teased her tongue when she traced his jaw with hungry kisses.

"Do you have any idea how long I've waited for this moment?" he asked, his voice husky and thick with desire. He pulled her closer, sliding his hands to cup her bottom and tugging her hips forward.

A pleasured sigh escaped her throat. She leaned into him, and her breasts nestled against the hot skin of his chest. "About five years?"

He sank his fingers into her hair, combing the damp strands away from her face before cradling her head in his palms. "Longer. It feels like forever."

He tipped her chin up with his thumbs and licked the drops of water from her lips before covering her mouth with a deep, soul-searing kiss.

She curled her fingers into his back, clung tighter as waves of dizzying pleasure washed over her. She angled her mouth to capture his more fully, and his tongue swept inside to tangle with hers.

Oh, but the man's kisses were devastating. How could she have forgotten the way his lips took control of her senses? How his mouth could tantalize and please, coax and seduce her? Her brain may have tried to banish the memory, but his kiss woke sensations her body remembered with startling clarity. Every cell was alive and alert, clamoring for his touch.

Cal skimmed one hand over her hip, strummed the ridge of her spine then dragged his fingertips down her back. His caress elicited tingling sparks that sizzled through her blood.

He moved his kiss south, his tongue tracing the curve of her neck, sipping the water droplets collected on her skin. As he had with their wedding, he left no detail unattended. His thoughtful attention to little things had benefits beyond the everyday, she discovered as he feathered shivery kisses along her collarbone.

She arched her back, offering her breasts for his questing lips. The warm spray of the shower rained down on her when he dipped his head to draw a nipple into his mouth. The water streams teased the tight peak of one breast while his tongue flicked the other. Heat coiled low in her belly, pulsed through her in throbbing beats.

Libby wound her fingers in his thick, wet hair, reveling in the sweet torture of his mouth suckling her breast. Cal was the only man she'd ever trusted enough to allow such intimacies. He was the only man who'd ever gotten close enough to touch her soul. The only man who could seduce her with a look, drive her wild with his kiss, send her body skyrocketing with his touch.

Cal nudged her leg with his hand, and she opened to him. He slid his palm down, nestled against her heat.

She couldn't breathe. Could only gasp when his fingers moved. He began with a sultry stroking, testing before probing inside her. Her body gripped him, and a fresh spasm of pleasure pushed her toward the edge of control.

"Cal!" she cried, and he abandoned her breast, brought her upright so he could claim her lips again. The water began to grow cooler as it rained down on them, yet her body burned. He kissed her with the same desperation that clawed inside her. Feverish. Impatient. Long overdue.

She raised her leg, hooking it around him. She wanted him nearer, wanted to climb inside him. Her hands roamed restlessly from his shoulders to his buttocks, memorizing every ridge of sinew and rock-hard plane.

His breathing, like hers, was ragged and shallow, and she could feel the thundering of his heart beneath her palm.

Moving his hands behind her thighs, Cal lifted her. He turned to pin her between his body and the shower wall. With a groan, he burrowed himself in the V of her legs, stroking the sensitive flesh there until she was ready to fly apart.

"More," she gasped, rocking her hips forward, straining toward him and the fulfillment her body craved.

Again he insinuated a hand between her legs, from behind this time. His fingers worked their magic, knowing just where to stroke, exactly how to bring her to the edge of sanity and keep her teetering there for what felt like eons.

Then, like a lightning strike, she shattered.

She bit down on his shoulder, a half moan, half scream tearing from her throat as she careened into her climax. She gripped him tighter with her legs, holding on for dear life while shuddering contractions rippled through her, pounding her with mind-numbing bliss.

As her last tremors faded, Cal smacked the water off and shouldered the shower door open. His wet feet slapped the bathroom floor as he carried her into the bedroom with long, hurried strides.

He followed her down onto the unmade bed, covering her, kissing her.

"Don't move," he murmured between kisses.

When he levered away from her, cold air nipped her wet skin. She shivered, missing the heat and weight of him on top of her.

"C'mon," he grumbled as he wrestled his wallet from his jeans pocket and removed a foil packet.

A condom. Of course Cal would think of protection, even when her own mind was hazed with desire. His dedication to protecting her made warmth swell in her chest.

Then he was back. Surrounding her with his heat. Filling her. Driving her back to the brink of ecstasy with the slow glide of his body inside hers.

This was what she'd missed. For five years. The sweet feeling of holding Cal while he was buried deep inside her. The sensation of their two bodies joined as one. The fusion of flesh. The union of souls. The completion of mind and body.

No wonder she'd hurt so badly when he'd left. He was a part of what made her whole.

She moved with him in the timeless dance of lovers. His body trembled with restraint, and his muscles knotted as he moved.

With her hands on his hips, she urged him on, encouraged a faster pace as tension swirled and collected inside her.

"I want—" she whispered, breathless. "Now…together."

"Libby…" Her name was a groan, a prayer, a release.

She held him, clung, as they were swept into the maelstrom. She couldn't separate his shudders from her own, carried higher by the power of going together. As one.

He collapsed on her, wrapping her in his arms and holding her close. He pressed tender kisses on her brow while she gathered her breath. The peace and security of lying in Cal's arms settled into her marrow. With Cal, she could let go, lose control and feel completely safe.

Chapter 14

He was in terrible danger.

Cal shifted his weight off Libby and rolled to his side, bringing her with him, keeping her soft body pressed close to his. When she snuggled under his arm and let her hand rest over his heart, he sighed his contentment.

Oh, yeah. Big danger.

Making love to Libby, being inside her, surrounded by her, in sync with her, had felt so unbelievably good, he'd let himself believe they could build a future together.

Too many old hurts and unresolved issues still lay between them to get his hopes up yet. They'd only begun to connect again. They'd barely scratched the surface of the history they needed to dig through before they could rightfully expect to move forward. And this time, he intended to get things right with Libby.

Hot, even-better-than-he'd-remembered sex was a step in the right direction, for sure. He'd rather kiss Libby than argue with her any day of the week. But they'd had great sex before. The problem was, so much had gone unsaid years ago that his leaving had caused deep scars, wounds that still needed to heal.

"Wow," she whispered and heaved a deep, happy-sounding sigh.

A smile tugged his lips. "You can say that again."

Cal ran his fingers through her damp hair and watched the strands fall back to her shoulder. Something had changed for her while he'd been at the fire scene, something that brought down her walls of resistance. He was almost afraid to ask her about it, afraid he'd break the spell or wake himself from an incredibly erotic dream.

Libby lifted her head and squinted at the bedside clock. With a disgruntled groan, she settled back down. "I'm due at the office in just over an hour."

"Call in sick."

She thumped his chest lightly. "I can't do that! I have things on my desk that need my attention."

"You have a husband in your bed who needs your attention," he murmured while insinuating a hand between her legs.

Her breath hitched. Her eyes widened. And in one fluid motion, he rolled her back onto her pillow and caught her lips.

A protest rumbled in her throat, and she pushed against his chest in an unconvincing show of resistance. Soon the rumble melted into a purr, a moan, and her hands slid around his neck and pulled him closer.

He lost track of time as one sizzling kiss led to another. His hands explored her silky skin, relearning every dip and swell of her womanly form. Her nipples budded for him, and he savored each sweet peak, rolling it with his tongue, tugging with his lips. She arched her back and mewled her approval, and her response spun liquid fire to his groin. Hating every second away from her, he sheathed himself with his last condom. Then, gathering her near, he pressed home. The grip and heat of her body engulfed him, sent him soaring for the stratosphere. But he gritted his teeth and held himself back.

Her legs circled his hips, and she strained to get closer, to draw him deeper.

He kissed her forehead, and she angled her eyes to meet his.

"Easy, Lib. I'm not going anywhere without you."

She smiled, and something sweeter than passion, deeper than desire, lit her eyes. His heart somersaulted.

From now on, he wanted Libby right beside him. He wanted the future that they'd had to put on hold before. And it started in this moment, while he was buried inside her, his gaze locked on the mahogany depths of her eyes.

Her fingers dug into his back, and he felt the first pulses of her climax milking him. With a roar, he joined her. The heat that flashed through him burned hotter than the wildfire he'd fought hours ago. It had always been that way with Libby. More fire, more intensity, more emotion than he'd ever known. And still he wanted…more.

He wanted her faith. Her trust. Her love.

As he lay beside her, his body still quaking with the aftershocks of their lovemaking, he knew he had to take the first step. He'd been the one to break off their relationship the first time. He'd been the one who'd filled her gaze with doubt and resentment. The one who'd called his character into question when he'd lost control, unleashed his anger on an easy target and landed himself in prison.

He held her tightly and allowed the memories and regrets to invade his bliss. Restitution for the pain he'd caused her, the debt he owed. There was no easy segue from passion to penance, but he had to try. A cold twist of regret tightened his gut.

"Have I said I'm sorry yet for the pain I put you through when I married Renee?"

She stiffened in his arms, and he squeezed her arms, drew her closer.

"Not now, Cal. This isn't the time to—"

"It is time. And it's overdue." He kissed the top of her head and wound his fingers through the hair at her nape. "I wish I could take away the hurt I caused you. God knows, I was hurting, too." An echo of that old pain rolled through him, and he sighed. "I should have married you back then, tried harder to find a way to be there for Ally and Renee without losing you in the process. You had every right to resent me."

Tilting her head back, she snapped her gaze up to his, and her eyes danced and sparked.

"I saw it. When the judge ruled on my plea agreement. You looked across the courtroom, and I saw pain and resentment in your eyes. That dark look was more devastating than if I'd been sentenced to life in prison. I knew I'd lost you. Your love."

"Oh, Cal." Her brow pinched, and her fingers curled against his chest, clutching. "I was so worried about you going to prison. I'd heard terrible things about conditions for inmates."

He clenched his teeth, fighting to block the flood of memories, his personal horror stories of life behind bars.

Shadows shifted in her gaze. "I wanted to do something to help you, but I couldn't. It could have cost me my job. I knew Stan was bent on making a point with your conviction, drawing a definitive line between defense and assault for future cases."

Cal's mind reeled with what he was learning. Was it possible she'd never lost faith in him at all? That *he'd* been the one whose distrust had been unearned?

"Stan may have been tough, but the fact was you crossed the line from defender to aggressor. You broke the law." Conviction and determination molded her features, set her mouth in a firm line. "And the law said you had to pay for your actions."

He grunted his disagreement then narrowed a querying gaze on her. "How'd you convince the D.A. to let you take David Ralston's case?"

She grimaced and sighed. "It wasn't easy. Nothing about that case was simple. I fought tooth and nail, but Ralston's lawyer always seemed a step ahead of me. In the end, the jury found him guilty but let him off with only a slap on the wrist."

Cal fisted his hands as the injustice raged through him. "Free to beat the next unsuspecting woman to cross his path."

Libby flopped back on her pillow and stared up at the ceiling. "Probably. The guy had a juvenile record as long as my arm that I couldn't, by law, introduce. I had testimony from friends of his ex-girlfriends that showed a pattern of violence. But it was all hearsay. None of the girlfriends would say anything about his mistreatment of them. Meanwhile, his attorney paraded professors from Louisiana Tech who extolled his abilities and his intellect. His co-workers all said he was a hard worker, an affable guy. His boss bragged on his skill and reliability."

An uneasy prickle scraped the back of Cal's neck. Something Libby had said set off alarms in his mind, but he couldn't pin his odd intuition down. "Skills. In what?"

She furrowed her brow and pinched the bridge of her nose as she thought. "I don't remember exactly what he did, where he worked, but he had an engineering degree from Tech. Top of his class. Seems like he built things or fixed industrial machines or something highly technical. A real brain."

Cal grunted. "Yeah, well, my stepdad was a cardiac surgeon. Didn't stop him from being a loser in his private life."

She rolled to her side, her eyes darkly intense. "I didn't realize your mother remarried after your dad died."

"It didn't last long. Thank God. Just long enough for—" He stopped as a wave of nausea gripped him.

"Cal?" She perched over him now, lines of pain and worry framing her incisive gaze. "What happened?"

He struggled for a breath, memories crashing down on him. He wanted to lock the ghosts from his past away again, but they clamored for attention, haunting him.

Besides, he owed Libby an explanation. He wanted no more secrets, no more misunderstandings. He looked deep into her dark eyes and found the strength to speak the words that left a foul taste in his mouth. "He hit my mother. He battered her."

Libby paled, grew still. "Oh, Cal…I never knew."

He swiped a hand over his chin, restless now as the images from his adolescence pounded him. He swung his legs out from under the sheets and rose to stalk the room. "Because I never told anyone."

Cal shuddered recalling images in black and blue. The scar on his chin seemed to burn, taunting him. "He always waited until I wasn't home. So I couldn't stop him. I wanted to kill him when I found out the truth. That mom's injuries weren't accidents." Guilt slithered through him, clammy and cold. He clenched his teeth, forcing oxygen past the knot of fury and self-censure.

He should have realized what was happening sooner. Should have stopped the man who was hurting his mom.

Libby wrapped the sheet around her and sat up. He had her undivided attention, a silent show of support and encouragement.

"When I finally did put it all together, I went out looking for him. At his office. My mom begged me not to go, pleaded with me." He stopped pacing long enough to meet Libby's gaze. "See…she was afraid for *me*. Afraid of what my stepdad could do to me." The sick irony of his past taunted him. "At the time, he outweighed me by eighty or so pounds and had several inches on me in height. I was just fourteen. Skinny, all bony arms and legs. But he'd hurt my mom. And my dad had taught me to defend a woman, to protect my family. I couldn't do nothing."

Libby drew a shaky breath. "Go on."

He gave her a short, bitter laugh. "Well, he broke two of my ribs, blackened both my eyes and put me in a coma for thirty-six hours." He rubbed his scarred chin. "This was my souvenir."

Libby's hand flew to her mouth, and a fat tear slid down her cheek. Her haunted eyes reminded him so much of his mother's the day he woke in the hospital and found her hovering by his bed.

"All I'd done was cause her more worry, more suffering. She left him after that, but not for herself. She left to protect me." He scowled and gritted his teeth with frustration. "I hadn't done a thing to help her. Even when I finally figured out what was going on under my nose, I was completely useless to her. I'd failed her. I'd failed my father. I've never felt so…helpless, so frustrated, in my life. I couldn't even defend my mother's honor without nearly getting myself killed and hurting her even more."

Libby climbed from the bed and crossed the floor to him. Nestling beside him, she stroked his cheek, and he turned his face into the comforting caress. Years-old pain and recriminations battered him and made his lungs feel stiff and heavy. The misery he'd known as a fourteen-year-old punk knifed through him again, and he bit down so hard his jaw ached. He settled a hand at her waist and drew her closer, resting his forehead on hers. He needed her near, needed to feel her in his arms. He absorbed her comfort and strength like a dry sponge.

Her thumb glided over the tensed muscles in his cheeks, and she pressed warm lips to his temple. "When you saw David Ralston beating a woman that night at the bar…"

His heartbeat slowed, burdened with guilt, waiting as she filled in the blank.

"You thought of your stepfather."

A statement, not a question. A logical conclusion after what he'd confessed. He confirmed her assertion with silence.

In the moment of silence, the niggling intuition, an incomplete thought like a name on the tip of his tongue, teased him again.

"David Ralston bore the brunt of your anger and frustration," Libby said, redirecting his thoughts. "All the years you'd blamed yourself for not protecting your mom."

He nodded then met her eyes, even though the raw emotion in her gaze cut him to the marrow. "Ralston was scum. But that didn't justify what I did. I know that now."

"At least I understand now how the man I knew and loved could have done something so…"

"Stupid."

She winced. "No. Not stupid. Just…unfortunate. Ill-advised." She cupped his cheeks between her hands, her gentle expression softening the sting of her words. "Even though you carried it too far, you had good intentions, understandable motivation." She shook her head, consternation puckering her brow. "But that doesn't make it right."

He caught her chin in his fingers and rubbed the tip with his thumb. "I'm good at making mistakes. I'm bound to make plenty more along the way."

A puzzled look crossed her face. "I don't expect you to be perfect. Everyone makes mistakes."

He nudged her chin higher, bent toward her lips. "My biggest mistake was letting you go."

Her soft sigh fanned his skin as he sealed his mouth over hers. He drank in the sweet taste of her lips, reveled in the promise of a thousand more mornings like this one with Libby in his arms. He lingered with his kiss, in no hurry to go anywhere, in no rush to let her go.

Until the jarring trill of the phone made her pull away. When she moved toward her nightstand to answer the call, he sidestepped her and grabbed the receiver.

"Hello?" He didn't bother hiding any of his annoyance at the interruption.

After a brief hesitation, a male voice said, "Walters...let me talk to Libby."

A prickling suspicion crawled up his spine. "Who is this, and what do you want?"

Libby watched him with a curious knit in her brow.

"Since when did you start screening her calls?" the caller tossed back, irritation rife in his tone.

Cal squeezed the receiver tighter. "Since now. I'm her husband, and I'll protect her any way I see fit."

Libby reached for the phone, and he waved her away. Blowing hair out of her eyes with a huff, she turned and marched out of the room. His eyes gravitated to the sleek curve of her bottom and her long legs as she walked out. A spike of lust arrowed through his preoccupation with the hostile caller. The woman had one gorgeous body....

"Listen, Walters, I don't appreciate you interfering with—"

"Hello?" Libby came on the line. The kitchen extension.

"Libby? It's Stan. If you'll call off your pit bull, I've got to go over some questions with you on the Hildebrand case."

"I'll be in the office in half an hour. We can talk then."

Cal pinched the bridge of his nose. So much for his plans to spend the day in bed making love and clearing the air between them. This morning's discussion had been a start, but he needed to be sure where Libby stood, what she was thinking and feeling.

When she returned to the bedroom and started dressing, he climbed back on the rumpled sheets and propped himself against the headboard to watch her.

Jewel sauntered into the room, clearly under the impression that if the humans were out of bed, it must be breakfast time. The cat eyed Libby then hopped up on the bed and plopped down beside Cal's hip. He scratched Jewel behind the ear then turned his attention back to his wife.

"I'd hoped we could spend the day together," he said to

Libby's back as she let a silky slip slither over her curves. "Maybe talk some more."

"Sorry. Can't. Like I said, I've got a pile of things waiting at the office."

If she'd bothered to give him more than a glance, she'd have noticed his scowl, his disappointment.

"I'd make it worth your time to stay home." He infused his comment with more than a little suggestive overtone.

She paused in the act of buttoning a conservative white blouse. "Cal, I have to—"

"Work. Yeah, I know. Business before pleasure." He grunted and bunched the sheet in his hands. Jewel decided he was playing with her and pounced. "Some things are more important than work, Lib. Home. Family. Your happiness."

She sent a sharp look over her shoulder. "My job does make me happy. It's fulfilling."

"I can fulfill you if you let me. Your job can't give you comfort or understanding. Protection. Companionship when you're old and gray."

"Cal…"

Nudging Jewel aside, he shifted off the bed and stepped behind Libby, meeting her gaze in her dresser mirror. "Haven't you been on your own long enough? Let me in, Libby. Let me be there for you."

Chapter 15

Let me in, Libby. Let me be there for you.

Libby propped her elbows on the conference table at the D.A.'s office and rubbed her temples while Cal's words resounded in her head. His plea had preoccupied her throughout the morning meeting with the D.A., and she was certain she'd missed something important. Hopefully Stan could fill her in on the things she'd missed during her mental lapses. But she had to stop thinking about Cal and get her brain on work.

"Any questions?" her boss asked, tossing down his fountain pen and casting his gaze around the assembled attorneys. "If not, then we're adjourned."

Yeah, she had questions. Plenty of them. But none that anyone at the office could answer for her. How did she trust Cal enough to open her heart to him again? Why had she thought she could allow him into her bed and not be vulnerable to the flood of emotions that came with making love? And what did she do now that she'd opened that Pandora's box of regrets and expectations?

Libby pushed her chair back and rose. After five years of celibacy, her body was mildly sore from Cal's passionate lovemaking, but it was a wonderful ache. Yet along with the physical imprint his body had left on hers, she felt spiritually naked, exposed. The last time she made herself this vulnerable to Cal, he'd crushed her.

The little girl who'd always been in her mother's way, who'd never had anyone but herself to rely on and who'd never had the unconditional love every child craves, had offered Cal her heart once. And had her love rejected. Pushed aside. Shut away to make room for a higher priority.

Leaning close to her, Stan whispered, "Hey, are you okay?"

She forced a smile and hoisted her briefcase. "Just dandy."

He studied her through narrowed eyes. "The police called me about the incident at my cabin. Sounds like your stalker is getting too close for comfort."

Nodding, Libby glanced at Stan. A shiver raced through her, remembering yesterday's inauspicious start, and she rubbed the goose bumps that popped up on her arms.

"Are you sure you shouldn't just leave town for a few days until the cops can catch up with this guy?"

"I'm not the sort who hides from problems, Stan."

Liar, her conscience screamed. She shook her head, hoping to rattle the disturbing thought from her mind.

Stan shuffled a stack of papers into a file and slapped it closed. "I understand they lifted a few good fingerprints at the cabin."

Libby blinked. "They did?"

"Yep. If the guy's in the system, and no doubt he is, they'll have a match soon. Until then, go somewhere safe."

Safe. She'd felt safe in Cal's arms this morning. Safe and happy. She longed to crawl back into his embrace and pick up where they'd left off.

"I'll be fine, Stan." She patted his arm and headed for the door. "But thanks for your concern."

Conflicting emotions tangled in her heart. Confusion buzzed in her ears and weighted her chest. How did she make sense of the tumult in her life and find direction? If only relationships came with a set of rules.

Stan followed her to her office. Though preoccupied with her own problems, Libby didn't miss the sappy smiles, the heated looks, that passed between Stan and Helen as they walked by her assistant's desk. A grin tugged the corner of her mouth. "Gee, Stan, and here I thought you stopped by my office so often to see *me*. On business. I'm hurt."

"Huh?" He gave her a puzzled frown.

Helen chewed her bottom lip, a guilty flush in her cheeks. Were her feelings for Cal as plainly written on her face when he was around?

"I'm happy for you two."

Stan opened his mouth as if to make denials, then snapped his mouth shut. "But you know the policy on office affairs."

Of course. Interoffice romances were strictly forbidden.

A shadow of disappointment and torment stole the light from Helen's eyes. A pang of regret spun through Libby. "So what are you going to do?"

"What can we do?" Helen asked, and Libby felt the young woman's ache to her bones.

"Nothing for now," Stan said firmly. "Neither of us can afford to risk our careers by letting this get out." He shot Libby a pointed, plaintive look.

"Hey, mum's the word. But how long do you really think you can keep your relationship secret?"

"Until we figure out a workable solution, we have no choice." Stan crossed his arms over his chest and sighed.

"I keep telling him that I can find another job somewhere else," Helen said. "But how often do you find true love?"

Stan's cheeks colored as he gave Helen an embarrassed grin.

She swiveled her chair to face Libby. "Some things are more important than office policies or jobs. Don't be surprised if I turn in my resignation before long."

Stan groaned. "But this is your dream job, Helen. You don't get this kind of opportunity every day. You don't—"

"But you're more important to me. I'll find another job."

Her assistant's sacrifice and determination touched Libby. "I'll be sorry to see you go. But I'm happy for you." She turned to include Stan in her congratulations. "Both of you."

Stan headed toward Libby's inner office and cast a worried frown at Helen. "We'll talk later. Don't do anything rash."

Libby's assistant lifted her chin and spun her chair to resume working at the computer. "I'll have the information you wanted on Mr. Hildebrand in a moment. It's printing out now."

"Thanks, Helen." Libby gave the young woman a sympathetic smile then followed Stan inside. As she sat behind her desk, Libby raised an eyebrow. "She's right, you know."

Stan grumbled. "Can we change the subject?" He angled his head and narrowed his eyes. "Perhaps you'd like to tell me why Cal Walters answered your phone at the crack of dawn."

Libby turned up a palm. "Why shouldn't he? He lives there, too. The call could just as easily have been for him."

"I know that. It's just..." Stan fidgeted then leaned forward, propping his arms on her desk. "I'm your friend, Libby. I was there the last time he ripped your heart out, and I don't want to see you hurt again."

"Who said Cal would hurt me this time? Maybe this time we'll finally get it right and have a future together."

"Oh, God." Stan grew very still, his expression stricken. "You've fallen in love with him, haven't you?"

Libby's stomach flip-flopped. "He's my husband! What's wrong with that?"

He pushed to his feet with a sigh and paced across the

room. "Nothing's wrong with falling in love. God knows you deserve to be happy. But why this guy? Why Cal Walters?"

Bristling, Libby straightened her spine and flattened her hands on her desk. "Why not Cal? What's your problem with him?"

"I don't trust him. He dumped you for another woman last time. He's served time for beating up some drunk. He admits he had a grudge against you while he was in lockup. I'm just having a hard time seeing how you can ignore all that!"

Libby stood and squared her shoulders. "He had good reason to marry Renee. He did the honorable thing. I respect him for making the tough choice in order to be a father to his child."

"Even though he broke your heart in the process?"

"It broke his heart, too. He never wanted to leave me. But he sacrificed what he wanted for his daughter's sake. That's the kind of man I want fathering my children." As soon as the words tumbled out, Libby caught her breath. What was she saying?

The idea of having babies with Cal, raising a family together, crashed through her thoughts. A tender ache blossomed in her chest. She wanted Cal's babies to grow inside her, wanted him rocking her children to sleep and crying at their weddings. Her knees shook.

Stan sent her a challenging stare. "You want an ex-con raising your children?"

Defensiveness pricked her, and she curled her fingers into her palms. "His only crime was letting memories of an abusive stepfather override his restraint. He came to a woman's rescue, and somehow, in all that ensued, he was punished for that. And despite everything, I know if he were in the same situation today, he'd still put himself on the line to save a woman from abuse. So, yes, that's the kind of man I want as a role model for my sons." *Sons with Cal's dark, wavy hair and laser-blue eyes.* Her pulse pattered.

"And what about the grudge he admitted having toward you? That doesn't bother you?" Stan took a few steps toward her, meeting her glare with an unshakable, all-business expression molding his features.

"If you believed someone you loved had sold you out, wouldn't you nurture some hard feelings? Some people would call it quits after someone lets them down. Some people can never forgive. Some people don't love enough to work through the misunderstandings and hard feelings."

And what kind of person are you? a little voice taunted. She silenced the needling question and rounded her desk to meet Stan from a more superior position. "Cal found me when he got out of prison and fought for a second chance to make our relationship work. He'd didn't let his hurt and anger kill his feelings for me, and he never gave up hope that we could work through the problems from our past. He's been patient and gentle and supportive of me these past weeks. More than any man could be expected to be, considering how I've kept pushing him away."

Again, Libby realized what she'd said and stiffened. *She* had been pushing *Cal* away. In self-protection. He may have left her five years ago, but he'd still cared. She was the one standing in the way of their future this time.

Stan took another step, closing the distance between them. "And that's the kind of man you want to spend the rest of your life with. The kind of committed man you could give your heart to. Right?" His tone was calm, nonargumentative, and his hazel gaze softened.

Libby blinked, her head spinning as she tried to process the change in Stan's demeanor. Not to mention the truths behind her defense of Cal. "R-right."

He put a firm hand on each of her shoulders and met her dubious gaze. "You build a strong case, Counselor. Very persuasive arguments." Behind his wire-rimmed glasses, Stan arched an eyebrow, and his eyes glimmered with satisfaction. "But who were you trying to convince? Me…or yourself?"

Libby rocked back on her heels, would have fallen over if not for Stan's steadying grip on her shoulders. "I—"

"If you believe everything you just so passionately argued, then why should it matter what I, or anyone else, think of your relationship with Cal?" His mouth hitched up at the corner.

The tension in her muscles unfurled with a rush of warmth. She returned his grin, rolled her eyes. "I think I just found out how witnesses feel after you finish your cross-examination." The man could push a hostile witness in a corner and drag incriminating admissions from even the most hardened criminals.

He tapped the end of her nose. "Ding. Vanna, tell the lady what's she's won."

She raised her arms. "I'd settle for a hug."

Stan enveloped her in a tight embrace. "Be happy."

Libby exhaled deeply. "Thanks, friend. I think I will."

Cal beat Libby home from work and was already in the kitchen making grilled-cheese sandwiches when she bustled in with her overladen briefcase. "Hi, honey, I'm home!"

He turned to grin at her, and she crossed the kitchen in order to drop a quick kiss on his cheek. Cal had other ideas. Snagging her around the waist, he planted a deep, knee-buckling kiss on her mouth. "Good day?"

She sighed contentedly. "Getting better all the time. How'd you manage to get in so early?"

"Foreman on the road crew heard about me being at the fire scene last night and how little sleep I'd gotten, and he sent me home to nap. Said he didn't need sleep-deprived men wielding a jackhammer or operating heavy machinery on his crew."

She ran her fingers down the line of buttons on his shirt, freeing enough of them to work her hand inside to the warm skin of his chest. "So then…you're all rested up?"

Cal arched an eyebrow and lifted a corner of his mouth. "Depends. What did you have in mind?"

Rising on her toes, she nibbled his lips and nipped at his chin. "I've been thinking about you all day." She slid her hands around his neck, under his collar, and leaned into him. "You can be quite distracting."

He anchored her body firmly against his and cradled her cheek. "Likewise, my dear."

His lips found hers again, followed by the light caress of his tongue. She opened to welcome him, greeting the sweep of his tongue with her own. She languished in the intoxicating pull of his kiss, the heat of his body pressed flush with hers, the anticipation of the evening ahead, lying in his arms. She lost all sense of time and place, everything except Cal and his kiss.

Until she smelled smoke.

The acrid scent jerked her back to the here and now, and she wrenched from his embrace. "Cal, the sandwiches!"

He spun to snatch their blackened dinner off the burner. Groaning, he fanned the smoky air with his hand and cast her a sideways glance. "Forget distractions. You're a fire hazard, lady."

With a smirk, she sauntered toward the hall, letting her suit jacket slide down her arms slowly. "Meet me in the bedroom and maybe we can burn up the sheets together, hot stuff."

Cal laughed then sent her a smoldering look. "You're on. You have two minutes while I clean up this mess, then look out."

"I'll be waiting." She started peeling off her work suit and shoes as she made her way down the hall. Her heart drummed an expectant rhythm, and her nerve endings crackled.

She had plenty she needed to tell Cal about the decisions and discoveries she'd made today. With Stan's nudging. But talking could wait. First she wanted to satisfy the thrumming physical need to join her body with Cal's.

She sat on the edge of the bed and rolled her stockings

down her legs. The sound of Cal's voice drifted down the hall, and she smiled realizing he was talking to Jewel.

The man was even nice to her cat! As responsive to the feline's needs as he was to hers. A smile touched her lips, a slaphappy grin probably not unlike the one Stan had worn this morning around Helen. And by the time Cal strutted through the bedroom door, that smile was all she wore. She opened her arms, and blue fire leaped in Cal's eyes.

They fell back on the rumpled sheets together. Frantic hands roamed over heated skin. Hungry mouths fed on the taste of each other. Eager bodies tangled and writhed.

And when the right time came, Libby opened herself to Cal's penetration and took him inside. Into her body, into her heart, into her soul. Right where he belonged.

Holding Libby felt so good, so right, he hated to move. But as darkness swallowed the day out her bedroom window, hunger pangs rumbled in his stomach. He'd burned a lot of calories in the past couple hours, and he needed refueling. He had plans for a long, active night ahead.

He brushed a sweat-dampened lock of hair from her cheek and tucked it behind her ear. "Can I interest you in a snack? Maybe a ham-and-cheese omelet?" He quirked a frown. "Assuming we still have any cheese after the sandwich disaster."

She chuckled and rubbed her hand over his chest. "Sounds good. Need any help?"

He lifted her fingers and brought them to his lips for a light kiss. "Not unless you hear the smoke alarm."

She laughed, and the musical sound gripped his chest. He'd missed her laughter, the spark of mischief and joy in her eyes, the sense that he could be completely at ease and unguarded with her. He could be goofy or serious, be quiet or talk openly, whatever the moment demanded. He had back the

Libby who had stolen his heart five years ago. Warmth spread through his chest, expanding until it was difficult to breathe. He shifted to his side and gazed into her glowing eyes. "I've missed you, Lib. The connection we have."

She grew still, and her smile sobered. For a moment, he feared she would retreat, pull back behind her defensive walls. He clenched his teeth, fighting off the swell of disappointment.

Instead, her eyes misted, and a bright intensity lit her mahogany gaze. "Cal, I've done a lot of thinking today. And I realized a lot of things about myself."

He stroked a knuckle over her cheek. "Like what?"

"For starters, I realized how—"

The impatient trill of the phone interrupted. Her gaze darted to the obnoxious machine.

"Ignore it. What were you saying?"

She sat up, pulling the sheet around her breasts. "It could be important." She reached past him for the phone.

He caught her hand. "Let me."

The shadow that flickered over her face told him she understood what he'd left unsaid—her stalker was still on the loose, getting closer.

"H'lo?" He sensed Libby was finally ready to open up to him, to reach an understanding, a truce. To move forward.

"Cal? It's me."

He recognized Renee's voice. And the panic quivering in her tone. "What's the matter, Renee?"

"Oh, God, I'm sorry," Renee sobbed. "I'm so sorry. It's all my fault!"

He tensed, squeezed the receiver. *Ally.*

"What is your fault? What's happened?"

"I fell asleep. I didn't hear anything until too late."

Cal's gut churned, and bile surged upward in his throat. "What happened?" he snarled, already climbing from the bed and fumbling to put on his pants.

"It was only some w-weed, Cal," Renee choked out. "I…I really am trying to c-clean up my act, but—"

"What happened!"

"Ally's gone," his ex squeaked.

Icy dread snaked through him. "Are you sure? Have you looked in her closet?"

Libby gasped, and he raised his gaze to clash with the fear filling her eyes.

"She's not there. Someone took her. They left a note."

"A note?" A terrifying suspicion crawled through him. Libby's wan expression reflected the same chilling conclusion.

He forced his constricting throat to work. "What'd it say?"

"He has d-demands. He wants something. It says…he'll be calling L-Libby to arrange his ransom."

Cal felt the blood drain from his face. Rage pumped through his veins. Terror twisted his lungs. "Have you called the cops?"

"I…not yet. I called you first."

"Do it. Now."

Renee hiccupped a sob. "Cal, why would someone take Ally? And wh—why would he call Libby about the ransom?"

"I don't know." But he feared he did. And the answer scared the hell out of him.

His baby girl was in the hands of Libby's stalker.

Chapter 16

Libby jumped when the phone rang, even though the call was expected. Her nerves jangled with dread and frightening images of Cal's daughter—*her stepdaughter*—in the hands of a madman.

Cal pounced on the phone. "Yes?" he snapped, his own fear and tension palpable.

Guilt wrenched her gut. She'd drawn Cal and Ally into her nightmare. She should never have gotten involved with Cal again while she had the stalker's threat hanging over her. If anything happened to Ally…

"Listen here, you scum." Cal's face contorted in a mask of fury and loathing. "If you hurt one hair on my daughter's head, I'll hunt you down and make you wish you were never born!"

Tears burned Libby's eyes, and she pressed her fingers to her mouth to muffle the whimper that squeaked from her throat. Numb and silent, she and Cal had both dressed as they'd waited for the ransom call. Libby had used her cell phone to call the police—just in case Renee still hadn't.

Now, trembling and heartsick, she stepped closer to Cal, hoping to give him strength with her presence. Needing to draw strength from him.

She smoothed a hand down his back. His muscles bunched and vibrated with the fear clearly written in his eyes. What would Cal do if he lost Ally because of her? And it would be her fault. She'd brought the horror of her stalker into his life and his daughter's.

Please, God, spare Ally. I'll do anything…

"You're a sick bastard," Cal growled.

Libby winced, shook her head. "Don't make him angry."

Cal met her worried gaze. His cerulean gaze clung to hers. "No. You're crazy. No way."

"What?" she mouthed.

Cal closed his eyes and shuddered.

"Listen, I'll give you money. Name your price. Just give me back my little girl. Safe and sound."

Cal listened again and bit out a scorching curse. "Where? Where are you?" Pause. "I can't promise that."

Pain and frustration laced Cal's tone, hummed from his tight, quivering muscles.

Libby moved in front of Cal, trying to read his expression. What had the creep asked for?

"Tell him yes. Whatever it is he wants! We have to get Ally back!" she begged.

"No!" he shouted into the phone, but she couldn't be sure if he was answering the stalker or her. He circled her waist with his free hand and hauled her in close, clutching her to his side like a life preserver in a stormy sea.

Her tears soaked his shirt, concern for precious Ally choking her.

"Wait! Don't hang up! Let me talk to Al—"

She hugged him tighter as another shudder rolled through him.

With a roar, he threw the phone across the room. It smashed into a vase of dried flowers with a jarring clatter and crash.

The echoes of his outburst reverberated through the bedroom and settled around them like an ominous fog.

Libby swallowed, wetting her arid throat. "What does he want? What won't you give him?"

Cal's arms tightened around her until she couldn't breathe. "You, Libby. He wants you."

"I'm going after her." Cal levered away from Libby even though he wanted nothing more than to hold her, protect her, until the stalking scumbag was caught.

But Ally was in danger. He had to do something, had to try to save his daughter.

Libby clutched his sleeves as he pulled away. "Going after her? Where are they?"

"Lake D'Arbonne. The cabin where you went yesterday."

Libby knitted her brow over dark eyes brimming with tears. "Stan's place? Wh—why there?"

"You're the prosecutor. Why do you think?" He worked his arms free of her grip and headed for the dresser, where he'd left his truck keys earlier. Libby's cell phone lay beside his keys, and he took it, as well, shoving it into his pocket.

She drew a shaky breath. "The cabin's isolated. But…we know how to get there."

Cal didn't know how to reach the cabin, but he didn't say as much. He had a good idea how to find out.

"He wants us to come," Libby added, "but he wants privacy."

"Bingo."

Libby trailed behind him as he marched down the hall. "Cal, wait! You can't go after them! This man is dangerous."

"Which is exactly why I can't leave my daughter out there

with him a second longer." He opened the front closet and took out his jacket.

Libby grabbed his arm again, squaring off in front of him. "We'll call the police back and tell them where the cabin is. They have hostage negotiators and tactical experts to handle things like this."

He pried her hands from his wrists. "You do that. Meantime, while they get someone dispatched and the directions sorted out, I can be halfway there."

"Cal, please! You're not trained for situations like this. What do you think you're going to do when you get there? What if you make him angry and he hurts Ally?"

As he stalked through the living room toward the back door, the gleam of metal caught his eye.

A gun.

Libby's gun. Still on the coffee table from this morning.

Cal picked up the weapon and turned it over in his hand.

"No," Libby whispered hoarsely. "Put it down, Cal. Please."

He shoved the gun in the waist of his jeans, at the base of his spine, and closed his jacket. "Just a little backup."

Turning, he started for the door again.

Libby bolted past him and blocked his way. She stood in front of the door with her arms spread. "I can't let you do this. I *won't* let you do this. Cal, I know you're scared. You're worried about Ally. So am I! I'm worried sick. But going off halfcocked, maybe getting yourself killed, is not the answer."

Frustration boiled inside him. "I can't sit here and do nothing!" *Like I did with Mom.*

"I know you want to do something, but there are legal channels, rules, proper procedures to follow—"

"Libby, he's got my daughter! I have to help her!"

Tears spilled onto Libby's cheeks. "And how is breaking your parole going to help her?"

His parole.

A fist of anguish and futility punched him in the gut, and he tensed. Biting out an ugly curse, he plowed his fingers through his hair.

Libby stroked a gentle hand down his shoulder. "D'Arbonne is outside your parole jurisdiction. You can't leave the parish, and you can't be found in possession of a gun."

Cal gritted his teeth, clenched his fists. "Hell, I *know* that."

She held out her hand, palm up, clearly waiting for him to return her pistol.

He didn't move. In his mind's eye, he saw Ally, locked in some cretin's grip, maybe with a gun to her head. White-hot fury burned in his veins.

The sound of his own labored breaths joined the loud tick of the kitchen clock. Seconds of precious time clicked off while he hesitated. He was wasting time debating this with Libby.

"Get out of my way. Please. I *have* to go."

"If you break your parole, you'll go back to jail. Don't you understand what you're risking? Think of all you could lose. Ally. Your freedom." She hesitated. "Me. Cal, I need you. I don't want to lose you again."

The thought of losing Libby yanked a knot in his chest. But the immediate threat to Ally bore down on him with more frightening power than the forest fire he'd battled last night.

He framed Libby's face with his hands and lifted her lips to his. "God knows I don't want to go back to prison, Lib. I just got you back."

She wilted against him, obviously believing she'd won.

With her guard down, he pushed her aside and jerked open the door.

"Cal! You can't! The rules of your parole—"

"Libby, that bastard has Ally. My flesh and blood. My baby. I love her more than anything. More than my freedom. Even if it means I spend the rest of my life behind bars, I have to go to her. I have to try to save her." He gave Libby a quick kiss. "I'm sorry, Lib. But love doesn't follow rules."

He pivoted on his heel and stalked out to his truck.

Libby dogged his steps. "At least leave the gun, Cal. Or take me with you. Maybe if I'm there—"

Cal spun around, aimed a finger at her. "Hell, no! You're his target, Libby. If you go up there, you're as good as dead."

"Not necessarily. Maybe we can use me as bait to stall him until the cops get there."

"No." He climbed in his truck and slammed the door. "Not a chance. You stay here. Stay safe."

She crossed her arms and glared at him as he backed out.

Let her be mad. Better mad than dead.

He turned his truck toward the highway, toward Lake D'Arbonne. And toward the parish line.

If you break your parole, you'll go back to jail. Don't you understand what you're risking?

Libby's gun gouged his back. He leaned up in order to pull it from under his jacket and set the weapon on the seat beside him.

Next, he pulled Libby's cell phone from his pocket. He jabbed a few buttons and found Stan Moore's home number stored in her address book. Cal punched the call button and lifted the phone to his ear.

"Yo," a groggy voice answered.

"Stan, this is Cal Walters. I need directions to your place at Lake D'Arbonne. Libby's stalker has my kid."

Libby wrapped her arms around her waist, fought the wave of nausea pitching in her stomach. Without her coat, the damp winter chill in the night air seeped to her bones. But it was Cal's words that made her tremble, made her heart ache.

I love her more than anything.

Earlier today, she'd told Stan she respected and admired

Cal's unlimited love and commitment to his daughter. And she did. But…

More than anything.

Once again, she risked losing Cal because she was somehow less important, less worthy of his love. And it hurt.

Damn it, she knew it was selfish. She knew Ally came first. But the sting of being pushed aside by someone she loved, someone she had trusted with her heart and soul, still raked through her, digging up old wounds. Her mother's easy dismissal of her as unimportant. Jimmy's cruel treatment because she'd been an inconvenience.

The cold and her tears made her nose run. Libby swiped at her damp cheeks as she stumbled back into the house.

Some people would call it quits after someone lets them down, she'd told Stan that morning. Some people. But not Cal. This morning, she'd asked herself what kind of person she was and pushed the thought away. Now the question begged to be answered.

What was she willing to risk for the people she loved?

You're his target, Libby. You stay here. Stay safe.

A plan began to take shape in her mind. There was a chance she could help save Ally. A chance she could save Cal from going back to prison.

She was the stalker's target. She could use that to their advantage. Without stopping to analyze what she was doing or the repercussions, Libby grabbed her purse and hurried for her car.

Maybe she could still prevent a disaster.

Cal cut his headlights and engine at the end of the gravel driveway leading to Stan's remote cabin. He let his truck roll to a stop behind a line of tall bushes. Out of sight.

Even with Stan's directions, the place had been nearly impossible to find, the turns unmarked. He'd wasted precious minutes doubling back when he missed the road leading to the cabin. He prayed the cops would be able to find the turns.

The lights were on in the cabin. Through a window, he saw movement, a shadow on the far wall.

He wrapped sweaty fingers around the gun lying beside him on the seat. Checked that the chamber was loaded. Flipped the safety off.

He left his truck door open. The slam of closing it would signal his arrival. His heart pumped, shot full of adrenaline, like a rookie's at his first fire.

But unlike a rookie dragonslayer, he had no backup. No one covering his back. And he was fighting a different kind of enemy.

Crouching low, he crept across the dry leaves, the slippery pine straw and loose rocks. Trying to be silent. Praying he wasn't too late.

A twig snapped beneath his foot. The crack reverberated in the quiet woods like a gunshot. He froze, held his breath. But no one emerged from the cabin to investigate the noise.

He exhaled slowly, collecting his focus. He couldn't blow this. Ally's life was at stake.

He wouldn't fail her the way he had his mother. Failed to protect her. Failed to see the true nature of his stepfather until it was too late. Failed to properly defend himself when he confronted the bastard about his abusiveness.

Inching forward, he pressed his back to the outside wall of the cabin. He eased up to peek in the window, careful not to be seen. By Libby's stalker or by Ally. He couldn't risk Ally giving him away.

In the distance, an owl hooted. A low, haunting call.

Tension screamed in his muscles. His pulse thumped in his ears. His hand flexed and tightened around Libby's gun.

He surveyed the interior with a sweeping gaze. Ally huddled on the double bed at the far side of the room. Her black hair tangled in a halo around her pale face. His chest tightened with the longing to pull his baby into his arms and shield her.

Cal's eyes darted to the other occupant of the cabin. A hulking, fair-haired man paced the floor, jostling a lethal-looking revolver in his hand. His daughter's captor strode toward the window, and Cal shrank back, plastering himself to the wall.

A fleshy, scowling face appeared in the pane above Cal. Hatred churned in Cal's gut. He aimed Libby's pistol, ready to take a shot then and there. Ready to kill the lowlife who'd dared to touch his daughter. The scum who'd terrorized Libby, tried to kill her in the elevator.

Cal curled his finger around the trigger and drew a deep breath. He aimed for the cretin's forehead, right between the eyes.

And hesitated.

Don't you understand what you're risking?

Grimacing, Cal let his arm drop to his side. Sure, he could kill the dirtbag. But then what? Spend the rest of his life in prison for murder?

He'd lost too much the last time he let his frustration and rage guide his actions. When he'd taken his wrath for his mother's abuse out on David Ralston two years ago.

Ralston's face flashed in his mind, at first smug, and later battered by Cal's fists.

And that image merged with the glowering face in the window.

Cal's heart tripped.

The images were the same. The man holding his daughter hostage was the same man he'd pulled off a woman in a bar two years before and beaten.

David Ralston.

But why? What did the man have to gain by taking Ally? Stalking Libby?

Cal's mouth went dry. Revenge? Libby had said she'd gone

after Ralston with both barrels when she prosecuted him for his assault on the woman at the bar. Was *that* what this was about?

Ralston stepped back from the window and barked something at Ally that made her whimper.

Cal heard the thump of footsteps as the man stomped across the cabin's wood-plank floor. Fresh claws of anger slashed through Cal.

Time to act. Time to get Ally out of there. Time to put this man's days of terrorizing women and children to an end.

Get low and go.

Following the firefighter's strategy for entering a burning building, Cal moved toward the front door.

Leading with Libby's gun, he kicked open the front door and swung inside. "Freeze, you scum!"

Ralston spun. Raised his revolver.

"Daddy!" Ally sprang from the bed and charged toward Cal.

"Ally, no!" He motioned frantically for her to stay put, stay out of the line of fire.

Ralston snaked an arm around Ally's waist as she scampered past. He hauled her close and pressed the end of his gun to Ally's head.

Icy horror slammed into Cal, stealing his breath.

No! No, no, no, no! Damn it, what had he done?

Why had he charged in without thinking through all the repercussions? His rash reactionism may have cost Ally her life.

"Checkmate," Ralston growled.

Chapter 17

Libby peered into the darkness, scanning the side of the highway for the turnoff to Stan's cabin. Anxiety beat a panicked rhythm in her chest.

Please, please let her get there in time!

When she spotted the narrow gravel driveway, she eased off the main road and followed the black tunnel through the dense woods. She found Cal's truck, driver's door still open, and tensed.

Where were the police? Why hadn't the local sheriff arrived yet?

Impatience fluttered in her throat, kicking up her pulse. Clearly Cal hadn't waited for help to arrive.

Damn it!

Parking behind Cal's truck, she climbed from her Camry and scanned the night-shrouded forest.

Stan had bought this cabin because of the privacy of the thick woods. Now Libby cursed the isolation, the miles that separated her from civilization. From help. From a hospital.

Shivering, Libby refused to consider the possibility Cal or Ally could need medical help. She started toward the cabin, where the windows glowed with a dim yellow light. As she stumbled over the roots and rocks in her path, she took her can of pepper spray off her key chain and readied the vial for use. Slipping the can in her slacks pocket, she jogged across the cabin lawn.

The murmur of voices stopped her at the foot of the wooden porch steps.

"Let her go!" Cal said, fear and anger thick in his taut tone.

"I don't think so," another male voice chortled.

Libby heard a plaintive whimper that wrenched inside her. *Ally.* The sweet little girl was an innocent in this nightmare. Libby bit her bottom lip to keep from crying herself. She had to stay in control long enough to help Ally. Help Cal.

"Listen, Ralston, I don't know what your game is, but my daughter has nothing to do with it. Please…let her go."

Ralston?

Libby muffled a gasp. David Ralston had been stalking her all this time?

"The girl means nothing to me. Except as a means to an end," Ralston said.

Reaching in her pocket, Libby grabbed the pepper spray. And wavered. The spray was only effective if she could get close, had a direct shot at her opponent's eyes.

As quietly as she could, Libby climbed the stairs, hoping to assess the situation through the door that gaped open.

"Where's the woman?" Ralston asked.

You, Libby. He wants you.

Fear choked her, and she struggled to swallow. To breathe. This was her fight. Her stalker. Her responsibility.

Her fault.

"I told you," Cal answered. "You can't have Libby. She's not here."

"Then I guess I'll have to settle for this little thing until you bring me the lawyer."

Libby balled her fists.

Where were the police?

Edging to the door, she took in the scene inside.

Cal held her gun, aimed at the large blond man across the room. Ralston, in turn, had Ally in his grip, his own gun kissing Ally's temple.

Libby's knees buckled. *Oh, no!*

She sent up a silent prayer. For guidance. For strength. For Ally's and Cal's safety.

For the police to arrive before it was too late.

"You harm my girl, and you'll be dead before you can blink," Cal snarled.

No! Don't make him angry! Not while Ally's at risk! Libby longed to scream.

Why didn't the cops hurry? What was taking so long?

"You sure about that?" Ralston said, his tone overconfident. The smug sound of a man who had nothing left to lose.

Things were escalating fast. Too fast.

Inside, a gun clicked as it was cocked.

"No!" Cal shouted.

"Wait!" Libby screamed, throwing herself through the door.

Three startled gazes flew to her, but Libby focused on only one—the man holding the life of her stepdaughter at the end of a deadly weapon.

"Libby, get out! What are you doing?" Cal's panic rang in his voice.

She ignored the urge to look at Cal, even for a second. Holding her hands up, she walked toward Ralston. "It's me you want. Not Ally. Please. *Please,* don't hurt her."

Confusion and suspicion shifted in Ralston's eyes. A muscle jumped in the man's jowl, and he jerked Ally closer. "Is this a trick? I warned you! No tricks, or the girl buys it."

She heard Cal suck in a sharp breath.

Libby shook her head, took a cautious step forward. "No tricks. Me for the girl. I'm the one you want. But you have to let her go. Unharmed."

"Libby…" Cal's voice sounded strangled, hoarse.

"Closer." Ralston waved the gun, motioning her forward. "You come here, and I let the girl go."

Libby wiped her sweaty palms on her slacks, eased her hand toward her pocket.

"Keep your hands where I can see 'em!" Ralston said.

Her heart thundering, Libby raised her hands again. She searched her brain for a plan B. She wasn't good in situations like this. No plan, no guidelines, no rules.

She'd have to trust gut instinct.

Fear scampered inside her, a cold sweat beading on her lip. She moved closer to David Ralston on leaden legs. Closer.

She chanced a quick glance at Ally and met the child's wide, blue gaze, damp eyes, bright with terror yet so full of trust and hope.

And Libby knew why she was doing this. She loved Ally. Cal's daughter was her priority, too. Her family. A bittersweet pang unfurled in her chest.

"C'mon, lady. Quit stalling." Ralston waved the gun impatiently and glowered at Libby.

She took the final steps toward her stalker, unwilling to try anything to save herself while Ally was still in his grasp. A grasp Ralston had to release in order to grab Libby's arm.

Libby's stomach lurched as Ralston hauled her against his stout chest and trained his gun on her.

"Ally!" Cal spread his arms.

The little girl scrambled across the floor and flung herself into her father's embrace. "Daddy!"

Cal lifted Ally, hugging her close while his gaze gravitated to Libby's. Moisture gathered in his eyes as he clutched his daughter to his chest. Relief and gratitude warred with a new, keen anxiety clouding his expression.

Why? his eyes asked.

Libby found her voice. "Get her out of here, Cal. Go!"

He hesitated. "Libby…"

"Go!" she repeated, then mouthed, "I love you."

Cal jerked as if punched in the gut. His eyes, a brighter shade of blue than she'd ever seen them, held with hers as he edged out the door. His reluctance to leave her wound through her heart, a small comfort that Libby latched on to as Cal left.

Reaching across her chest and keeping Libby's back pressed tightly to his chest, Ralston dug his fingers into her arm. He yanked Libby backward, dragging her toward the bed. "Looks like it's just you and me now, Counselor." The man's hot breath smelled of onions, alcohol and evil. "Shall we get down to business?"

Yes. Time to get down to business.

Steeling herself with a deep breath, Libby stomped her captor's instep. Hard. She followed quickly with a backward kick in his kneecap.

Ralston grunted, his grip loosening, and he stumbled back a step. "Ow! Damn bitch, you'll pay for th—"

Spinning, Libby aimed a roundhouse kick for the hand holding the gun. The weapon flew from Ralston's grip and skittered across the floor.

Quickly adjusting her stance, she capitalized on Ralston's brief distraction. A front-snap kick to his groin.

Picture the face of that someone who has really been getting on your nerves this week, and let 'em have it! she heard her kickboxing instructor say.

Ralston raised his head, a stunned, pained expression pinching his face.

Libby zeroed in. Uppercuts. Left, right, left.

Blood spurted from Ralston's nose. He wobbled.

Charged with adrenaline, Libby landed another round-house kick to his kidney.

She had Ralston on the defensive. Had him shaken.

But could she continue to fight him off until help arrived?

Damn it, where *were* the police?

Cal peeled Ally's arms from his neck and set her on the front seat of his truck.

She whimpered and fought to climb back into his arms. "No, Daddy! Hold me! Don't let that man get me!"

His heart wrenched. "Baby, you're safe here. The police will be here in a minute." *He prayed.* "Right now, I have to go help Libby."

"Daddy!" Her lip trembled.

"Stay here. Understand? Stay right here. Get down on the floor and stay out of sight. Please, kitten. I have to go help Libby now."

Ally bobbed her head and scrambled to the floorboard.

"Good girl." Cal blew Ally a kiss and turned to run back to the cabin.

I love you. His mind whirled, tangling around images and emotions. Libby had sacrificed herself for his daughter. The idea humbled him. Terrified him.

Ralston had Libby. *Oh, God!*

Hang on, Libby. Hang on!

If he'd ever doubted Libby's priorities, he didn't now. And he had no doubt he loved Libby. Completely. Deeply. Unconditionally.

The sounds of a struggle echoed from inside the cabin.

"Libby!" The pistol ready, he leaped over the front porch steps and plowed through the front door.

In a stuttering heartbeat, he assessed the situation. Ralston's battered face. Libby's attack pose, feet braced, fists up.

And Libby's startled glance toward the door. Enough time for Ralston to lunge for her, tackle her. Together, Libby and Ralston crashed to the hard floor.

Breath stuck in his throat, Cal watched the twisting, grappling limbs.

Just as Cal moved to pull the man off Libby, Ralston reached for his ankle. Metal flashed as Libby's attacker raised a hunting knife to her neck.

"Get back!" Ralston screamed.

Cal froze.

Libby's thrashing caused the tip of the blade to slice her skin at the base of her throat. Crying in pain, she stilled, knowledge of the new threat to her life bright in her eyes.

Holding the pistol between his hands, Cal waited for a clear shot at Ralston. But he couldn't risk hitting Libby.

Like a horror movie from his past, played out in slow motion, Cal watched Ralston drag Libby to her feet.

The helplessness and rage he'd known discovering his mother's abuse flooded back tenfold. Ralston's knife hovered by Libby's jugular. Drops of crimson seeped from the gash just above Libby's collarbone, marring the silken skin he'd savored just hours ago.

Fear balled in his gut.

Libby's chest rose and fell in quick, shallow breaths. Her frightened gaze found Cal's.

"Easy, lover boy," Ralston gloated. "Just a flick of the wrist and your lady is history."

Sweat trickled from Cal's forehead and stung his eyes. But he didn't flinch. Didn't take his eyes off Ralston for an instant.

He couldn't risk Libby getting hurt. As much as he hated to admit it, as long as Ralston had that blade pressed against Libby's neck, the madman had the upper hand.

* * *

Libby blinked to clear the blur of tears from her sight. Unless her eyes were playing tricks on her, something blue had flickered in the trees out the window behind Cal. Blue lights.

The police. Finally!

Relief threatened to turn her legs to jelly. But in deference to the sharp knife edge under her chin, she steeled her muscles. She only had to hold on a little longer. Until the police could surround the cabin.

Cal. If the sheriff deputies found him holding the gun on Ralston, they might assume he was the enemy.

The flicker of blue lights disappeared. With any luck, Ralston hadn't seen the evidence of the arriving law enforcement.

Tension quivered through her body. She had to signal Cal without tipping Ralston off to the help that had finally come.

Libby drilled Cal with a hard look. When he met her glare, she shifted her eyes to the window with a slight nod, a subtle lift of her eyebrows.

"If I were you, I'd put the gun down. Nice and easy, pal," Ralston said, his breath hot against Libby's ear.

"Do it, Cal. Please. Put the gun down." She tried once more to signal him, but his focus had returned to the threat of the man behind her. How could she make him understand? "Cal, there are better ways to handle this. Proper channels. Don't take *the law* into your hands."

Cal frowned, his blue gaze darkening to the color of deep water. Fathomless. Troubled.

Ralston jerked suddenly, shifted, craning to look outside.

Damn. He must have spotted the men outside.

Panic clambered inside Libby.

With a grumbled curse, Ralston yanked her around and headed toward the door. He shoved her forward, clearly hoping to make a run. To escape.

"Ralston!" Cal shouted.

"Cal, don't!" she screamed.

"Sheriff's department! Drop the weapon!" came a shout from just beyond the door.

Ralston abandoned her, made a dash for the woods.

A uniformed man pursued and tackled Ralston at the edge of the circle of light spilling from the cabin's open door.

Turning, Libby watched Cal's shoulders drop in relief. But not the gun.

"Drop the weapon!" an officer outside repeated. The man's no-nonsense tone sent shivers skittering up Libby's back.

"They mean you, Cal." She barely recognized her own voice. "Put the gun on the floor and step back. Keep your hands where they can see them."

She knew the moment Cal understood exactly what was happening. She saw the pain, the fear, the defeat, that swirled in his gaze. Slowly, he set her pistol on the floor and straightened, hands up.

Two officers swung through the front door, their own weapons drawn and aimed at Cal. Dread grabbed her lungs and squeezed.

"Are you all right, ma'am? You're bleeding," the older of the two men asked.

She nodded stiffly. "Fine. It's not a deep cut."

"Put your hands behind your head!" the same officer ordered Cal, then moved forward to handcuff him.

"Libby, tell them who I am." Cal's eyes beseeched her. "Tell them I'm not their man."

"Ma'am?" the younger deputy, named Edison, according to the badge he wore, cast a sideways glance at her.

"The man outside, the one who tried to run, is your main concern. His name is David Ralston, and he kidnapped the little girl outside. You'll probably find her in the Chevy truck."

Cal nodded affirmation.

"Her name is Ally," Libby continued. Her head spun, and

her legs quivered in the aftermath of all that had happened. She braced a hand on the wall to support herself.

"And you are?" Deputy Edison asked Libby.

"I'm Assistant District Attorney Libby Hopkins."

"Walters," Cal corrected.

"Be quiet," the older deputy warned. "Let her talk."

Cal scowled. A muscle in his jaw worked as he clenched his teeth.

"And who is he?" Edison asked, nodding toward Cal.

"Her husband," Cal said, earning a jerk on the handcuffs.

"His name is Cal Walters. He's my husband and the girl's father."

Edison nodded, spoke into the radio transmitter hooked on his shoulder, summoning the dispatcher.

Libby hesitated. She knew what would come next. How it would look if they tried to conceal the truth. Especially since she'd told them her position with the D.A.'s office. She had a duty. She'd sworn an oath.

Her heart thundered. Her throat closed.

"Sir…" She couldn't look at Cal, though she felt his stare burning her. "Cal is a parolee from Lagniappe."

A pregnant silence filled the room for the space of a heartbeat.

"Oh, really?" Edison said, clearly intrigued by the new information. "Then he's in violation of his parole?"

She heard Cal's sigh, but avoided the accusing glare that nailed her. Her stomach pitched. "Yes, sir. He's outside his jurisdiction and in possession of a weapon."

Cal swore under his breath, his tone rife with disgust and fury.

She dragged her eyes to his. The accusation that blazed in his returned glare riddled her with guilt. "They would have found out as soon as they ran your name through the computer, Cal. It was better to be forthcoming. I have a duty to my office to—"

He told her in colorful language what she could do with her duty. "I'm your husband. Doesn't that count for anything?"

Libby struggled to draw air into her constricted chest. "Cal, try to understand. I had to—"

"No, I don't understand, Libby!" His anguish reverberated through her. "I will *never* understand why you think you have to hide behind your strict interpretation of the rules. What are you scared of? Why wasn't the love I gave you enough?"

A sob ripped from her throat.

"Okay, pal. Enough. Let's take a ride." The older deputy pushed Cal toward the door.

Libby tried to catch Cal's eyes as he walked past, but he kept his gaze looking ahead. His face was molded with disappointment, defeat. And hurt.

A razor-sharp ache sliced her to the marrow. A pain more devastating than any damage Ralston's blade could have inflicted. She could easily lose Cal again. This time for good.

And it was her own fault.

Chapter 18

Cal staggered numbly toward the patrol car waiting beside his truck. As he approached, the driver's side door popped open, and Ally scampered out.

"Daddy!" His little girl ran to meet him.

He cursed the handcuffs that prevented him from lifting his baby into his arms. Would he ever get to hold Ally again?

He was on his way back to prison. Any hope he'd had of skirting his parole violations had gone up in flames. Thanks to Libby. Her betrayal rose in his throat with the bitter taste of bile.

He dropped to his knees, and Ally threw her arms around him. "It's okay, baby. Everything's going to be okay now."

His gut churned. He hated lying to Ally. Nothing would be okay.

Going back to jail meant he'd lose his shot at custody. He'd lose the right to have his record expunged. He'd lose the chance to get his firefighting credentials reinstated.

Why, Libby? Why!

Hearing the shuffle of feet on the gravel, he raised his head and watched another sheriff's deputy shove Ralston against the end of the patrol car.

At least Libby's stalker was in custody. She would be safe. A small victory.

But no comfort for the sting that penetrated to the core.

The evening air carried the scent of mountain heather even before the sound of footsteps signaled Libby's approach. Even knowing how she'd betrayed him, the sweet scent filled his senses and made his body hum. He'd have to live with the fact that Libby was, and would always be, a part of him. Woven into the fiber of his being.

Libby stalked toward Ralston.

"You got off with a light sentence last time. But never again. I'll make sure you go straight to prison for this and that you stay there," she growled.

An evil glower darkened Ralston's face. "At least lover boy will be going with me. Maybe there's justice, after all."

Libby stiffened, glaring at Ralston. "What do you mean?"

"I could hardly believe my good luck when Walters entered the picture. When the SOB who caused all the problems I'd been through married the wench responsible for ruining my life. It was too perfect. I could get my justice against both of you at the same time."

"Justice? For what?" Cal said, his tone dark and disbelieving. "You didn't serve time. You got off with a slap on the wrist!"

Ralston snorted. "I lost my job because of that conviction! A good job. But that was just the start. My whole life went to hell, one piece at a time. All of the fines and legal expenses drained my bank account, and without any income, I finally had to declare bankruptcy two months ago, and I lost my house to the bank. Do you know what it does to a man's pride to tell the world you're broke?" He narrowed a lethal glare on Libby. "It's humiliating. Goin' broke was the last straw. If I had to suffer, then the scum who did this to me had to suffer, too." Ralston pulled against the restraints on his arms, snarling at Libby then Cal. "All because *you* didn't mind your own friggin' business."

The sheriff's deputy who'd brought Ralston over to the patrol car put a restraining hand on the thug's shoulder. "Settle down!"

"Your hitting a woman was my business." Cal knew he was pushing the officers' patience, but he no longer cared.

"She was a lying, smart-mouthed slut," Ralston growled.

Libby stepped forward, squaring off in front of her stalker. "That doesn't give you the right to hit her."

"I had every right! Just like my daddy did. Women need to learn their place around men!" Ralston snarled like a pit bull on the end of a short leash. "Like you, lawyer bitch! Women belong at home, not in the man's world."

"All right, let's take this mess downtown and straighten things out there." The older officer pulled Cal to his feet.

Ally continued to cling to his neck and wrapped her legs around Cal's waist with a whine.

Libby smoothed a hand down Ally's back. "Honey, your daddy has to go with these men. I'll take you home."

Cal flicked his gaze up to Libby's. She'd put her life on the line to save his daughter. He had no doubt Ally would be in good hands with Libby.

Steeling himself, he murmured, "Go with Libby, kitten."

Libby cradled his daughter in protective arms and continued to stare at him with pain swirling in her dark eyes. "Cal, I'm sorry. I had to—"

"Save it." He turned abruptly and lowered himself into the back seat of the patrol car. He didn't want Libby's excuses. She'd made her choice.

With a resounding thud, the deputy closed the door, locking Cal in the patrol car. The sound vibrated with an ominous finality in Cal's soul.

"Cal's in jail? Why? What did he do?" Renee clutched Ally to her chest and gaped at Libby with wide eyes. Eyes that were bloodshot and puffy from crying.

"He violated his parole when he went after Ally. He left the parish, and he took my gun with him." Libby stepped into Renee's apartment, where a small amount of clutter was strewn about and the hint of marijuana still hung in the air. Overall, though, the place was considerably cleaner than the last time Libby had been there. Renee's boyfriend was nowhere in sight.

Frowning over the top of Ally's head, Renee narrowed her eyes. "Did Cal shoot someone?"

"No, but even being in possession of the gun breaks the rules of his parole."

"So…they're putting him back in jail because he tried to save his daughter's life?" Renee dropped her mouth open again. "Is that some screwed-up system or what?"

Libby drew herself up and took a calming breath. The whole night had been chaotic, emotional, confusing. A roller coaster ride. "There are good reasons why laws regarding parole are written the way they are. They aren't just arbitrary dictates."

With a sniff of disagreement, Renee turned and marched into her kitchen with Ally still in her arms. "Well, if you ask me, it's stupid to punish someone who's just tryin' to protect his family. Cal and I had our problems, but I never doubted for a minute that he was a good man, deep down." She set Ally on the counter and bent at the waist to meet Ally's eyes straight on. "You want a snack? How 'bout some chips and milk?"

Ally rubbed her eyes tiredly, pouting. "I want my daddy."

Renee let her chin fall to her chest, and her shoulders heaved as she drew a deep breath. Then, raising her head again, she stroked Ally's head. "I'm sorry about tonight, punkin. I'm gonna do better, though. I swear it."

Hope blossomed in Libby's chest. She walked closer to the kitchen to listen, wanting to believe, for Ally's sake, that Renee would keep her promise. "Do you mean that?"

"Mean what?" Renee reached into the cabinet and took down a bag of corn chips.

"That you want to change. For Ally."

"Well, sure. Tonight was horrible. I was so scared." Handing the bag to Ally, Renee got a plastic cup next and poured her daughter some milk. Once Ally was snacking, Libby took Renee's arm and pulled her into the front room.

"If you really want to change, you need to get help. Professional help."

Renee wrinkled her nose. "Like a shrink?"

"Like a rehab center. You need to get clean. Stay away from drugs."

Renee hesitated, staring at Libby with a dubious frown.

"Think about it, Renee," Libby pushed. "If not for the drugs, would you have ever let that man get near Ally?"

The young mother's face crumpled in regret and self-disgust. "Cal was right. I've been a terrible mother. I cared more about my next hit than my own baby. That's not right. There's no excuse for it."

Libby tugged the corner of her mouth up in a reassuring grin. "You made a mistake, but you've seen where you went wrong and know what you have to do to change things. That's a start."

"If I hadn't gotten stoned tonight and passed out, Ally would have been safe. That guy just walked in and took her 'cause I was so out of it." Recrimination darkened Renee's face. "While I waited for some news about Ally, I kicked

Gary out. He was a leech, anyway. And I promised myself, promised God, that if He'd bring my baby back alive and well…" Her voice cracked, and she paused to clear her throat and swipe at her eyes. "I want to be a good mom."

Libby touched Renee's arm, squeezed. "Then get clean. I can help get you into a good rehab center. If you're willing. You have to be committed."

Renee gave a jerky nod. "I am. I'll do whatever it takes. I love Ally. I do!"

"I know you do." Libby smiled and gave Renee's arm an encouraging pat. "I'm proud of you. The first step is often the hardest. I know a good clinic in Shreveport. I can call them tomorrow and make arrangements for you to check in right away."

Renee scowled and looked toward the kitchen, where Ally munched chips straight from the bag. "I'd need someone to take care of Ally." She frowned. "But if Cal's in jail, then—"

"I'll do it," Libby said without hesitation. Accustomed to taking a long time to make major decisions, Libby waited for the flicker of doubt and second-guessing that should have followed her split-second decision. But the doubt never came.

"You will? But…" Renee's skepticism was written in the wrinkle of her nose.

Libby squared her shoulders. "I'm her stepmother. And I love her. I want to help."

Renee blinked. "What about Cal?"

An arrow of guilt shot through Libby. "What do you mean?"

"What's going to happen to him? This whole parole thing. Don't they make exceptions to those rules you were talking about? Ever?" Renee tucked a bare foot under her as she flopped down on the sofa.

Libby sat beside her. *Exceptions to the rules?*

She'd been so focused on calming Ally on the drive back from D'Arbonne, so mired in her guilt for having turned Cal in to the authorities, that Libby hadn't had time to really think how she might get Cal out of this mess.

In the past, Libby had considered exceptions and loopholes as cop-outs. She'd never dared to look for a way *around* the law.

"It would be up to his parole officer whether he wants to pursue the violations or excuse them," she told Renee. Her heart picked up an excited tempo against her ribs as an idea formed. "If Boucheron doesn't press the matter, Cal could be released."

Renee sat forward and grabbed Libby's hand. "His parole officer just *has* to release him. Cal did what he did out of love for his daughter. The man has to see that!"

Love doesn't follow rules.

Libby stood and paced across the dirty shag carpet to a window with a view of the parking lot. She turned the budding plan over in her head, looking at it from all angles.

The law was very clear about limitations on parolees. And she was an officer of the court. Wasn't upholding the letter of the law her obligation?

I'm your husband. Doesn't that count for anything?

"I turned him in," she thought aloud.

"You?" Renee appeared beside her, her expression incredulous. "Why? I thought you loved him?"

"I do love him!" The same panic that had choked her at the cabin clamped down on her chest again. "But the deputies saw Cal with the gun when they arrived. They would have run his name through the computer anyway and seen for themselves that he was in violation of his parole. It would have looked bad for him if he tried to conceal the truth. It's much better for his case that we laid it all out up front."

That much was true on the surface, but something still nagged her, chafing her conscience.

I will never understand why you think you have to hide be-

hind your strict interpretation of the rules. What are you scared of?

Libby sucked her bottom lip in and bit down.

Losing control scares the hell out of you, doesn't it?

Cal had seen through her from the start. She'd clung to the only security she'd ever known, hidden behind the structure and predictability of rules because the alternative was too frightening. The instability of her childhood had scared her. And she was still hiding.

"Libby…" Renee narrowed her eyes and crooked an eyebrow. "You sure you weren't just covering your own butt? Your job with the D.A.? I'm sure it would have looked bad for you if it appeared you were—what's it called—aiding and abetting?"

The pressure in Libby's chest doubled. Breathing was impossible. "Maybe a little." She forced air into her lungs, struggled to steady her voice. "All right, a lot. I've worked hard to get where I am. My job is important to me."

"More important than Cal?"

Libby fell back a step, as if pushed. Blood roared through her ears, and her spinning thoughts coalesced into one pinpoint of light. Why hadn't she been able to boil it down to such a simple, straightforward question? Her dilemma wasn't shades of gray at all. She loved Cal. Period.

The constriction in her chest loosened. The one real certainty in this whole situation was that she loved Cal. *That* was black-and-white.

"Will you and Ally be all right tonight? Do you need anything?" Libby asked as she turned and made her way to the door. She had something pressing to take care of, something that wouldn't wait until morning.

Renee followed Libby to the door. "I guess not. You're sure about keeping Ally when I go to Shreveport?"

"Positive. I'll call the clinic in the morning and stop by first thing tomorrow to get Ally."

Renee quirked a lopsided grin. "Thanks. For everything. And, uh…tell Cal, if he gets this parole thing straightened out—" Renee rubbed her arm and raised her chin "—I'll work with him to arrange joint custody. Something that will give him more time with Ally."

Libby's smile broadened. "Thank you, Renee. I'll tell him."

On her way out, Libby detoured by the kitchen long enough to get a milky kiss from Ally and give her a tight hug. "I'm gonna get your daddy out of jail, kitten. I promise."

No matter what it took.

Hearing the jangle of his jailer's keys, Cal sat up on the thin mattress in the holding cell and rubbed his eyes. It had been a long night with no sleep. He'd been transferred to the police station in Lagniappe within hours of being taken into custody by the D'Arbonne department.

While he was being processed at the Lagniappe facility, the police had brought in a handful of thugs netted in a drug raid. Including Roach. From the snatches of conversation he'd heard between Roach and the police, Renee's dealer was in deep trouble. He'd be behind bars for a long time.

Just like me.

Cal would have an arraignment hearing today, but the court appearance was a formality. His fate was sealed.

"Walters," the cop at the cell door called. "You can go."

"Go?" His ears were playing tricks on him.

"You're cleared for release to the custody of your P.O."

The hearing. Had to be. But it seemed awfully early for that. He pushed to his feet and shuffled along behind the officer to the room where he'd been processed last night.

Boucheron was waiting for him. Cal gave his parole officer a grim nod, feeling he let down the man who'd tried to help him get back on his feet. The man who'd showed faith in him by pulling strings to get him on with the volunteer fire department.

Call gritted his teeth. He'd let a lot of people down.

Including Libby.

Although her reasons for turning him over to the deputies made more sense to him in hindsight, her actions still pricked him, still cut deep.

But the consequences of his actions were his own fault. She'd tried to warn him, begged him not to break his parole. He'd made his decision and had to live with it. Even though it meant losing his freedom, losing his daughter. Losing Libby.

She'd probably divorce him the way Renee had. Being married to a convict would put her reputation, her career, in jeopardy. An A.D.A. had to be above reproach.

The police officer behind the desk in the processing room handed Cal a bag with his belongings: watch, shoes, wallet.

"Well, you don't look too happy for a man who just got sprung from jail," Boucheron said in his booming voice.

Cal shrugged then hesitated when the P.O.'s word choice sank in. "Sprung? I thought I was going to my hearing."

"No hearing. No need. I'm not filing anything on what happened last night."

Cal stared at Boucheron, whose rumpled shock of white hair gave the impression the P.O. had also had a long night. Cal hesitated, not sure he'd heard correctly. Behind his bushy mustache, the man wasn't smiling.

Did he dare hope that he was actually free to go?

"I'm…not sure I understand."

"Well, let me see if I can explain a little better." Boucheron rocked back on the heels of his worn cowboy boots and hooked his thumbs in his pockets. "About four o'clock this morning, way too early for sane folks to be up and about, someone pounded on my front door. Now mind you, I'm used to getting woke up at all hours of the night on work-related emergencies, but…never by a gorgeous brunette."

Cal's pulse stumbled. A gorgeous brunette? Libby?

"Seems a certain tigress from over at the D.A.'s office needed to speak to me about one of my parolees. She told me an involved story about a stalker and a kidnapping and how this parolee—who was first and foremost a loving father—had left the parish, toting a gun, to try to rescue his little girl."

Cal held his breath. Anxiety did a tap dance in his chest.

"Anyway, I won't bore you with the details, since I'm sure you know how the story goes." Boucheron's mouth finally peeked out from his white mustache in a grin. "But suffice it to say, this brunette presented *quite* a case in my parolee's defense."

In his *defense*.

A ribbon of warmth unfurled inside him, loosening the grip of nervous tension.

His barrel-chested P.O. stroked his chin. "I can imagine she's a top-notch litigator and a boon in the D.A.'s office."

Pride nudged Cal, and cracking a smile, he nodded. "I imagine she is."

"So, I asked this pretty thing just how certain she was that this parolee deserved a second chance. If I was going to put my job on the line, going to bat for this young man, I wanted to know someone else—someone, say, from the D.A.'s office—would back me. That she was also willing to stake her job on such a potentially controversial decision."

Cal tensed again. Would Libby really put her career on the line defending him? A seed of doubt planted itself at the forefront of Cal's mind. He curled his fingers into fists as Boucheron continued.

"I mean, this guy was clearly in violation of his parole. The case could be construed as open-and-shut."

"Yes, sir." Cal clenched his teeth, struggling for the patience to hear out his loquacious, good-old-boy P.O.

"However, this lovely A.D.A. was so passionate in her belief that this man deserved his freedom, and that the circumstances surrounding his violations were at the very least understandable and forgivable, that she convinced me to take a risk." Boucheron flicked his hand in dismissal. "As far as I'm concerned, this is one case where the circumstances make it possible to excuse the breach of regulations."

Blinking his disbelief, Cal searched for his voice. "Are you saying…I'm not going back to prison?"

"That's what I'm saying."

Another thought popped into his head, dimming the elation budding inside him. He drew his eyebrows together in a frown. "What about my standing with Act 894?"

Boucheron shrugged. "I'm not filing any paperwork on what happened. There will be no record of any of it. Your slate is still clean." His P.O. aimed a stout finger at Cal. "But don't let me hear of anything like this ever happening again. You'd better be clean as a whistle from here on out, or I'm coming down on you like the wrath of Hades. Got that?"

Despite Boucheron's stern warning, Cal couldn't suppress the grin that tugged his lips. "Got it. Thank you, sir. Thank you very much."

"The one you need to thank is that sweet thing waiting for you outside." Boucheron hitched his thumb toward the door to the lobby. "That's quite a wildcat of a wife you've got, Mr. Walters. I'd take good care of her if I were you. Don't let her get away."

"I don't intend to, sir."

With a nod, Boucheron turned on his boot heel. "That's all. I'm goin' home now and tryin' to get some sleep. See you at your next regular check-in." He paused in the door. "Oh, and tell Libby to lock that gun up. I'd hate to have to confiscate it."

"Yes, sir."

Numbed by the whirlwind of the unexpected new direction

his life had taken, Cal dropped onto the bench along the wall and pulled on his shoes.

Libby had tried to explain herself, her actions, last night, and he wouldn't listen. He'd let his old hurts color his reaction.

I love you. He recalled the emotional wallop her mouthed confession had landed when he'd had little time to process it. He'd been too involved in getting Ally to safety and getting back to help her.

Help her? He knotted his shoelaces and grinned. When he'd gotten back to the cabin, Libby had been kicking Ralston's ass. Where had she learned those moves?

If not for his distraction…

As it had last night, a fist of horror and guilt grabbed Cal by the throat. Seeing Libby at the business end of that knife still sent icicles through his veins.

"Daddy?" The quiet inquiry brought his head up, made his heart pound.

"Ally?" He spread his arms, inviting his daughter to receive a hug.

She assessed him from the doorway with an adult knit in her brow.

"It's okay, kitten. Everything's going to be all right now."

With that assurance, Ally dashed across the floor and flung herself into his arms.

"What are you doing here? Where's your mom?" he murmured, while inhaling and soaking in the sweet scent of baby shampoo.

"Mommy went away. She's going to get well."

He sensed more than saw Libby standing in the door, and he looked up, his heart in his throat.

She gave him a hesitant smile. "Renee checked into a rehab center in Shreveport this morning. You have Ally until she's discharged, and then Renee has promised to find a custody agreement you both can live with."

An unexpected relief and joy swelled in his chest, and he closed his eyes. Hugging Ally tighter, he savored the moment, reveled in it.

Until a thread of doubt and uncertainty threatened to unravel all the happiness and resolution this morning had brought. He snapped his eyes up to Libby. "*I* have her? Don't you mean 'we'?" The shadows shifting in Libby's gaze struck him with a clammy knot of dread. "Libby? What about us?"

"I…" She licked her lips and drew a slow breath. "I wasn't sure you still wanted me. After…I turned you in."

He kissed Ally's forehead then set her down. Rising to his feet, he stepped toward Libby. "I was hurt at first. Because I didn't put enough faith in you. I should have trusted you more, and I'm sorry."

"You're sorry? I'm the one who almost got you sent back to prison!" She shook her head, and lines creased her forehead. "You were right when you said I was scared. I was using rules and legalities as a shield, to protect myself from getting hurt. If I didn't let anyone get close, I couldn't blame myself and what I lacked when they left."

"What you lack? Libby, you are the most wonderfully complete woman I've ever met. You're intelligent and brave. Compassionate and hardworking. And sexier than any lawyer has a right." He gave her a mischievous grin. "Do you have any idea how much I love you?"

She smiled sadly and ducked her chin. "I know you care. And, after Ally, I hope I'm pretty high on your list, but—"

"Whoa! Wait a minute. *After* Ally?" He put his hand under her chin and lifted her face to meet his gaze. "Look at me." He held his hands in front of him. "Here's Ally." He wiggled one hand. "And here's you." He wiggled the other hand and held it at the same height in front of her. "Even. I love you two differently, but just as much. You two are everything to me. My whole world."

Tears sparkled in her dark eyes, and she grinned. "Really? I've never been someone's whole world before."

He slid a hand around to cradle the back of her head and pull her closer. "Yes, you have. You were my whole world five years ago, even when I left. And all through my years in prison. You're a hard woman to forget, and an easy woman to love."

Her smile brightened. "I love you, too. More than I can say."

"I think what you did this morning, arguing my case to Boucheron even at the risk of jeopardizing your position at the D.A.'s office, says a whole lot." He kissed her lightly. "Thank you."

"It was the least I could do. I couldn't stand the thought of losing you again." She eased closer, until her body pressed against his. She wove her fingers through his hair and rose on her toes to kiss him. Not until Ally sidled up to them and wrapped an arm around each of their legs did Libby pull away.

"I think we should get this little kitten home for a nap. She had a rough night." Cal stooped to lift Ally in his arms and shifted his gaze to Libby. He gave her a heated grin. "And then, what do you say we work on giving her a little brother or sister?"

Libby snuggled under his free arm and wrapped him in a hug that included Ally. The warmth and love that flamed in Libby's eyes zinged through him, like fireworks celebrating his freedom, his family, his future.

"I'd say, yes. Most definitely, *yes.*"

* * * * *

INTIMATE MOMENTS™

A WOMAN WITHOUT A PAST

A MARK THAT BECAME A DEATH WARRANT

A MAN WHO WAS MORE THAN A STRANGER

Let award-winning author

KYLIE BRANT

show you how animal attraction and heart-stopping danger explodes in

The Business of Strangers

Intimate Moments #1366, May 2005